MY SISTERS MADE OF LIGHT

MY SISTERS
MADE OF LIGHT

JACQUELINE ST. JOAN

PRESS 53
Winston-Salem

Press 53
PO Box 30314
Winston-Salem, NC 27130

First Edition

Cover design by Sonya Unrein

An earlier version of Chapter 13, "Islamabad, 1996" was published as a
novel-in-progress excerpt entitled "Meena" in *F Magazine*, Issue 8, 2009.

Library of Congress Control Number: 2010936842

Printed on acid-free paper

ISBN 978-1-935708-06-3

This book is dedicated to Samantha, Elizabeth, and Nico
—and all our children made of light.

Contents

Pakistan

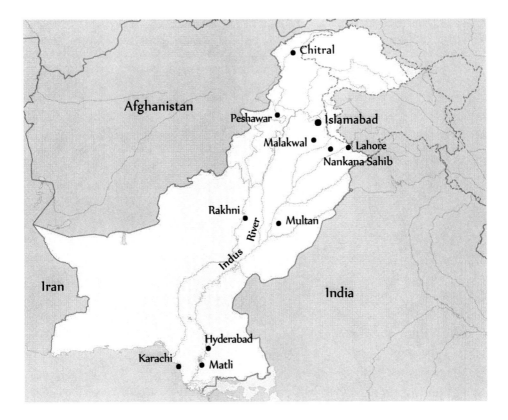

Family Tree

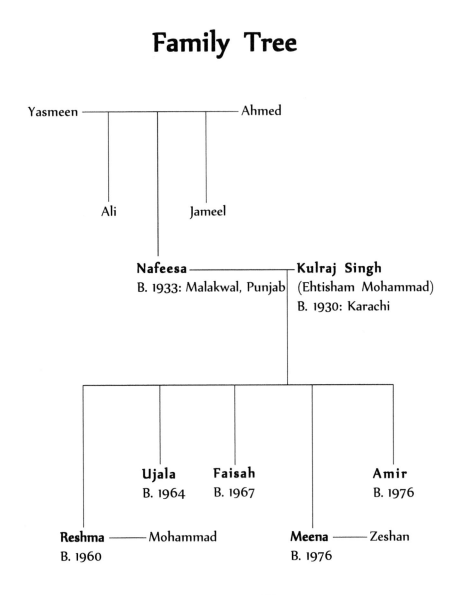

Yasmeen —————————— Ahmed

Ali   Jameel

Nafeesa —————— **Kulraj Singh**
B. 1933: Malakwal, Punjab | (Ehtisham Mohammad)
B. 1930: Karachi

Ujala   **Faisah**   **Amir**
B. 1964   B. 1967   B. 1976

Reshma ——— Mohammad   **Meena** ——— Zeshan
B. 1960   B. 1976

1

ADIALA PRISON, 1996

Prison is freedom. Outside? *That* is prison to me." Meena drew the newborn close inside her shawl. "Here my daughter and I are safe."

Ujala was dreaming about Meena again. She could hear a voice calling, whispering, coaxing her to open her eyes.

"Ujala," it sang. "Uji."

It was a woman's voice. Perhaps her mother was leaning next to her ear and would soon touch her arm, kiss her hairline. Or was she only dreaming of a voice? Ujala willed her mind to stay put, waiting for the speaker to reveal herself.

"Your friends in high places must feel sorry for you," the voice said, and Ujala awakened to a shadow looming. "To my office," demanded Rahima Mai, the Women's Prison supervisor. Ujala heard the turnkey unlock her cell and saw the back of a wrapped figure moving away, far down the corridor.

"Yes, Madam," she replied, rising from her string bed. Her shoulder blades were wooden planks ramming the soft tissues of her neck. But Ujala was pleased, excited by this abrupt shift in the prison's endless routines. Jabril Kazzaz must have pulled some strings, she thought, hurrying behind Rahima Mai. As Ujala padded forward, she glimpsed a bare foot wiggling its toes through the bars of a cell they passed. Next, the muffle of someone clearing her throat. Then, a scraping noise.

"Silence!" Rahima Mai shouted, and the clatter ceased. Ujala faced the vestibule door while Rahima Mai tightened her mouth and fingered the pocket of her polyester uniform. She found the key and slotted it into the lock. "Straight away," she said, poking a finger between Ujala's shoulder blades, "and keep moving."

To Ujala walking was a joy—to be able to move her legs and hips again was like floating. She had been in Adiala Prison for six weeks, and for four of them she had been confined to solitary.

A month earlier Rahima Mai had announced Ujala's reassignment to a solitary cell. "Your fame has created a security risk in the open detention area," she had insisted, tapping the end of her pencil against the desk blotter. Her voice softened and she backtracked. "Of course, solitary rooming is not a punishment, but merely"—she searched for the right word—"an administrative precaution for your protection."

Ujala had wanted to argue. *Those women are no risk to me, nor am I a risk to them.* But, she thought, there is no point disagreeing with a bureaucrat who has made up her mind.

"Stop there!" said Rahima Mai, and Ujala halted in front of another closed door. Its cardboard sign read WOMEN'S ADMINISTRATION. OFFICIAL CLEARANCE REQUIRED. Rahima Mai placed her index finger on the intercom button and leaned her considerable weight onto it. "Rahima Mai and Resident Number 482," she announced to the box. She twisted her face toward the ceiling camera, and a barrage of squawk and static emitted an indiscernible reply. A bolt withdrew from its chamber, and the door clanked open.

"Push it!" Rahima Mai ordered, and Ujala pressed her open palms against the sticky, metal grate. She could smell Rahima Mai's armpits as she passed ahead of her. Ujala stepped over the concrete threshold and looked around.

On the wall behind a large gunmetal desk, someone had tacked up the usual framed photo of clear-eyed President Jinnah in his lambswool cap. On either side of the photo were hand-printed posters: A CLEAN MIND IN A CLEAN BODY: CLEANSE WITH PRAYER AND

WATER. The desktop held a telephone, an adding machine, and a Royal typewriter, along with remnants of carbon paper. An adjacent table was covered with thousands of index cards. Attached to one wall was a row of hooks on which shawls, broom handles, and plastic shopping bags dangled. A green filing cabinet with a long face stood in the corner. Its bottom drawer jutted out.

Ujala heard the swivel chair groan as Rahima Mai settled into it.

"My office," Rahima Mai said with a sigh. Somewhere between those two words and her sigh, Rahima Mai had inhaled and exhaled into a personal tone, the first human interaction Ujala could count for the week.

Ujala thought that Rahima Mai was not a bad-looking woman. The prison supervisor looked solid under the polyester prison garb: a worn blue shalwar kameez—the loose pajama-style pants and overshirt worn throughout Pakistan—and matching dupatta—the veil that covered her head and breasts. Rahima Mai's cheeks dominated her long face, and the lines around her mouth suggested sadness or, perhaps, resignation. The circles beneath her eyes darkened under the overhead tube lights.

"We will be spending a lot of time together now," said Rahima Mai. "I have my orders. We can no longer keep you in confinement, nor can we put you back into the general population." She curled her mouth and looked into Ujala's eyes. "So! You will be spending your days right here—with me."

"Yes, Madam," Ujala said, looking down. She tried to disguise her thrill at release from solitary. The supervisor continued describing her plan.

"Yes, this may work out quite well. We are educated people, you and I," she said, thereby elevating her social class to Ujala's. "Just imagine how expensive it is to operate this reformatory." Rahima Mai never used words like *prison*, or *guard*, or *inmate*. Instead, it was *reformatory*, or *staff aide*, or *resident*. "Just think of the costs of staff and repairmen, food, waste removal, uniforms. The list is endless." She gestured toward the adding machine tape that was spilling onto the floor. "With so little help from the central office, how can we afford medicines, school supplies, and sewing materials for the girls?"

"Yes, Madam," said Ujala. She wondered where Rahima Mai's thoughts were taking them.

Suddenly there were two raps on the door and a sergeant-guard entered. The guards wore short dupattas as a safety precaution. Years before, a guard had been found hanging on a clothesline pole from her own dupatta. The guard handed Rahima Mai a folded paper, they nodded to one another, and the guard reversed direction in military fashion and left the office.

"So," Rahima Mai said, "if we can't afford the basics, how can we afford the office assistance we need?" She looked as though she expected Ujala to reply. "Hmmmm?"

"I don't know how you could," Ujala agreed. She dared not let Rahima Mai know how she craved the work assignment for fear it would become a pleasure to be confiscated.

"So that is where you come in. If you can read, you can file. If you can add and subtract, you can do bookkeeping. If you can write, you can answer the phone and take messages."

"Yes, Madam," Ujala replied, curtseying, facing the floor.

From Sundays through Thursdays, Ujala worked like a good servant, with reverence and thrift. In her cell on Fridays she wrote letters and, for part of the day, met visitors. She dreaded Saturday's fruitless hours. Within weeks she had organized the files and bookkeeping into an efficient system. Sometimes she wanted to go further than the assignments she was given. She would have liked to tackle budget reports and problems that Rahima Mai seemed unable to manage. But she did not. She stayed at her station. She was a small, low-flying shadow that Rahima Mai began to believe was her own. When Rahima Mai was tired, Ujala would pour her a cup of tea. If her neck ached, Ujala would massage it.

One day Rahima Mai reached beneath her desk and pulled out a pile of folded clothes. With one hand flat on top and one hand underneath, she pushed the stack toward Ujala.

"My mending," she said and laughed out loud for the first time. She was in a generous mood. "Carry your own cup tomorrow, and you may have tea as well," she said, blowing on the steaming surface. They sat in plastic chairs with a low table between them. "This is how my husband and I used to make the transition from work to home. With a nice cup."

This was the first time Rahima Mai had mentioned her husband. Ujala passed the plastic sugar bowl across the table and folded her hands in her lap. As usual, she was silent, but her heart was quickening, as if it were anticipating something. What is it? she asked herself. Suddenly Rahima Mai reached for her and her fingers squeezed Ujala's chin, lifting it, forcing her to look directly into the supervisor's face.

"Explain this to me," she said. Her voice had dropped into a lower tone. She cleared her throat. "I was reviewing your file the other day." She let go Ujala's chin.

Again Ujala's heart began to race.

"A long way from Clifton to Adiala, my dear, isn't it?" Ujala could not read Rahima Mai's attitude. Was it contempt? Curiosity? Cruelty? Ujala remained silent as Rahima Mai continued. "The file explained your arrest and the complaint against you, but it did not tell me what I really want to know." Then Ujala heard a flat bitterness enter Rahima Mai's voice as she posed her question: "How did a thirty-two-year-old, unmarried, upper-class girl like you end up in Adiala Prison anyway?"

It was a question Ujala had asked herself often, a question that caused her usual sharp focus to fade, her memories to blur into the people, places, and years of her past. She could never recall a coherent version of events—only moments. The day her mother died and she became the family's new mother. The day Yusuf left forever. Bilqis on fire. Khanum on the train. Taslima in a pool of blood. Chanda dancing. The women she had rescued, or failed to rescue, over the years—the ones who helped Ujala discover who she was. Or was that discovery of herself, as her father would say, simply the hand of God pushing her out into the traffic? She was uncertain, but no longer demurring.

"I don't know exactly how I ended up h—"

"Yes, you do," Rahima Mai interrupted, then waited for Ujala's response. "We all know how we ended up here."

Ujala squirmed.

"The way one thing leads to another, it is difficult to know where anything begins," said Ujala.

"Then begin in the middle. It doesn't matter. We both know where the story ends up, don't we?" Now Rahima Mai was both taunting her and making a request, but she was patient. She was used to getting her way inside these prison walls. And, thought Rahima Mai, here is an interesting girl for a change, somebody new, somebody to talk to. There was no question Ujala would tell her what she wanted to know. So she waited.

Suddenly, Ujala's dark eyes widened. She inhaled and faced Rahima Mai.

"You are right," she said. For the first time, Ujala matched Rahima Mai's gaze. "It is a long way from Clifton to here. The story ends in Adiala Prison, but it starts in the famous suburb of Karachi. It begins in Clifton.

"Karachi was a city filled with concrete and constant motion. Traffic was heavy and dominated life at all hours. The presence of the Arabian Sea did little to slow people down; it was another commodity, a vehicle, a field. There were always industrial odors hanging in the air to overpower the scent of orange blossoms that smothered the courtyards of Clifton. In Clifton our courtyard was filled with bougainvillea and jasmine, and the air always was sweet. Our childhood was like that, too—my brother, my sisters, and I— we lived wrapped in the shawl of our parents' love.

"Until eleven years ago—when our mother died, when the shawl dropped open and the family scattered." Ujala hesitated, recalling the changes in her life that the death of Ammi had meant. "Ammi's soul flew to heaven, to be with her parents—they were killed on the Lahori train during the Partition. She lost her entire family. She was the only one to survive."

Ujala continued, "My younger sister, Faisah—she entered law school in Lahore. Once Ammi was gone and we were grown, my father wanted the simple life of an observant Sikh. He took the twins, Meena and Amir, with him to Nankana Sahib, the birthplace of his root guru."

Rahima Mai's brow lifted.

"Yes. My father is a Sikh," said Ujala, matter-of-factly. "My oldest sister's life changed the least. By then Reshma was married. She remained in Karachi with her sons and her husband—Reshma is quite a scholar in her own right. My father wanted me to go with him and the children to Punjab, of course, but I had a different idea. And I needed his permission."

◆ ◆ ◆

"I have been asked to be a traveling teacher-trainer," I told Abbu one night. We were on the upstairs verandah, reading the newspaper together, the way he and Ammi had often done. "With the Women's Aid Society," I said, nonchalantly.

He rattled the newspaper down into his lap with force.

"Traveling? Alone? Women do not travel alone in Pakistan." He sounded stern—not at all like himself. I continued speaking as if what I was asking was nothing unusual.

"Perhaps I can make a contribution to the education of women, Abbu. I will live with groups of women teachers in each place. And I will visit you often. I promise." I smoothed the front of my kameez and looked into his eyes. "Please say yes."

He looked as if I had slapped his face.

"You are begging?" he asked, sounding disgusted.

"It is my life."

I watched the skin on his face drop into the hollow between his cheekbones, and I waited. I knew it was best to wait. In a matter of seconds he had let his fear shrivel up and blow away. I had seen him do it many times. Suddenly his eyes lit up.

"Yes," he said with certainty. "Of course. Your mother prepared that path for you."

My mother was one of the founders of the organization I eventually worked for—WASP, the Women's Aid Society of Pakistan. At that age—I was only nineteen—I felt unprepared to teach. I had no training in how to run a school. I'd done only a little informal teaching with a friend. But later I learned a great deal about teaching women and girls. We worked on basic Urdu—both reading and writing. Eventually we added computer training, micro-credit projects, and even legal assistance. It was a productive, creative time. Many families opened their doors and took me in. I became Baji Ujala—everyone's older sister—wherever I went. But it was when I discovered a truly godforsaken place— the desert of interior Sindh— that I began to feel deep inside of me the forces that eventually led me here to Adiala Prison.

How slowly life moved in the heat of Sindh! Even at daybreak, milk buffaloes sought out the thin shade of a kikar tree. The boys with their sticks poked the beasts' hides to get them up. It was still early in the day, and the worst was yet to come. By midmorning smoke was the only thing moving in the sky. By midday brick particles stung our lungs. By evening the place smelled like it was on fire.

The kilns' smokestacks were as plentiful as minarets. During the merciless dry season, the children worked from dawn to dusk, scooping the mud with ungloved hands, then patting the dampened clay into identical steel molds, each one labeled with the landlord's logo. During the winter months, when school was open, we helped those same small hands with their tiny fingernails trace letters and numerals—hands without even a pocket to protect them.

The children were paid less than a rupee for each brick, but they preferred making bricks to lugging loads of onions from the field. Their families owed the company store, not only their own debt, but also the debt of their grandparents that they had inherited, plus interest, plus fines, plus, plus, plus. There was no end to the debt, so the people became virtual slaves. They had to get permission to leave the work site or else they'd be beaten or jailed. The headman would yell, "Bend over. Let your children witness your beating."

Only the headman could afford a brick house for himself. The villagers, on the other hand, collected dung, shaped it into patties, and slapped them onto the sides of rocks. The dung pies baked all day to be used for constructing homes or for fuel. The grandmothers would spend their days scavenging and, if they were lucky, they would find a few sticks of wood. Sometimes a home would have a small kerosene cook stove . . . *kerosene* . . . the smell of it, the cold tin cans sloshing. Ugh! It makes my stomach sting just thinking of what kerosene can do.

You know, in Sindh carnivals still travel from town to town, the way ancient caravans journeyed with poets, musicians, and clowns. Two years ago—was it only two years ago?—when the carnival arrived in Matli from Karachi, I recognized one of the girls. It was Bilqis—a Christian girl—whose father had been a teacher in Clifton. Bilqis had been just five years old when I left Karachi ten years earlier. I remembered her well because her father left her in my care one time when her mother was ill.

Bilqis had been a skinny thing, but strong, and she loved to climb.

"See, Baji?" she smiled up at me with bright eyes. Her arms were suspended like vines from the branch of a young neem tree. "I am part monkey."

I had to laugh. "Which part?" I asked.

"The lively part," she replied without hesitation.

"The banana part," I said, playing with her.

"The curling tail part," she continued swinging, trying to touch the top leaves of the tree.

"The long arms part," I said, smiling. She liked that. I wondered if she could keep up with me.

"The monkey sounds part," she said. "Woo. Woo." I tried to think of what to say next.

"The funny face part," I said, and Bilqis stopped swinging. Tears formed in the inner corners of her eyes. I had hurt her feelings.

"My face is not funny!" she said.

"Did I say funny?" I asked her. "I meant the *sunny* face part." A wide smile spread over her face. "Sunny face."

"Oh," she replied, not quite sure what had just happened. "Sunny face!"

Early one evening, Bilqis and I hastened to the local school so she could climb on the jungle gym there. It was the hour when women are supposed to be at home. So I wrapped her in a blanket and carried her like she was my baby. We hurried along the street to avoid anyone questioning our being unescorted. When we turned the corner into the wide-open field, Bilqis peered out of the blanket. The silent streets were deserted.

"Are we in a story?" she asked. I looked around at the dry ground, the empty windows, and perfect light. She was right—the scene looked like a picture from a storybook. It was eerie.

"What do you think?" I asked, putting her down. I wanted a glimpse of what she was thinking—how a child tries to distinguish what is real from what is imagined.

"I don't know," she said. Bilqis handed me the blanket, grabbed hold of the sliding board, and clambered to the top. Her bare feet squeaked against the metal surface. "But I think I know how the story ends," she said.

"How?" I asked. "How does it end?"

"Nobody knows," she laughed. "Nobody ever knows how the story ends." She reached the top, twisted her torso and slid down, landing by my feet.

"Not even a monkey like you?" I asked. "Tell me how the story ends," I pleaded. I bent over and looked her in the eye. She turned away. I had ruined the moment with my probing. I wanted to know too much, more than she could tell me.

"I told you, Baji, I don't know. Nobody knows."

A policeman passed the schoolyard, and the light changed.

So I remembered Bilqis well ten years later when she visited her grandmother in Matli, where I was teaching in interior Sindh. She was turning fifteen, and the teachers wanted to give her a birthday party.

"Bilqis!" I said when I opened the door to her and her auntie. But when she felt my enthusiasm, she lowered her eyes and withdrew into her dupatta.

"Salaam, Madam," she said formally. She did not remember me.

"Salaam," I replied, "Not Madam. Call me Baji Ujala." I put my hands on her head, and she stretched up to kiss my cheeks.

"How beautifully she carries herself," one of the teachers remarked. You know, Sindh is not like Karachi or Lahore. A Sindhi girl rarely leaves the house, so on the rare occasions when she does, she doesn't know how to interact naturally. But Bilqis knew the social graces—how to introduce herself to others, how to sit comfortably and engage in small talk, and even how to tell a few jokes. With a tambourine and bells, she performed traditional folk dances for the teachers. Then, the next day, while I was overseeing spelling exercises in the courtyard, the carnival manager drove in, blasting the horn of his old truck. It was quite a noise and drew me to the gate.

"Is the world on fire or something, Shams?" I called to him, not hiding my annoyance that he was interrupting the girls' lessons.

"Yes, Madam," he said, "The world *is* on fire. It is Bilqis. She has been burned. She needs you at the hospital. You know the nurses there."

"Burned? She's been burned?"

I left at once and climbed into his truck. I brought along the young boy sweeper to sit between us. Shams hesitated and drew a breath before he ground the truck's gears into their rightful places.

"They say the stove burst," he said, squeezing the corners of his mouth to let me know he doubted the stove had actually burst.

Someone had set Bilqis alight!

Outside the clinic, I inhaled the stink of burned flesh. Inside, Bilqis lay wincing. Her whole body was an open wound. The outside edges of her arms were blackened and peeling. Her torso was covered with one thin layer of gauze, its slight weight keeping her skin attached to her organs. Her eyes, and many of her teeth, had been entirely burned out.

I had to lean into the wall to keep from fainting. The nurses took scissors to the loose flesh on Bilqis' leg, where the skin hung in defeat, like a torn flag. They snipped close to the raw pulp of her blood vessels and bones.

I pulled a folding chair up next to the bed. I wanted to comfort her, but how?

"Who did this to you?" I whispered, and an awful sound erupted from her mouth. I could not understand what she said. Her upper lip was missing. Then she called out again with what must have been all of her strength.

"Allah!" she cried, but she was looking at me. A sound cracked from deep inside her, "K-k-kill-e-eee."

She was begging me to kill her. In her eyes I was the merciful

God who could stop her suffering. Even now, recalling that scene, I feel nauseous. The moment shines in my memory, as if from a great distance. My soul was plummeting and groundless. Eventually, when Bilqis fell into unconsciousness, the nurse spoke to me.

"This is not a burn unit, Baji Ujala. The child's blood cannot move the drugs efficiently. If an infection sets in—and it will— she will not live more than a few days."

I prayed her agony would not last that long.

"How did this happen?" I demanded.

The nurse shook her head. "They say a kerosene stove blew up while she was making tea," she said. I wanted her to tell me what she knew. I caught her glance and held it. We stood in that clean moment until finally she said, "Ask someone else. I have to live here."

I went looking for Shams. It was time for Zuhr, midday prayers. He was with a small group of men, prostrating on their rugs. I felt a fire smoldering in my brain as I watched them lined up like that. *How can they pray five times a day and be indifferent to this girl?* When I saw Shams folding his prayer cloth, my mind's embers caught fire and I shouted out.

"Shams, Shams, why do stoves burst only on women? Do men not also light stoves?" I asked the question to all of them, to the crows on the wires, and to the glare of the sun. I did not care who heard me. I was on fire.

"Don't say it out loud, Madam," Shams said, pulling me aside.

"I knew Bilqis' family," I said, my voice as loud as ever. "Her oldest sister was in my class—among the few Christians who could afford the convent school." I lowered my voice. "I know the grandmother, too, and I know this was no accident. I have been inside that house. They have no kerosene stove there."

"You are right, Madam," Shams said. "The elders say her uncle heard a rumor that she is pregnant. He tied her to a bed, poured kerosene from a can, lit a match and locked the door." Shams choked. He could hardly speak and neither could I. Finally he said, "It was an honor crime. No one could rescue her. No one even tried."

"No one even tried!" I was horrified. "Do they not love their daughters, Shams? Do they not worry when they are sick? Are they not happy when their daughters are happy?" I still shiver when I recall his reply.

"Yes," he said. "They love their girls, but who does not love his honor more?" Shams turned his back to me. I was naive in those days. I argued with him.

"Not everyone loves their honor more," I said. "My father is not like that. He loves his children more than anything." Shams looked at me over his shoulder.

"But did you ever break any of your father's rules?" he asked, and doubt tore into me with its probe. Who knows what would happen if I did break his rules? I had never tried.

I could see that Shams was eager to leave, but I begged him to go to the police.

"Police are no friends of women, especially Christian women," he said. "They look the other way, or attack women who complain."

"But we have to do something. You're a man. Come with me. We'll make them listen to us."

The long look on Shams' face told me that we would not be able to make them listen. It was hopeless. A woman's word would never match that of a man. Shams was only an itinerant entertainer who came to this village once a year. He was unknown both to the civil authorities and to the bradari, the local council whose word was law. I watched Shams' dry lips split with his final words.

"We will stay in our camp until Bilqis' parents arrive from Karachi," he said. "Or until she dies. Then we have to move on. I have others I am also responsible for. And this could mean trouble."

How heavy my body felt as we stood there in the heat of midday, abandoned by any benevolent power whatsoever.

"Then I'll go to the police alone," I said, as if I were threatening him. He kept sifting through the belongings in the bed of his truck. "And, Shams," I said. "What do I tell the other women about the men who pray five times a day? What do I say about that? Where are they when we need them? What can we do?"

The whites of his eyes reddened and their corners creased. When he spoke, his voice was angry.

"How should I know?" he bellowed. "Tell them we pray because we don't know what to do either. Because the men on the prayer mats are afraid, too."

I returned to the infirmary where the sharp odors of death were baking. Bilqis faded in and out of consciousness, moaning. Her grandmother stood by the window blocking the blinding sunlight. With a straight back, wrapped and veiled entirely in black, she shaded Bilqis. I closed my eyes to the sounds of whimpering and the clicking of the grandmother's beads. The old woman hummed a missionary's lullaby:

Too-ra-loo-ra-loo-ra
Too-ra-loo-ra-li
Too-ra-loo-ra-loo-ra
Hush now, don't you cry

Minutes after Bilqis died, the ground shook. Officials said the earthquake registered 6.0 on the Richter scale. Poets would have said that fire itself rebelled against its use in destroying beautiful Bilqis. People gathered first at one house, and then at the next, to rebuild their mud huts that had collapsed in the upheaval. They soon forgot the gossip about Bilqis. But I was unable to forget. When I smelled breakfast steaming, the spices stung my nostrils like needles. When I heard the rooster crowing, I held the palm of my hand over one ear and turned the other to the pillow. I was haunted by the demand that I speak, but I was afraid—afraid of backfire at me, the school, the other teachers and students. If I registered a formal complaint, what proof did I have? If the police arrested Bilqis' uncle, would the women in his family be jailed along with him? Would they have money for a bribe? There was just no telling how the sands might shift in such a storm.

Finally, I decided not to involve anyone else from the school. I would go for condolences and talk with Bilqis' grandmother about filing a complaint herself. I would assure her that I could arrange funds for a bribe, if necessary. I would get money from my father.

I walked into the village completely veiled. I recognized Bilqis' brother, Daniel, and her older sister, Nahida. When I touched Nahida's hand, she smiled.

"Salaam," I said, "May her soul rest with God. May God bring peace to you."

"Salaam," she whispered and hugged me.

Daniel nodded and walked away. I could see through the gate that people had gathered with Bilqis' family. Women were repairing fallen bricks around the water pump. They worked in a sad silence.

"We are grateful for the comfort you gave her at the clinic," Nahida said. "Such a horrible way to die." She shivered.

"She never deserved what your uncle did," I said, and Nahida faced me at once.

"But my uncle had nothing to do with it," she insisted. "In fact, he tried to save her. The stove exploded. It was an accident, or didn't you know?"

"No one in the village believes it was an accident," I said. I didn't want to argue, but Nahida and I had been friends once, and I wanted her to know the truth. Her jaw fell open with disbelief. "Ask your grandmother," I said. "She was there. Better for you to hear it from her."

"Grandmother? Why are you saying this? Our grandmother is the one who described the accident to us. She said my uncle tried to help. Why would he do such a thing to Bilqis?"

"They say he thought she was pregnant. A matter of family honor," I whispered, immediately regretting that my words sounded as if I were blaming both Bilqis and her family.

"That is impossible, shameful, ridiculous," Nahida said. Now she was angry with me. "The Lord came early and unexpected for Bilqis. It is the will of God. If what you say were true, the police would be involved. Where are they? Do not make trouble for my family. What are you doing here anyway?"

She paused.

"Perhaps you should leave."

The carnival left the next day. For three days Bilqis' family mourned, and in the end, her uncle was one of the men who carried her coffin behind the priest to the tiny graveyard. Her father was the first to throw dirt onto the slab that weighed down her crisp ribs and fixed her bones into the soil. On the fourth day, the family drove out of the village and returned to Karachi.

After Bilqis' death, I had trouble sleeping. More than once I awakened from nightmares of fire. In one dream her uncle burst into flame in an open field. In another, her grandmother and I patted the uncle's face of clay into identical brick molds. We loaded them into the cart, and our donkey hauled them to the kiln.

I would approach the door of the police station, determined to make a report, but then I would keep walking, pretending I was shopping. At the fruit stall I would turn over a melon and see Bilqis' face on the other side. I was haunted by the stench of flesh, so I stopped cooking meat.

Oh, how I longed to be with my family! Travel was long, expensive, and difficult, and required being away from the school for many days. But are there any secrets in a small village? My friends had noticed the change in me. They could read my thoughts.

"Baji, go home," the other teachers begged. "Get some relief, then come back to us."

On the day I left Matli, the wind was arriving from the sea. The radio reported that a cyclone had upended palm trees along the beach before sending its blistering sand northward, invading from all directions, filling holes and cracks in mud houses. The people covered every centimeter of themselves and their windows with red-and-black printed Sindhi cloth. Then they retreated inside until the storm passed.

Except for the farmers, who endured the assaulting sand and the directionless wind. They laid plastic sheets over their frayed crops. When the wind whipped the sheets out of the men's control, the boys chased the plastic around the fields. Once caught, they folded it against their bodies, locked arms with each other and pushed back into the fury. Then the boys laid their bodies down along the edges of the plastic while the men dropped heavy stones.

I boarded the bus to Hyderabad where I could transfer to the train to Punjab. Fat raindrops slapped the windshield, but the expected downpour never occurred. During the ride, I watched a dozen crows on a radio tower fight like politicians for the top rung. In a field a woman carried a wrapped load on her head, moving gracefully in her flowing cotton veil. She was like a tall yellow and orange bird. On the outskirts of Hyderabad, two white egrets waded at the edge of a cesspool in front of a bleached-out mosque. An immaculate swan swam in an open toilet of garbage.

The noisy city sped by me on that sweltering day. Police appeared everywhere, some shouldered Kalashnikovs, others had simple revolvers in their belts. Horns from the motorized rickshaws blared. I felt lonely, remembering busy Clifton, thinking of home. Was it Yusuf I missed or the protection his love implied, the refuge where I longed to rest my head?

I confess that phantoms of my middle-class upbringing inhabit my psyche whenever I travel. I did not want to interact with the tea vendors, shouting, "Chai, chai!" I did not want the dry palms of lost women cupping mine, calling "Baji, Baji," pleading for a coin or two. I was disgusted by my own elitism, yet at the same time, I retreated into it.

As a woman traveling alone, I was given the preferred aisle seat, of course, rather the window seat that was always open and dusty. The porter placed my valise overhead, while I tucked my book bag, food basket, and purse under my seat. Sitting alone, directly across from me was a sleeping young woman in a pale green silken shalwar kameez embroidered with gold. Her skin shone as her head rested on her own shoulder.

Then I noticed a bright red spot on her sleeve and a line of dried blood smeared across her wrist.

My heart sank.

Over the years I had heard the stories of burst stoves and other "accidents." I had seen the slit wrists, the scarred faces, unmarked graves. After all, I worked in Sindh, where two women are burned to death every day. I recalled the day years earlier when three students had rushed into my classroom, in the same way Shams had done to tell me about Bilqis.

"Baji, you must come right away," they said.

I followed them into a neighborhood of mud huts and an open sewer line. There, lying in the gutter, was the body of a woman. It was impossible to know how long it had been there. The dark flesh was swollen with wastewater and death. Insects swarmed around her eyes and belly. Her dupatta barely covered her face.

"Does anyone know this woman?" I called out to the people on the street.

No one responded.

"Has anyone called the police?"

Silence. The neighborhood women covered their noses with the edges of their dupattas. The men looked at their feet.

"It was an honor killing," an old man said finally. He leaned on his cane. "The police are not involved."

No family. No police. It looked like God, too, had abandoned this poor woman, I thought. I did not know what to do.

"Will someone take her body for burial?" I asked. "For the love of Allah?"

Two men with gray beards and a donkey cart stepped up.

"Five rupees," the tall one said.

"Three," I replied, and they nodded.

The men slogged barefoot into the sewage, one grabbing the ankles, the other grabbing the wrists. Her thin, stiff body was soaked and heavy; the once-colorful dress was now brown. They tossed the body into the back of the cart.

"Where is the cemetery?" I asked the neighbors.

"Not the cemetery, Madam," the driver said. "The mullahs have declared her kari—black. She cannot be buried in holy ground. Just follow us."

The two men mounted the front of the cart. The gray donkey inched down the road, and the neighbors formed a small procession.

I began to recite prayers with the students, when suddenly the cart stopped. We had not gone thirty meters from where the body had been found.

"Here," the old man said. "We will bury her here. On the side of the road."

The men began to break up the ground with some sticks. Two boys brought shovels. The women watched in silence, listening to the sound of metal piercing earth.

I could see that the schoolgirls were frightened.

"To bury her along the side of the road! It is treating her like an animal," one of the girls whispered.

The old man had heard her.

"We will flatten the ground over her body and walk on her forever," he said. Then he directed the boys to drop the body into the pit. The boys began to toss in big rocks from a distance, one at a time. Some were making a game of it. Others aimed intentionally, as if stoning the body again.

What could this woman have done to deserve this? I wondered. Whatever had struck her down still electrified the atmosphere.

The women did not stay to watch the burial, and I sent the schoolgirls away. But for myself, I felt compelled to stand there to the end, to be a witness to this horror that I did not completely understand. When it was finished, the roadside looked as it had before, except that dirt had been disturbed, as if sewer workers had just finished their job.

"To Allah we are born, and to Allah we shall return," I prayed aloud.

"There," the old man said, spitting on the ground behind him. He turned to me with his palm extended. "Three rupees, Madam."

After Bilqis' death, all my senses were keen, unmitigated by thoughts or reason. The blood on the wrist of the woman sitting across from me on the train was a taste my mouth recognized. I asked God, Why have you placed another broken woman in front of me? Life's hardships were accumulating; a wave of nausea rolled through my body and I gagged.

I wanted to move to another seat, but I did not. It was quiet where I was, and moving to another seat would change nothing. I looked out the window into the darkness as lambent light diffused throughout the valley and the train penetrated the tunnel of evening. If Abbu were here, I thought, he would say something noble like, "We are living in a time when rulers are butchers, and the spirit has left us the way eagles disappear in a drought. We must take care of each other." To me, my father's words seemed like cotton candy on a paper cone. What was the use of repairing endless broken bodies and torn hearts? I thought that a person who would spend a lifetime trying to fix such wrongs must be a fool.

Suddenly, all of the fluorescent ceiling lights blinked on. The harshness jarred me and woke the sleeping woman.

"Assalam aleikum," I said. *Peace be with you.*

"Walaikum salaam." *And to you, also*, the woman replied, tugging the sleeve to cover her cut wrist.

I unwrapped the food I had brought with me. I offered her sea bass cooked in onions and tomatoes and a small disc of chapati, flatbread I had spiced with coriander. She accepted gladly. Around us women were passing dishes of Sindhi cuisine and cups of cold chai. A small Kholi woman in soiled clothing leaned across the aisle. She handed me cooked dodo flour and garlic-mint chutney. I gave her a sweet pancake spread with lentils, mung dal.

Flies swarmed as the compartment filled with strong aromas—garlic, hot peppers, fennel, turmeric, saffron, onions—and we swatted at them half-heartedly. It was not long before the agitation caused by the long train ride was soothed by the fullness of our bellies. Children curled up, two to a seat, and fell asleep. When women ventured to the toilet from time to time, they watched one another's children. The train swayed; "tuctuc—tuctuc—tuctuc," it said. Someone switched off the lights, and the horn of the locomotive cried into the night.

I learned that the woman across from me was named Khanum Wazir, and she was traveling to Rakhni with her husband, who had taken a seat in the men's first-class compartment. At first, after she awakened from her nap, Khanum was tense, but with all the eating and chatting, she relaxed. Her hair had fallen loose from its clips during the ride and had become messy like a little girl's. Her skin was the color of roti, lightly toasted bread, and her eyes were large and inky. She had a classic nose—strong and straight like royalty—with a ruby stud in her left nostril. When she smiled, her eyes crinkled easily, as if she were suppressing a laugh.

"We were in Hyderabad for a funeral," Khanum said. "And you?" Her question seemed more courteous than curious.

"Going to Lahore to see my family. My brother has been studying in London, but now he is home on holiday. I am excited to see him. It has been a long time."

"And what has kept you away from your family?"

It was an intrusive, personal question, the kind of oblique inquiry I heard often. The real question was *where is your husband?* I explained my work as a teacher-trainer.

"How lucky you are," she said, "to be a teacher. My husband will not let me work. Actually, he won't let me do anything at all." When I told her about Faisah's legal aid work, Khanum leaned forward and whispered, "Maybe your sister can help me."

I knew then that she was about to tell me about the blood on her wrist. And, by this time, I was ready to listen. Food, and time, and the rocking of the train were fortifying.

"I am from Sibi in Balochistan. Married for just six weeks. My uncle sold me to my husband for a herd of cattle and a small plot of land. Now I live in my husband's house in Rakhni." She fell silent, and I waited. A trace of her soul stared out from the back of her eyes as she whispered. "This old man never leaves me alone. He makes me do things I do not want to do. It is worse than it was with my uncle." She stopped and sucked on her teeth before she continued her grievances. "I am trapped in the house all day," she said. She spoke as if her words were backing up in her mouth and she had to spit them out, or choke. Then she looked me in the eye and spoke slowly, deliberately, so I would not misunderstand her meaning. "I will no longer get down on my knees for that man," she said, and I believed I heard a promise she was making to herself. She turned over both of her wrists to show me the proof of her intention, scars of self-destruction I had noticed earlier.

"Can you help me get away?" she pleaded. "I cannot survive this. I am not surviving. I just happen to be alive."

Then something amazing happened.

"Yes. I will," I said. "I will."

And, unlike the broken promises I had made to myself to go to the police about the murder of Bilqis, I knew this was a promise I would keep.

Khanum gestured to the back of the train, and we moved to vacant seats as far from the others as we could get.

"My address," she said, handing me a piece of paper. "When you can do it, come to Rakhni. When you get to our district, hire a taxi and tell the driver to take you to this house. Come any day, except Friday. Come between one and three o'clock. I will be ready. You will see."

Her eyes shone, revealing something opening up inside of her, powerfully, naturally, the way leaves unfold in spring.

"Are you sure you will do it?" she kept asking.

Each time I would nod, yes. I felt the same power spreading throughout my body.

"Are you sure?" she asked again.

"With Allah as my witness," I swore. "I do not know when, but, yes, I will come some day and help you to get away. Soon. I promise."

At first light the train passed into Punjab, where the greening riverbanks reminded me that prosperity and plenty still existed. As the locomotive snaked its way along the valley floor, it seemed as if the fading moon were sliding from one side of the train to the other. By midmorning the train pulled into the Multan station. Through the window I watched Khanum step onto the platform and trail behind her husband and the porter. Soon they were swallowed up by a bevy of cab drivers and their automobiles.

Through open windows at the station I purchased oranges and paratha for breakfast and cotton dhurries as gifts for my sisters and Amir. I sunk a thumb into the vertex of the fruit and peeled it open. Cooking oil from the parathas greased my fingers as I made my plan. I would take Khanum to another part of Pakistan where her husband could not find her. But where? And how to do it without harm coming to either of us? I popped an orange section into my mouth and sucked its sweetness.

Entering Lahore has always been a thrill for me—to be at the crossroads of South and Central Asia, roads a thousand years old. I knew my father would be at the rail station, standing back from the crowds that swarmed. He raised his hand to get my attention, but he need not have signaled. I recognized that soldier's posture he maintains under all circumstances. I had not seen Abbu for many months. He was past sixty, and thinner than usual. The skin around his eyes was loose and freckled, and his entire beard was the color of ashes. I felt my heart hesitate at the fact of his aging, as if it were stopping to consider whether or not it could ever go on without him.

He kissed the top of my head.

"Ujala," he said. "My daughter made of light." His teeth gleamed. "Bless the train that brought you home to us."

"Still the infidel, Abbu?" I teased him. "You worship too many gods already—but, really, the Pakistan Railway?" He laughed, but I could see anxiety in his puffy, electric eyes.

"God brought you back to us just when we need you most," he said as he drove the Toyota out of traffic and into the countryside. The fine leaves of kikar trees shaded both sides of the highway, and the light of the oncoming evening cast long shadows. "I have failed your mother," he said with resignation in his voice. "I've not been able to find even *one* husband for *any* of her daughters. Now it is time for Meena to get married. I'm not getting any younger, Uji, and neither is Meena. I tried to get Faisah to help me, but she said it was not her cup of tea—." His voice hardened. "Uji, you must do it," he said. "After all, you are the mother of this family now."

"It will not be difficult to find a willing man," I said, squeezing his hand. Abbu's eyes moved from the road, to my face, and back to the road. His back and arms remained tense throughout the drive.

Old men rode bicycles with cloth bundles of mustard plants tied to their backs. Schoolgirls in gold shalwar kameezes and maroon cardigans carried baskets for collecting guavas. Strings of colored lights illuminated the stencils on the commercial truck ahead of us. Metallic red and gold Arabic script exclaimed, "Allahu akbar!" *God is great!*

Our family was living where we live now—fifty miles west of Lahore on the edge of the temple grounds in the Sikh quarter of Nankana Sahib, birthplace of Guru Nanak. When Abbu left Clifton years before, he joined dozens of Sikh families who had returned there to reclaim their founder's temple that had been destroyed during the Partition.

That house is also a long way from Clifton. No more family compound with verandahs and wide gates. Instead we have a one-story, U-shaped mud-brick structure with a small interior courtyard. The front door is directly on the road. Inside, an open sitting and dining area is backed by a kitchen and bath. A tiny shrine room adjoins the sitting area. Abbu's bedroom and Amir's room are in the east wing—the men's quarter—and the women's quarter, with one large bedroom, is on the west. The courtyard faces a field of sunflowers and a patch of cauliflower and tomatoes. Jacaranda and ivy geraniums drape from window boxes.

In front of the house a row of multicolored hollyhocks struggled through the cracks between the house and the road. I saw Amir walking toward me, smiling. He had grown into a long and lean man, like Abbu, and even from inside the car I could see the light in his eyes.

"You look so much like Abbu now," I said, stepping out of the Toyota and moving toward Amir. Abbu stayed with the car to check some wires under the hood.

"Oh, I'm much prettier than Abbu, don't you agree?" teased Amir.

I had to laugh. Indeed he was pretty.

"Don't be so vain, my boy," I said.

"And I'm richer than Abbu."

"Now you're bragging," I said. While Abbu had been deepening into the spiritual plane, Amir was moving quickly into the material. In London he had become an entrepreneur while still an engineering student.

"Well, I am president of PakBrains, Unlimited," he said, "the first mobile computer repair service on the West End." It was hard for me to know how to respond to Amir—so proud was he of himself and his bank accounts.

"Good, maybe you can come back and start a business here. Employ some of the locals."

"I doubt if anyone in this area would know a USB from a SUV," he laughed, finally taking a bag from my shoulder. I had no idea what he was talking about.

My sisters stood in the doorway—Meena, light-skinned, tall and slim, like her twin, Amir—and Faisah, dark and plump. Meena had plaited her light brown hair into a single braid as thick as her wrist. Faisah's hair was cropped close to her scalp. As different as my sisters are, they and Amir all have the same wide smile. And on this day, the three of them were wearing matching aprons.

"Just in time for tikka," said Meena.

"But with bean curd instead of chicken," said Faisah. She shifted her eyes in Abbu's direction and mouthed to me, "Veg-e-tar-i-an."

"And I made the chapati," said Amir proudly. Flour dust coated his big hands.

They sounded like three children in a storybook tale. I let them carry my bags, bring me cool water, and usher me to the most comfortable chair. I had forgotten the privileges of being the "mother" of the family, and I could not remember the last time I had felt so happy.

For the first time in his life, Abbu was doing his own house cleaning and yard work. At sunrise he carried a tray of fresh flowers, water, whole fruits, and sweets in small, shiny bowls and laid them before the guru's image in the home shrine. And every afternoon he prayed at the Gurdwara, the sacred Sikh temple.

The next day I accompanied him to the temple gate. As we walked on an old donkey path, I told him about Bilqis.

"You sound distraught, Uji," he said. "Lonely."

"Not lonely, Abbu. Distraught."

Then I told him about Khanum.

"Abbu, as soon as I heard myself tell Khanum that I would help her, my distress disappeared. I think if I save her life, I may save my own."

"The only one anyone can save," said Abbu.

We walked in silence. I was thinking about how to ask his permission to take this trip to Balochistan to rescue Khanum. I had been on my own for so many years, so it seemed out of place to be asking permission, especially for the "mother" of the family, but I knew it was disrespectful not to give him the opportunity to give me permission.

At the temple he slipped his feet out of his open-back shoes. I realized then that he was going inside to pray without saying anything about my going to Balochistan.

"Abbu?" I said. He turned and took my hands into his own.

"What you intend to do brings the sour taste of fear into my mouth, Uji. My advice will be wiser if I pray first with that old friend." I felt then—as I had many times—that he had been reading my thoughts. I kissed his cheek.

"And, Abbu, next I will fulfill my promise to you—and see a sister about a husband." I grinned and handed him two lemon-colored sunflowers I had picked along the road. He smiled. "One for you and one for the Guru," I said.

He took my offerings and opened the gate.

At home Faisah was mopping the kitchen floor and Meena was squatting, mixing water and flour in a metal bowl. She had laid out three onions and jars of spices on the enamel shelf. Meena and Faisah had greatly simplified taking meals together. When our mother was alive, she had made great efforts to present several dishes every evening—and always an assortment of chutneys, breads, drinks, and desserts. Now the family ate one dish, a plate of chapati, a pot of mint tea, and sometimes a dessert.

I washed my hands at the pump and took a sharp knife and a plate from the drawer. Kneeling on the concrete floor next to Meena, I began mincing onions.

"I wish Reshma were here," Meena said with a sigh. "It has been more than a year since I saw them in Karachi. The twins are almost teenagers now."

"And I miss Ammi," Faisah sighed as if arguing with Meena. She returned the mop to its spot behind the door. I knew that Faisah did not miss Reshma. Faisah had lived with Reshma's family during her final year of college. She especially disliked Mohammad, Reshma's husband. A student of an obscure Islamist scholar, Sayyid Hamri, Mohammad measured everyone against Hamri's teachings. "And I don't miss Reshma one bit," Faisah continued. "They let their boys criticize me—their own auntie—when the twins were only four years old!" Faisah mimicked the boys. "'You should cover yourself. You should not cut your hair. You will burn in hell for it.'"

Meena's back stiffened. Following our mother's death, Abbu had chosen me to be the family's mother, yet truly Reshma had been more of a mother to Meena than I. But Meena was familiar with Faisah's ranting, and she let her vent. As I reached for another onion, Meena handed me a soft cloth to wipe my stinging eyes.

"Abbu wants me to help you find a husband," I said.

"Well, don't cry about it, Baji. It's not that hopeless, you know."

I laughed, then Faisah jumped in.

"I offered to place a personal ad on the Internet for her," she said. "Single light female…"

"Seriously, Meena," I said, "What do *you* want?" Meena turned away from me, but I continued. "When Ammi wanted to find a husband for me—right before her first stroke," I said, "I had mixed feelings about arranged marriages, and I secretly hoped for a love marriage." I felt a twinge in my chest about all that had occurred between Yusuf and me—our dream that I would be a scholar and raise our children, and he would be a writer. "Sometimes I wish things had gone differently," I said aloud.

Suddenly Meena put her knife down.

"I do not want a love marriage," she said. "Iffat's sister had a love marriage. Then her parents threatened to kill her if she admitted that she had gone away with her husband willingly. Now the police are going to arrest her husband. It's a big problem. But I do not want to marry a stranger either." For a moment, Meena looked desperate. "What would Ammi say?"

"She would expect you to be yourself, Meena," I said. "And me—she would expect me to let it be known in the village that you are available. She would host a dinner party for each boy's family, and then you would decide."

"I might not want to stay in this town," Meena said quickly. "I might find someone in Lahore, and you don't know anyone there to invite for dinner."

"My, my, ladies," Faisah said. "I think that Meena already has her eye on someone in Lahore!" Meena burst into a wide smile.

"Yes!" she shouted. "Yes!" The three of us giggled, hugged, and danced around the kitchen—knives, onions, and all. My hip knocked a metal plate onto the floor. Clang! Meena picked it up. "His name is Zeshan Shaheed," she told us. "He's on our board of directors at the orphanage—our accountant, actually. A good family, a devout Muslim."

"And good-looking?" Faisah asked.

"Of course. Dark and handsome."

"You mean he's short." Faisah gave me the eye.

"No, he's not," began Meena defensively. "Well, he's not as tall as Abbu, or Amir, but he is tall enough for me, and that's all that matters. And he is sweet and loves music. He makes me laugh."

I recalled how Yusuf's family had rejected me, and I worried that Meena might have the same problem.

"You know, Abbu is now Kulraj Singh," I said. "He is not Ehtisham Mohammad—not a Muslim any longer. Will this boy's family accept that your father is a Sikh? No longer a Muslim?"

"A Sikh-a Muslim-a Sikh," said Faisah, "a Muslim sandwich."

When I called to invite Zeshan's family, his mother, Abida, was effusive.

"We would be delighted to come. When shall we do it? Tomorrow? Tonight?"

Later, in our sitting room, she grabbed my hands and looked into my eyes with such intensity I wished I had a shield. She jabbed her thick elbow into my arm to get my attention, and her breath smelled like last night's lamb.

"I can see that Meena loves Zeshan," Abida said, pausing. "But I worry that if he is in love with his wife, he will become brokenhearted, like all the men in my family. My father—every New Year's he cries for the loss of his wife. So long ago! And my uncle—married only a year ago, now his wife flirts with other men! Love causes such heartache."

I nodded politely and leaned away. I wondered if Abida thought that Meena would be unfaithful to Zeshan, or that she would die young.

"I must admit that I have considered a number of young ladies for Zeshan, but until I met your sister"—she corrected herself—"your daughter—Meena—I was never certain any of them was right for him. Now I feel sure." Her eyes narrowed as she drew close to me again. "I want you to know that my family has tolerant religious attitudes. In fact, my husband's grandfather is an Ahmadi. As for us, we are devout Muslims, but we have never wanted to impose our beliefs on others, not even on our own children. Surrender to the will of Allah must be voluntary and personal, don't you agree? But, of course," she added, her hand pinning my forearm with force, "Zeshan's wife and children must be Muslims."

"Of course," I said. "Islam is not an issue. We are Muslims. Only our father is a Sikh."

At first I thought that Abida's comments were intended to assure us that they were tolerant of Sikhism. But then I realized that it could be the other way around. She was revealing in an indirect way that Zeshan's great-grandfather was an Ahmadi, a fact that could create a problem for Meena. Ahmadis are illegal, declared so first by the mullahs and then by the Parliament. Zeshan's family would not be pure enough Muslims for Reshma and Mohammad. They would consider them revisionist heretics.

But, despite all the problems, I liked Zeshan's parents. I couldn't help it. They were outgoing people, laughed easily, and admired Meena. It looked like Zeshan had inherited his parents' liveliness. I could see it in the momentary gazes and private humor that he and Meena already shared. They emitted saturating devotion and desire. Yes, they would enjoy their lives together.

I have to admit, I envied them.

After the party I found Faisah ironing clothes on a folded towel she had spread on the floor in the women's quarter.

"I notice you are in a hurry to find a husband for Meena, but not for me," she said.

"That's because you *are* a hopeless case," I replied. I moved the electric cord away from the door. When I heard no comeback, I realized she might be serious. I sat on the bed we shared and watched her fold the still-warm kameez.

"Faisah, is there somebody I should know about?"

"No, not really. I'd like a family someday, but right now I have more than enough with my friends at work and the family here."

I noticed that she did not return the question to me. She had been a few years behind me in college when Yusuf went away, but she knew our story well. We had not spoken his name in years. No point in bringing it up now.

"I need to talk with you about my latest plan," I said. "It's crazy, probably dangerous, perhaps even illegal. I need your help."

She unplugged the iron and gave me her full attention.

"And don't try to talk me out of it, because I've made up my mind. But I may need a good lawyer before I'm finished."

How prophetic my statement turned out to be! I told Faisah about Bilqis and about meeting Khanum on the train and my decision to help her escape. Faisah was full of questions.

"She's married, right? Not just living with this man?"

"She said she was married, but who knows?"

"She's locked in the house all day?"

"I think so. Maybe."

"So how are you going to get into the house without committing a crime?"

"I hadn't thought of that. I imagine the servants will let me in."

"And what if she takes something of value with her and later you are caught? How will you defend against accomplice charges?"

I had the feeling Faisah was just warming up with the what-ifs. I cut her questions short.

"What is the worst that could happen?"

"In Balochistan? Oh, they might tie horses to your limbs and ride away in the four directions."

"Faisah!"

"It could happen, Baji. More likely, they catch you, register a complaint of theft, jail you indefinitely, and hang you for some religious crime you've never heard of." She looked me in the eye. "Oh, and this would be after they stripped and stoned Khanum publicly."

Sometimes Faisah exaggerated her arguments, but I realized what she was telling me contained some truth. Stoning still occurred in places like Balochistan.

"I won't let fear stop me anymore, Faisah. I promised Khanum, I promised myself, with Allah as my witness—I am so sick of coming into the lives of women when they are dead or maimed. I want to do something to prevent it."

"I understand, believe me, I do," Faisah said. "But I can think of only one way you could do it, if you want my advice." She had that conspiratorial tone again. I knew I could count on her to have a foolproof scheme.

"What is it?" I asked. Then Faisah leaned forward and whispered, "Take me with you."

I found Abbu in the courtyard, transplanting herbs. The temperature was dropping as light winds tussled with the heat of the day. Little gusts lifted the limbs of the neem tree from time to time, and they bounced up and down. Abbu knelt next to an old pushcart he had filled with sprouted cuttings. I shook the balls of dirt that clung to the roots and handed them to him one by one.

"I have been thinking about the direction you see your life taking, Uji," he said. "It worries me if you try to do this thing—to rescue this woman." He turned to me. Tears were melding along the sill of his lower eyelids. "Still, if you and Faisah do this together, I believe you will be more careful—having responsibility not only for yourself and for this woman, but also for each other. I have tried to clear my mind so I can best advise you, but in the end, I have no advice. How can I? You know more about what you are doing, and about what God wants for you. You are a grown woman now."

Abbu speaking that fact aloud gave it power.

My fingers circled the edges of a basil leaf. He continued digging with a hand tool, placing the young beings into the earth, spreading the tendrils of their roots, and tapping the dirt around them. I took a tin can to collect rainwater that he saved in barrels solely for this purpose. I sprinkled each sprout.

"Many years ago when you and Faisah first visited Central Prison . . . remember that? In Karachi?"

I nodded.

"I tasted then the same dread that I taste now, thinking of what you want to do and why. And my response is the same: the Guru asks for our heads in order to recognize those persons destined to live like lions, an army that serves both the human and the divine."

"I am angry, Abbu," I said. "How can God abandon people the way He does?" Abbu stopped his digging and looked up again.

"Or do people abandon God?" He went back to digging. "It is no different now than it was in the time of the Guru. We were a clinging, fearful people then—like this woman on the train. Back then, it was soldiers that were needed, and so the Khalsa emerged. Today I believe it is people like you and Faisah who are the lions."

"Lions?" I asked.

"Many turn away from the suffering they see, but you and Faisah do not. What is divine in you keeps calling you to this path. Can I oppose what God wills?"

We stood facing each other in our muddy clothes. The sun was low and the heat had won its skirmish with the wind. It settled into the bricks under our bare feet. Finally Abbu put his hands on my head.

"You and Faisah have my blessing. Lions walk with God."

The night before we left for Balochistan was cold, and the dogs yapped and yipped. I lay awake listening to the wild geese squawking from the trash pond. The sound became one disturbing cry as hundreds of birds joined the din. What was it? Had the dogs swum through the icy water to grab a weak bird by the neck? Were the others watching, terrorized?

After a while the distress calls stopped. I nestled into the fleece and tried to sleep, but I could not. I watched darkness withdraw from the ceiling and light begin its entry. I took a last look at the sunflower field, now watery gray in the shade of the world before dawn. The sky paled to lavender and the color held. When the arc of the sun appeared, its rays shot to the apex of the sky—yellow, orange and, for just a moment, everything turned blood red.

I shook Faisah.

"It's time to go."

Abbu had hired a neighbor named Kramot to drive us to Rakhni, telling him only that we were going to visit a cousin there and we would take her to the nearby train station.

Faisah continued to worry. "What if Khanum turns against us and claims we kidnapped her? What if someone notifies the husband? What if we are followed?"

Finally, I shouted at her. "I can't answer all your questions!"

She glared back at me. "OK. But we'll have to leave Multan early tomorrow morning," she said. "We have to get there by three o'clock."

I let her have the last word.

The plans were for Kramot to drive Khanum and me to the train station in Rajanpur, then he and Faisah would return to Nankana Sahib. I would transfer to the Matli bus at Hyderabad, and Khanum would continue by train to Karachi where Robina would meet her. My sweet Robina! We started our first school together years earlier when my mother was still alive.

"Always room for one more at our place. We'll just add another cup of flour to the chapati," Robina had said when I telephoned her about Khanum. "But who is this girl?"

"Sometimes it's best not to ask too many questions," I replied.

"This isn't somebody in trouble with the police, is it?"

"No, nothing like that," I said. "She just needs to start over, and that's all I can say about it. Best to let her do her own explaining. Just tell the others she is a friend of mine. That's the truth."

"OK, Baji, but how will I know her?"

"She will be wearing a bright orange and pink dupatta. She's young, Robina, about seventeen, and she's scared."

Robina did not hestitate. "Don't worry. We'll find her at the station and take good care of her, at least for a while. She'll have to help out around here and find her own way."

Faisah and I rode in the backseat with the windows open, our legs curled under us, the floor full of bags and boxes. The wind flattened Faisah's hair against her head. I took the jaws of a clip to mine, fastened it at the back of my neck, and wrapped up in my dupatta. We nibbled spiced potatoes and drank a flask of cold chai.

"OK, Baji," Faisah said to me in an undertone so Kramot could not hear. "Remember what we said last night?" She inhaled, "To review. What are the three basic rules?" She began to count them on her fingers as I answered.

"Number 1, we tell no one," I recited. "Number 2, we do nothing illegal." I stopped. I couldn't think of what number 3 was.

"Number 3, we don't get caught," she said aloud, smacking the side of my head. "The most important rule!"

It was half past noon when we entered Multan—that great blue-and-white-tiled city, the graveyard of imperial elephants—a city so old that historians still debate when it was founded. Kramot reached under the visor for a cassette and pushed it into the tape player. The alternating male and female voices of pop music sang out in a high pitch.

"Perhaps we should talk about rule number 4. What we do if we are caught," Faisah said.

"You're the lawyer. You can talk us out of it."

"Maybe. But what if I cannot?"

"What are you suggesting?" I asked, knowing that Faisah always had answers to her own questions.

"Maybe we should carry guns," Faisah whispered.

I shook my head. "I can't even drive a car and you want me to use a gun? Too dangerous. I wouldn't know how. And what would Abbu say?"

But Faisah tried to convince me.

"Well, first of all, if we are going to go on rescues like this one, we have to learn how to use a gun and how to drive. We could find ourselves in an isolated place, overpowered by a gang, or . . ."

I thought about how Abbu had said we were like soldiers, and indeed, in a way, we were placing ourselves in a war zone.

"So, do *you* know how to use a gun?" I asked Faisah.

"No," she admitted sheepishly. "But Amir taught me a little karate to use if a man comes at me!" Suddenly she poked her right knee in the air to show me the move she meant.

Embarrassed, I checked the mirror to see if Kramot had been watching, but his eyelids looked nearly closed, lulled by music. I was surprised that Amir would show Faisah such a move. Good for Amir, I thought. Every lion needs a few tricks.

That night we stayed with friends in Multan. At dawn we found Kramot on his knees in prayer. His clothes were wrinkled from sleeping in the car.

The highway to Rakhni became invisible in the powdery dust, and we rolled the windows up, even though the air was stifling. The rugged peaks at the Balochistan border looked like photographs of the moon, a place suspended in space and time. A long line of human history lay buried in the Makran desert, the ancient trade route between the Indus and the Euphrates civilizations. They say the Baloch language has one hundred words for camel.

Ours was the only vehicle on the strip of road that stretched ahead, except for an armed policeman on a motorbike speeding past in the opposite direction. When we came to a checkpoint, Kramot slowed the car.

"It's the tribal police," said Faisah, her elbow jabbing my upper arm. "I speak a little Balochi. Let me do the talking."

"As you wish," said Kramot.

Two men approached the car. AK-47s hung from their shoulders.

"Assalam aleikum," said the dark stranger with a thick moustache and bright teeth. His turban was wild and dirty. Kramot nodded in reply and Faisah lowered her window.

"Waleikum salaam," replied Faisah, keeping her eyes down, pulling her dupatta across her face.

"You are on the road alone?" he asked.

"Our cousin is with us," she replied, indicating Kramot.

"Where are your husbands?"

"We are meeting them in Rakhni. They are staying with family there."

"Your relative's name?" asked the man. Faisah's face went blank. Apparently she had forgotten.

"Wazir Hashmi," I spoke up. The guards looked at each other.

"We know him," he said. "We will escort you."

He moved the tail of his turban aside and peered into the car. We tried to decline his offer, but he insisted as only a Balochi can. Exquisite hospitality is their trademark, is it not? The matter was settled—we were indeed their guests. The two men mounted their motorbikes, one pulling in front of us and one tailing behind.

"You really talked our way out of that one," I said.

Faisah smirked, saying "Just hope they don't insist on meeting our husbands."

The hills surrounding Rakhni were barren. At the town's edge, acres of cattle, goats, and sheep were stuffed into pens. The animals moved together slowly like a distant ocean wave.

As Kramot wove the Toyota through the back streets, prayers blared through the loud speaker. Soon the tribal police motorbikes sputtered up to a solid double-wide metal gate, where a uniformed guard stepped through the human-sized door cut into it. The old man wore a military cap and had a pistol on his hip. He marched up to the motorcycle men and clicked his heels. They exchanged salaams.

"State your business."

"The home of Wazir Hashmi?" the policeman asked.

"Yes, Sir."

"Two aunties to see the family." He handed my calling card to the guard, who pulled open the wide gate and stood at attention while the police circled the courtyard and exited. Soon a servant returned with my calling card in hand.

"Please enter, Bibis," the woman said, bowing. When her fist opened to point the way, I saw that her fingers were as dark and thin as plum twigs. We removed our sandals and stepped onto cool marble. My feet shivered with pleasure. A hallway led to an interior courtyard surrounded by a filigreed portico. Intricate wall hangings and embroideries embedded with precious stones complemented the Mediterranean furniture and Persian carpets.

Khanum approached us from the portico, her shawl floating behind her like a ghost.

"Assalam aleikum," she said. I thought I could hear her effort to sound normal in front of the servants.

"Waleikum salaam," Faisah and I replied in unison. Our voices sounded like childish singsong, and suddenly the farce felt silly. I hugged Khanum and kissed her cheeks.

"We came without calling because we have urgent news," I said at once, while the servant was still present. "Sad news, really. Grandmother took ill during our return from Lahore. We took her to Central Hospital. She is asking for you and Wazir."

Khanum understood the ruse at once.

"Yes, of course," she said. "I will call Wazir to ask him to meet us there. I know how much he adores his grandmother's sister. Rest here while I gather my things." Without looking at them, she snapped her fingers in the direction of her servants. "Joseph will bring you some refreshments."

Faisah and I sat in identical carved mahogany chairs. We devoured the lemonade and all the food they brought us—sugared dates, mango slices, and balls of yellow almond paste rolled in coconut. I wrapped some in a napkin for Kramot. I wondered how seventeen-year old Khanum had learned her mistress role so completely and how she would ever adjust to Karachi. Outside the open window, in the branches of a lemon tree, a mynah bird let out a single shriek.

"Is that bird trying to warn us?" Faisah said, tapping her index finger on the arm of the chair.

I worried, too. It was getting late, and we had to catch the evening train. Women never travel on the road after dark, and we did not want to attract attention or trouble. Soon I heard Khanum's slippers shuffling against the tiles. She had changed into a simple dark cotton shalwar kameez and carried only a shoulder bag and a shawl.

"I spoke to Wazir. He says I should go with you now and he will join us at the hospital after his meeting."

As she stepped out the front door, I could hear birds chattering their good-byes. The guard opened the rear car door for her automatically. I sat next to Khanum, while Faisah climbed into the front seat next to Kramot. She held the dupatta across the bottom of her face. Staring at a vacant point in the distance, the guard saluted as we rolled through the gate. In an instant the Toyota turned the corner and we entered the anonymity of a traffic circle. Khanum squeezed my calling card back into my hand and did not let go.

"Fortunately, no one around here reads Urdu," she said, pointing to the card. "But you shouldn't have risked it."

"I didn't want to tell the servant my name," I said.

"True." She nodded. "They remember everything they hear."

Kramot threaded the car through the narrow streets and into the countryside toward the Punjab border.

"Mission accomplished?" asked Kramot innocently, his face looking at mine in the rearview mirror. I nodded and smiled behind my veil even though we could not relax yet.

"Quickly to the depot," I said, imagining that Satan had caught our scents. Who knew where Khanum's husband's relatives might be, or the extent of their power? Or their desire for revenge? Once we reentered Punjab, they could follow us, but it was less likely we would be found.

It was dusk. A thin layer of fuschia spread across the cloudless horizon. Headlamps of trucks shone on one another's metallic art, lighting up the highway. I heard the evening call: La illaha illa Allah Mohammad rasul Allah. *There is no God but God and Mohammad is His Prophet.*

Next to me Khanum's body hardened, and I feared she was beginning to crack. I looked to Faisah for support, but she had fallen asleep. Her head leaned against the doorjamb.

"Faster," I said to Kramot. "We must not miss that train."

"I'll never get away with this," Khanum whispered. "I belong to my husband."

"Shh!" I said. There could be no going back.

"I have shamed his family—dishonored him," she said. "There is still time to go back."

Faisah turned to us. Her eyes widened. I shook my head and kept hold of Khanum's hand.

At the Rajanpur station, we got out of the Toyota, careful not to speak in front of Kramot about where Khanum was going or why.

Tell no one.

When we approached the conductor in the station, Khanum squeezed my arm. I turned to see the most terrified face I have ever known.

"What is it?" I asked.

"Baji, should I do this thing?" she asked in fast, shallow breaths.

"It is already done," I said. "God is with us." I sounded more pious than I felt, pretending I was Abbu speaking with Sikh confidence. "The matter is settled." I watched her inhale my determination.

"I will not return to my husband's home; I am a widow. I will not return to the hills of Balochistan; I am an orphan," she said. "Now I will take care of myself."

Later, on the train, Khanum told me how she had prepared for that day, and how she separated her mind from her body when her husband used her in his ways.

"I lay on the sticky sheets reciting a mantra I invented," she said. "Aquamarine, emeralds, garnet, jade, lapis-lazuli, pearls, rubies, topaz, tourmaline. I put the precious words in alphabetical order, reversed them, then recited each letter of the word, and hummed them silently. I imagined colored crystals with light flowing through them—reds and blues, greens and white, all the shades of yellow and orange. Sometimes I pictured myself with plastic eye protectors, bending over an electric drill under a high intensity lamp. I cut jewels into hundreds of pieces of every size and shape. Some I placed into gold settings, using tweezers, or my fingers, or holding them in my mouth until they were hot, and releasing each gem, one by one, onto a pure white cloth, as if they were the souls of babies who were too good to be born. I named them: Lapis Lazuli, Pearl, Ruby, Topaz, and Tourmaline."

By day Khanum had been studying how to distinguish fake from genuine gems. Secretly she had removed and replaced throughout his house every precious stone in her husband's tapestry collection. Some gems she wrapped in cloth, and they became buttons for her purse. Others she sewed into the hem of her clothes and along the border of her shawl. On the day that I arrived, she had swallowed a small handful of pearls.

She showed me the bruises and burns on the inside of her arms. I remember the bitterness she spoke as she smiled.

"It does not matter to me now," she said. "His stink. I will never smell it again."

By the time the train slowed in Hyderabad, where we would go our separate ways—Khanum on the train to Karachi, I on the bus to Matli—we had constructed a credible past for her.

"And my future?" she wondered. I reminded her that she had told me on the train that she wanted to be a teacher.

"Talk to Robina. It is always difficult keeping women as teachers, so she may want to train and hire you." I pulled a bright pink and orange dupatta from my bag and placed it on her lap. "In Sindh they say that if you give a shawl to a woman, she is forever your sister and you have the right to protect her." I wrapped the dupatta around her neck. "I have mailed one just like this one to Robina. That is how you will find each other."

2

Adiala Prison, 1996

The evening call to prayer echoed through the narrow streets of old Lahore. Then Ujala knew that outside the prison walls her father and her brother were cross-legged on their prayer mats. And they were not alone. University students had spray-painted dupattas, transforming them into protest banners. "Free Baji!" they demanded in Urdu, Punjabi, and English. Throughout the evening a few protesters came and went. By midnight Ujala was asleep in her cell, and outside the square was deserted—except for one lean, gray-bearded Sikh in a white turban. Kulraj Singh kept watch all night long, until Meena arrived in the morning to take his place. Over the weeks, the size of the protest grew. By the time Faisah returned from New York, the press reported that fifty people were regularly present at Adiala Square.

Ujala complained when she saw Faisah enter the interview room. "I thought you would never get here."

"Baji!" murmured Faisah, nestling her face into her sister's shoulder.

A sergeant-guard assigned to observe their meeting leaned against the wall, dialed her mobile phone, and turned away. The sisters held hands across the table.

"I guess you could say I forgot the three rules," Ujala said at last. Faisah squinted.

"What?"

"Remember rule number 3?"

Faisah wrinkled her nose.

"Don't get caught!" said Ujala.

"Oh, right. Right," said Faisah. She realized she would have to be the ballast to Baji's rising energy. Just as Baji would lift up her spirit when she was low. They had been doing this for each other all of their lives.

"Are you getting enough to eat?" Faisah asked. She thought Ujala looked gaunt. The prison-gray shalwar kameez was so thin that Faisah thought she could see Ujala's skin glowing through the cotton.

"I'm OK. No longer in solitary, thanks to Jabril," Ujala said.

"Good!" Faisah was looking for any reason to reassure her sister, whose legal situation she had concluded was close to hopeless. "But what do you mean, exactly, that you forgot the three rules?"

Ujala smirked. It was fun to play with Faisah again, even if the stakes were so high.

"Well . . . I kept rule number 1. I told no one about taking the girl out of Chitral—except you, of course. And I kept rule number 2—I did nothing illegal. I merely defended myself from an acid attack. They tell me he has the scars on his hands from the burn, so he can't deny it—"

Faisah interrupted. "—It may be forbidden under Shariah, you know that—"

"But I'm not charged under Shariah."

"Not yet," Faisah said. "Yep. Rule number 3 is the one you broke. You got caught." She looked worried.

Ujala did not like that Faisah's tone all of a sudden had become solemn. "Any more questions for me, Counselor?" she asked. Ujala slipped the edges of her dupatta behind her ears and shifted the conversation. The sergeant-guard made another phone call. "I want to hear about New York."

"New York was extraordinary," Faisah began. "We were asked

to join a global leadership planning session—NGOs like Amnesty and the U.N. are starting to define violence against women as a valid human rights issue—right up there on the list with jailed journalists and political prisoners. The argument goes that violence is the one issue that unites women everywhere."

"It doesn't take Americans to tell us that," Ujala said. She worried that maybe Faisah was moving on without her. Forgetting Pakistan, the way Yusuf had.

"Of course it doesn't," Faisah said, squeezing Ujala's hand. "But they want to fund our media project—a radio network to link Central and South Asian women's NGOs—in Singapore, Delhi, even Katmandu." Faisah's voice came alive. "Baji, you don't realize it, but you are becoming a celebrity. They asked about you in New York. We are getting calls and letters every day—from health care workers, shelters, legal aid, women's resource centers, even the media. Wanting to know what is going on and how to help."

Ujala was not excited by her notoriety. This talk of politics seemed distant, irrelevant, counterproductive even. When she spoke, her voice was controlled.

"Faisah, remember how Ammi said that in the late seventies, when General Zia promulgated Hudood Ordinances, nobody resisted it because everyone's attention was diverted to Bhutto's murder trial?"

Faisah nodded. "Go on."

"Well, people become fascinated by the dramas of trials. We can't make the same mistake now." Ujala untwisted their hands, and a fresh smile spread across Faisah's face.

"At least we can expose the government in the press."

"And the press doesn't blow with the political winds?"

"When they learn how you rescued an innocent girl and how someone then tried to burn you with acid—well, everyone loves a hero, you know, and everyone loves a victim."

"For a while, they do."

"It's only the tabloids that are hostile—" said Faisah. She slowed down. She scratched her nose.

"I know," said Ujala. "I'm the schoolteacher with loose morals, a rowdy female who travels alone around Pakistan, packing a gun and hating men . . . It's a cowboy, or should I say, cowgirl image, Faisah." She laughed, imagining herself dressed like a Texan.

Now Faisah was annoyed by Ujala's cavalier attitude.

"Not so funny, Baji. The image of a violent, faithless teacher infiltrating the schools and corrupting girls strikes a fearful chord—and not only in conservative quarters."

"People distort facts to fit their own versions of reality," Ujala said. "What can we do?" She was tired of this dead-end conversation, but Faisah continued.

"Well, Amir is setting up our website, so we can get our version of events out in the public." She spoke quickly, before Ujala could protest. "And I found someone in New York who wants to help—it's Yusuf, Baji," Faisah blurted out. The back of Faisah's hand swept toward the door. "Yusuf Salman—he's right outside."

Ujala twisted her neck and stared at the door.

"And he wants to see you."

Ujala swallowed hard. *Yusuf?*

"Not now. Tell him I can't see him now, Faisah. I just can't. It has been so long, and I'm not ready. Just look at me—ugly clothes, my hair unwashed, even my fingernails are a mess. It's been more than ten years since we have set eyes on each other. I just can't."

Ujala's insecurities always surprised Faisah. She looked at her older sister and saw a beautiful dark woman—thin, yes, but with clear eyes, color in her cheeks, and shining shoulder-length black hair. She really doesn't know how lovely she is, Faisah realized.

"The clothes are bad, Baji, but for goodness sake, this is prison. And you—you look simply wonderful. In fact, you look better than I've seen you look in years."

"OK. I'm being neurotic, but indulge me, will you? Tell him that I do want to see him—next Friday. Tell him I'm not allowed visitors today—only lawyers—which is true, by the way."

The guard pointed to her wristwatch. It was time for Ujala to return to Rahima Mai's office. Faisah bent over and reached into her bag.

"Oh," she said, "I almost forgot. Yusuf asked me to give this to you. He said you would understand what it means."

She handed Ujala an ordinary orange.

"I am ashamed of Pakistan's failures as a nation, its pretentious and cruel customs, and its ruthless dictators," Yusuf Salman wrote in his departing *New York Times* commentary. "I hoped for a return to the Constitution of 1973, but now—my disillusionment is complete. The imprisonment of Baji Ujala is Pakistan's final betrayal."

Before the *Times* newspaper truck had dropped off the last copy of the final edition at the end of the line somewhere in Brooklyn, Yusuf was onboard a flight from JFK to the other side of the world—Islamabad. He took out his spiral pad and began to make notes:

Islamabad—where Islam abides, a city with one foot planted in the past, one stretching into the future.

White and spacious, shady boulevards, classic government buildings, gardens teeming with hibiscus and flaming jacaranda.

Heavy traffic, littered bazaars, unsightly slums kept apart from the showcase that is Islamabad.

In Lahore Yusuf was at loose ends, having to wait seven days before seeing Ujala. At the Women's Radio Network office, Meena was producing a program. She handed Yusuf a tape recorder and microphone and said, "Here. Make yourself useful. I've arranged for an interview with Rahima Mai, Women's Prison Supervisor— so far she has been quite helpful. At least it will get you closer to Baji."

At Adiala, Rahima Mai led Yusuf up the exterior staircase to a security platform. Yusuf noticed that she had difficulty climbing. She put both feet on each step before she moved them one by one to the next. The effect slowed them down, so she stepped aside, as if comfortable doing so, to let Yusuf pass. From the first landing he got a good look at this women's supervisor. There was a little pink in those cheeks—perhaps from the exertion of climbing— and a slight glint in those brown eyes. Her hair was cut short, and she was well-nourished. She smiled at him as she approached the landing, pleased that the press was interested in the women's prison. Together they viewed the interior courtyard, the center of Adiala's life.

"Virtually all of these women in here have been abused by someone," she said. "And those who are here for family offenses under Shariah, they are not really criminals. They may have run away with a neighbor, or killed their husbands, but they give us no trouble."

She pointed to a makeshift classroom in one section of the open area.

"Baji's volunteers are reestablishing our school programs—one for the women and one for the children," she said. "The prison has no funds for programs."

"So when Baji leaves, something will remain of what she has started?" Yusuf asked. It was the first time he'd referred to Ujala aloud as Baji, as everyone was now doing.

"*If* she leaves," Rahima Mai replied. Her eyes stared at the wall.

"Of course she will leave," said Yusuf. "Look at the public protests. And they have no evidence."

"Who knows what evidence they have?" Rahima Mai said, raising her eyebrows.

Yusuf saw her point.

"And," Rahima Mai continued, "protests could affect the outcome either way, could they not?" She glanced at his tape recorder and whispered, "Bringing volunteers inside could backfire, too."

"So which is she? Coconspirator, or government functionary?" Yusuf asked Meena when he returned to the radio station. But Meena was too busy to listen. She was poring over newspaper clippings that littered the room. She motioned him away while she finished what she was doing. As he waited, Yusuf examined the snapshots that covered the office walls. Photos of lawyers, writers, human rights workers in groups of three or four, each one posing, looking young, serious, committed. He was surprised how often Benazir Bhutto's creamy complexion appeared in the photos.

And I wonder what Benazir is up to these days? he thought. "What has Benazir done for women lately?" he asked aloud. Meena stood up and turned her attention to him.

"You asked if she was a coconspirator or government functionary? Who? Rahima Mai or Benazir?" She smiled at Yusuf, the Pakistani with the American accent who might have been her brother-in-law.

"Both," they said in unison.

"Benazir ultimately will be loyal to the ruling class from which she comes," said Yusuf. He wanted Meena to know his political stance. He wanted to impress her, the girl who might have been his sister-in-law. "Rahima Mai will be loyal to those who sign her paycheck."

"Maybe," Meena said, returning to her chair and to the clippings. "But Abbu says that God's will always prevails, it is just that we don't have His view, so how can we know what His will is? What would you say is God's class interest?"

Yusuf pressed his lips together.

"Intriguing question," was all he could say, but he wanted to scream. All this talk about God, he thought. Allah—the main character in the movie that is Pakistan. I'll have to get used to it again.

When Saturday arrived, Yusuf left his Levis in the closet and dressed like a Pakistani, in a white shalwar kameez and crocheted prayer cap. And when Ujala opened the door of the interview room, he was at the table wiping his wire-rimmed glasses with a handkerchief. He looked up at her smile, and saw the familiar gap between her front teeth.

"Assalam aleikum," she said, touching the back of the metal folding chair across from him. He grinned.

"And peace to you also," he replied. "My eyes are so happy to be looking at you again, Uji. Diamond happy."

Ujala's blood rushed through its vessels as if it could not decide where to go. She sat at the table thinking, here is Yusuf with his winning ways, already showing touches of silver in his hair.

"I wish I could hold your hand," he said.

Ujala blushed and held his gaze.

Yusuf thought she was even more beautiful now in these plain surroundings. Her dark hair fell to her shoulders, thick and shining, covered by a simple white dupatta. She looked feverish and saintly, like an ancient Sufi. He saw in her eyes the spark of fervor she carried for those she loved.

But Ujala was neither saint nor mystic. She could not stop looking at him. She said, "You look so mature, so elegant . . . so . . . so Pakistani." They laughed, and relaxed. Yusuf leaned back, tilting the legs of the wooden chair.

"Faisah has been telling me about your work, Uji—about everyone's work here in the trenches, while I have been safely ensconced in the U.S. I feel cowardly when I think of the many risks you have taken. You must tell me what I can do to be of use."

"If you've been talking to Faisah, I am sure she has given you assignments already. Or if she hasn't, someone soon will."

"Of course they have," he laughed. "Meena put me to work right away."

"Doing—?"

"Interviewing 'collaterals' to your story—the side people." He grimaced. It was difficult to believe that his Uji had become the story, was becoming an international celebrity, an icon for human rights. "It was not difficult. I've done some radio interviewing in the States. The recording equipment here is quite good." He did not know what she wanted to know, or if he should say what he wanted to say. He just kept talking. "I interviewed the women's prison supervisor the other day."

"Rahima Mai?"

He nodded. Ujala rolled her eyes. Now Rahima Mai would figure out who this Yusuf is to her.

"There is something you could do, Yusuf. I have been writing letters, but I cannot get them out. But, since you are a male and a reporter, they probably won't search you for contraband. But they might. That's the risk."

"Never mind that. I'll do it," he said.

"There is a letter in my pocket," she said. She maintained her focus on his face as she spoke. "When I stand up to leave the room—"

"Don't leave yet," he said. He could not get enough of looking at her.

"No, not now, but when I stand to leave, drop your book and papers as if by accident, and I will drop the letter at the same time. You can pick the letter up with your things. Take it to Faisah—to use on the radio, or the website, or however she likes."

Yusuf beamed.

"I love the intrigue," he said playfully.

She could see that he did not fully appreciate the perils involved. "But, Yusuf, be careful. This could be dangerous. This is real."

"Of course," he said. "I can be so blind."

"Blind?" she asked. "Better to be dumb, but keep your eyes open. See everything, but tell no one you have done this—there is no need to."

Tell no one.

"I can see you are used to plotting," he said, picking at the edges of his papers.

"We have to be."

"Yes, it is *we* now, isn't it, Uji? I mean Meena, Faisah, all of us." He paused. "But you in prison, Uji. I just can't get used to it. We will get you out of here. We will."

"I am counting on that," she said. Then she spoke the words she had spent all week gathering. "Yusuf," she began, loving the pleasure of speaking his name aloud, "so often I have wondered if you were living the life that we had planned for London." He looked away as she continued. "And if you were living it without me, then who were you living it with?"

Less than a second, only one heartbeat, less than a breath passed between her question and his response. In that moment, he flashed on the knowledge that the mistakes he had made in his life had been mistakes of missed moments, of not realizing what was rare until it was gone, or had become ordinary. He kept at bay others who wanted to be close to him. He failed to acknowledge intimacies that occurred. He had not been without offers, but he continued waiting, postponing, considering, evaluating, holding back, wanting something else, something more, wondering about the quality of the offers made to him. He recognized in the question Ujala was asking him, in its simplicity and truth, that his procrastination had come to an end. She was not trying to trap him or claim his banner for her own. This was not the usual power struggle. This was love.

"And I wondered about you, too, Uji," he replied, because it was the most simple and true statement in his heart. He slowed down to listen to what he would say next. "I lost track of your family after Clifton. I drove past your old home—it still has that purple bougainvillea over the front arch." They brought to mind together the place where they had last seen each other—outside of her family's home. "But you were not there," he said, and she heard a twinge in his voice. "The neighbors said you moved to Punjab, but they did not know where."

She was pleased. He had looked for her.

He swallowed the saliva in the back of his throat, adjusted his glasses, and rested his eyes again on her face. He said, "When I saw Bilal, he told me you were living with garbage-pickers somewhere outside of Hyderabad."

"Not exactly," Ujala said, "but close. We set up schools for the garbage-picking children there." She hesitated, wondering why he had stopped looking for her. "So, was it the children, the trip to Hyderabad, or was it the smell of garbage that kept you away?"

"I don't know, Uji. Maybe it was all three. I got a call from my editor, a new assignment, and I just stopped looking. I thought you would be married by now." Yusuf thought he saw her squirm, and he changed the subject.

"So Hyderabad is where you worked?"

"No," she said. But she was not squirming. "I lived in interior Sindh—Matli—for most of the time. Then I was in the Northwest Frontier, in Chitral. But now I am determined to stay close to home."

"Pretty independent, huh?"

She nodded. "I have learned to do without anyone's help. I enjoy the support of my family and friends, and . . ." She hesitated, shaking her head. "But Yusuf, my body has begun to ache for children. I feel they are wanting to be born." The words spilled out of her mouth, and she was relieved. She wanted Yusuf to know what she was thinking. Life is too short to hide the cards in this game, she thought. If it frightens him, so be it.

But he was not frightened. Her mention of the urgings of her body excited him, and drew him close to her. He asked, "And why have you never married, Uji?"

"I made a promise to my mother, to God, to be a teacher. That has been my commitment, and it is like a marriage vow. And I've had no mother to arrange a marriage for me." She looked at her hands in her lap. She did not want to be misunderstood. "Maybe I have just seen too much unhappiness between men and women."

Ujala hoped Yusuf would talk about himself, but he did not. He was waiting for her to answer his question. This time she was the one to move the conversation away.

"I'm not sure how much more time we have," she said at last, feeling disappointed and nervous.

"But you haven't asked me why I never married," Yusuf said. His tone had a challenge in it. She pressed her lips together. They felt as if they belonged to someone else.

"Tell me," she said.

"I almost married twice," he began. "One woman was an American friend of my sister. Another was a Pakistani I met in New York. But each time it came to setting a wedding date, I could not go through with it. Then I became afraid to visit Karachi because my mother might have arranged something for me with the daughter of one of her friends. Maybe I'm not the marrying kind. Maybe I'm an emotional coward. Maybe I just never could forget you."

"Time's up," the guard said. They both eyed her in shock. Her look told them she had been listening in. But Ujala no longer cared. She had not realized how much she had longed for this conversation.

"Oh, I brought you something," he said. He reached into his pack and handed her a twig from a lemon tree. It had two tiny lemon knobs attached.

She held it in her hand. "My mother always said that lemons . . ."

" . . . are oranges God created for those whose sweetness is a lie," said Yusuf, completing her thought. "I never forgot. It is why I sent you an orange. You will have to decide if this new fruit is delicious or tart, the truth or a lie."As the guard moved in their direction, Yusuf's arm swept his papers off the table and onto the floor.

"Tsk! I am so clumsy," he said, bending down to pick up his things.

"I met an old friend of yours," Rahima Mai said later that evening. She and Ujala were working late on the budget for the head office. "Yusuf Salman."

Ujala put her hands to her reddening face.

"So, he is the one!" Rahima Mai smiled. "The husband-to-be that got away?"

"Yes, Madam."

"Nice," Rahima Mai said. "Very nice." In fact, she was not so sure Yusuf was nice enough. Who knows what this young man is after? she thought. Time will tell.

Ujala was unruffled. So what if Rahima Mai knows who Yusuf is? she thought. In prison she was becoming free of the need to outsmart, stay a step ahead, be clever. In a way it pleased her that Rahima Mai was meeting the characters in her story. Ujala sniffed the air.

"Masala," she said.

"And I brought channa and saag paneer," said Rahima Mai. "Get yourself a plate." Rahima Mai unwrapped the cotton cloth she had tied around the two pots and began to stir the vegetables.

"Shukriah, Baji." Ujala said thank you and accepted a small plate. For the first time she risked using a familiar term, Baji—respected elder sister, and Rahima Mai allowed it. They were sharing work, stories, meals—just like a family.

They sat in plastic chairs in a comfortable silence, tearing the chapati into bite-sized pieces. Ujala served milk tea, wondering what Rahima Mai would ask next. She did not want the question to be about Yusuf, so she continued her story without waiting to be asked.

◆ ◆ ◆

A surprise was waiting for me after I left Khanum on the train and returned to Matli. While I was away, a former student, Taslima Rashad, had arrived at the school by bus from Jacobabad with her two young sons. I had not seen Taslima in many years, but she was a student I remembered well—a high-spirited beauty whose antics would send the other girls into fits of giggling.

Taslima had always been smooth-skinned and immaculate, but now her face was pockmarked and her dupatta was wrinkled, and the cloth's sunflower print had faded. She looked worried. Several years before, she had married a bad-tempered cousin. In a fit of anger, while she was pregnant, he had kicked her down the stairs. Three times Taslima had left him and returned to her mother's home with the children. But the third time, just when she was wanting out from under her mother's control and was preparing to return again to Rashad, he called and told her not to come back.

"He said he did not want me as his wife anymore," Taslima said. She spoke very fast. "He wanted a divorce, which made me happy. But our mothers, who are sisters, could not bear the shame of a divorce in the family. So we remained married and I lived with my parents. I was so lost and lonely. I could not return to him and I could not marry another. I was trapped."

Taslima tucked a strand of hair behind her ear.

"And the children?" I asked.

"My boys are suffering, too—nervous, not sleeping well. In Jacobabad they went back and forth between Rashad and me. He tells them to spy on me, then after they do, they feel they have to lie to me about it, which they do, but they end up telling me the truth, which they later admit to their father, and then he punishes them for telling me the truth. They are caught in the cross fire."

She wrung her hands like an old woman.

"I know I can be honest with you, Baji," she said. "After a time, I fell in love with a boy I have known since childhood—Ayman. He wants to marry me, but now my parents tell me that if I try to get a divorce so that I can marry Ayman, they will kill me. And they mean it." She searched my eyes to see if I believed her. "They have already threatened Ayman, and he has gone into hiding."

I was nervous about this Ayman. I wondered if he was hiding nearby.

"Baji, your sister is a lawyer. Perhaps she would help me?"

"I will ask her. But, Taslima, where is Ayman hiding?" Taslima had a pained expression on her face.

"I am sorry, Baji, but I cannot say. He told me to tell no one."

Faisah arranged for a lawyer in Hyderabad to meet Taslima the following Wednesday. After the meeting I met her at the bus station. Her two-year-old was sleeping on her shoulder. His arm tugged on her dupatta, exposing her long hair. She sat in the back of the car and spread the boy out across my lap like a doll. His eyes closed when she lay him down.

"Everything is going to be fine," she whispered. "Jina Awan is a knowledgeable lawyer and caring, too. She did not try to talk me into reconciling with Rashad, or moving back to Jacobabad. She said the courts there would have jurisdiction, and that I might have to go back there for the hearing."

Her eyes were dry and her voice rose.

"But I refuse to go back. It is too dangerous . . . I will have my life!"

She spoke as if she were having an argument with someone who was not there.

"Does Jina think Rashad will contest the divorce?"

"No. He wants the divorce. But the family is another matter. The grandmothers—they will want the boys, and they will want to shame me."

Taslima stroked Muzamal's damp forehead. She smiled for the first time since she had been in Matli. "But Jina called and arranged a settlement. I won't have to go back to Jacobabad. My mother will bring papers to Jina's office so I can sign them to make it official. And Jina has called a police official in Jacobabad who will review the papers to assure her that Rashad has already signed them. He told her that my family just wants me to be happy."

Taslima asked me to accompany her to Hyderabad. I was curious to meet the famous Jina Awan, and I was not disappointed. Dressed in a business-like tan shalwar kameez and white linen jacket, she had pleated her dupatta neatly and draped it over one shoulder. Her hair was long, dark, and straight, parted in the middle and pulled loosely into a knot at the nape of her neck. She had a streak of gray hair on one side of her head and wore large, square glasses. Her face was lovely without makeup, and her dark eyes lit up when I mentioned my sister, Faisah.

"That Faisah! What a lawyer!" Jina stood up dramatically. "I wish we had a thousand like her. A strong feminist—fundamentally committed." I imagined that I was getting a glimpse of Jina's courtroom style. "And I want to hear more about your literacy project in Matli," she said. She smiled as she lit a cigarette and exhaled out the corner of her mouth, directing the smoke away from us. "We can talk about it over dinner. Eh? A few colleagues will join us at my house later. I insist you stay with me."

Taslima's mother was late, and we were irritated and disappointed. Jina stood at her massive desk, flipping through her calendar book while she puffed on a Dunhill. Suddenly the door opened and a woman stood in the doorway. A bearded man appeared behind her, following the woman inside.

Taslima recognized them. She stepped backward toward the sofa. Fear was written on her face. Jina had seen it, too. It was Taslima's mother.

"This man, what is he doing here?" Jina demanded. "How did he get past the guards?" When Jina stood up, her chair spun on its wheels.

I began to panic. I felt as if my heart and my lungs were racing each other.

"My helper," Taslima's mother said. "I need assistance since I can't walk."

In the low, insistent tone of a person used to exerting authority, Jina instructed the woman—"Tell him to get out."

The woman did nothing.

Jina shouted, "Tell him to wait outside!" She buzzed her security guard again and again. We could hear the useless, distant hum.

"Assalam aleikum," the man said to Taslima, who was cowering on the sofa. He drew a pistol from his waistcoat and stood in front of her, taking aim with both hands. I did not move. I did not want to draw his fire. I wanted to disappear. In one unending second he squeezed the trigger and fired a bullet into Taslima's head. Then he stood there frozen, as if memorizing what he had done. Taslima lay twisted across the sofa, her head resting on a pillow embroidered with shards of mirrors. Her dupatta was pierced. A bloodless hole. On the other side of her head, pints and pints of blood began to pool on the upholstery.

"Yaqub!" Jina yelled to her security man. The name hung in the air like a cloud of gun smoke. We could hear scuffling and shouting outside the door, but no one dared open it. As Jina moved toward him, the gunman turned and fired again. Taslima's mother screamed, the door opened, and the woman disappeared through it imperceptibly. Two uniformed guards burst in with pistols drawn, and in the second they spent assessing the situation, the gunman found his next target.

"No!" I pleaded, but he grabbed me close, choking me with the crook of his arm while he backed away. The guards froze—eyes wide, hands at the ready. I heard rushing in the hall.

"Stand aside," Yaqub yelled to the guards. "Lower your weapons!"

The gunman pulled me into the hallway and down the back stairs. His muscles were like thick wire cables binding me.

"Leave me alone!" I said. "For the love of Allah, let me go!"

"Quiet!" he barked.

Then I heard Jina shouting, "Call an ambulance. Someone has been shot."

Jina was alive! All of my hope collected on that one fact. Jina was alive! If Jina could survive, I could survive. The gunman pulled me underneath the staircase and held the gun barrel to my head. He was squeezing the back of my neck with his left hand and gripping the pistol with his right.

At that moment my mind flashed on the day in my childhood

when Ammi had shown me the proper way to wring out a cloth.

"Not from the middle!" I could hear Ammi say. "Do it this way."

Ammi carried to the sink the sopping dishcloth I had been using to wipe the table. It dripped across the concrete floor. She put the tip ends into her fists and twisted and shortened the cloth at the same time. A flood of water was released with a flushing sound. Then she twisted and shortened the cloth again until her fists were almost touching, and it seemed a quart poured forth. Then Ammi gave me her happiest grin and did it one more time until the dishcloth would have cried out for mercy if it could have. She handed the knotted mess to me and I shook out a waterless, fresh cloth.

Recalling Ammi's victorious face, something inside of me rose up, like a fish arcs through a pool of calm. I gathered the tips of my dupatta bit by bit. The gunman and I could hear footsteps on the floor above us. As my dupatta slipped from my shoulders, I wrapped it twice around my fists. The moment he relaxed his grip to look around the corner, I bellowed like a cow in labor. In a flash I flipped the cloth over my head and wrapped it around his neck as if I were wringing steel. I shortened and twisted the dupatta and twisted and shortened it, and then wound it around his neck one more time. My fists pounded together, and my teeth sawed into to the bone of his wrist. He dropped the gun just as the policeman turned the corner and grabbed him.

I felt dizzy, elated, and more than pleased to leave the man on the floor with a pile of policemen stomping on him. What the police did not see was his pistol, the one that had probed my neck. I picked it up and ran back up the stairs to Jina's office, just in time to see the porters carrying Taslima's body away.

That evening forty people from the Human Rights Alliance crowded into Jina's house. Her wounded arm was in a sling. Men and women surrounded a large table, writing press releases and discussing strategies. They used their mobile phones to organize a protest march that would go from the hospital, where Taslima's body lay, to the provincial headquarters.

"You call the bar associations! I'll call the trade unionists! Asma can call the students!"

They pasted enlarged photographs of Taslima onto placards, assigned platform speakers, and practiced sound bites for the media. "Justice for Taslima! End police collaboration with honor crimes."

"We'll follow up with a petition to the provincial prosecutor," said Jina.

"Quick! Look at the television!" someone shouted and everyone crowded around.

"The parents of the deceased admitted their part in hiring the assassin," the newscaster was reporting. "And the arrested man confirmed it." A film clip showed the battered old man as he was put inside the police van. He shouted to the camera: "It is a father's right to kill his daughter if she disgraces his honor." The camera closed in on his twisted face. "The father was too sick to come to Hyderabad himself. As a believer, it was my duty."

"Oh, God!" said Jina. "The public will agree with him. The mullahs will back him, too. We have to send out a countermessage!" The possibility of suffering an honor crime is a seed sleeping inside every Pakistani, at whatever station.

They returned to their task, inspired by its importance, and by their own importance.

In Jacobabad, Taslima's husband enlisted his sons as his allies, taking them to his press conference to hear the Chamber of Commerce statement that the killing of their mother was justified by her disobedience.

"It is written," they said.

The mullahs marched in procession and damned Taslima as kari, black. They declared Jina Awan, kafir, an infidel, and issued a fatwa to kill her on sight. They condemned the Human Rights Alliance for leading daughters astray.

While the others ate biryani and drank tea late into the evening, I called Faisah.

"We have seen the news," she said, breathing hard into the phone. "You actually disarmed the gunman with your dupatta? Baji, is that true? Are you OK?"

"It is true, more or less. I'm shaky. And wish you were here. There will be a huge march tomorrow."

"Are you going?"

"Of course I'm going."

"What else can you do?" she asked. That was the question I had been asking myself: What else can I do?

"Faisah," I confided. "I could have stepped in front of that gun and stopped him, but I didn't. No one did. I hate myself that I could not protect Taslima . . ."

"Baji!" Faisah said. "Don't."

". . . and I could have killed him. When I had the chance, I wanted to choke him to death." I could recall every sensation of rage I experienced earlier that day. "And Faisah," I told her. "I'm keeping the gun."

"You should give it to them, Baji," Faisah said. Her tone sounded parental. "Give the gun to the police."

"Faisah, aren't you the one who said we should learn to fire a gun? Doesn't the scripture say an eye for an eye? Is it only men's eyes that deserve revenge? A woman's eyes mean nothing. A woman's teeth mean nothing. What would justice for Taslima be now? If the police won't even register a complaint against her parents, then exactly who is going to get justice for Taslima?"

"What are you saying, Baji?"

"They took her life right there in front of us, Faisah. They just walked into the room and took her whole life."

"Are you planning something?"

"I'm planning justice for Taslima."

"Baji, come home. Leave Sindh and come home now. We need to all be together," Faisah pleaded.

"Something has been set out of kilter today, Faisah. The wheel has turned, and I want to set it right. And, Faisah, I'm keeping the gun."

Another change happened that day. After many motherless years, I began to talk to Ammi. I needed my mother still and felt her presence near.

"Ammi, is this what you meant when you told me to teach them?

First Bilqis, beautiful, dancing, burned Bilqis, who wandered into someone's story—the story of my cowardice. Then, Khanum, the stranger on a train, another bartered jewel for a rich man. She is the first I would rescue, proof that I would no longer turn away. And now Taslima, who dared to fall in love. I almost died. I almost killed someone.

"Ammi, you said to teach them, and I have. To read and write, to sew, to think for themselves, to use a computer, to add numbers, to value what is unique in a conformist society. And then one student is shot for stepping out of line, the others hear about it, and our work is all undone. So we plant another seed, build another school maybe, or organize a demonstration, and hope sprouts again, until a can of kerosene goes alight or a bottle of acid splashes the bridge of a nose, a knife slits a wrist, and the merciless sun robs us again, taking all that there is."

I found a black-and-white photo of Ammi in the bottom of a box—not the formal portraits that memorialize her elegance—but a snapshot of her looking angry and determined. I do not know the circumstances under which it was taken. She was bending slightly forward. One hand gripped her hipbone, which was cocked at the photographer. What occurred after the shutter snapped could have been kissing or could have been spitting. There was no way to know.

I built a shrine around that photograph to invoke Ammi as my saint. I had the photograph enlarged to the size of a notebook and framed it in red walnut. I centered it on a table covered with white muslin, and I filled vases with whatever flowers I could find. I lit a candle at night and in the morning. I brought mementos to the shrine—the silk pouch in which Ammi had folded her underwear, a leathery Rumi text, the cotton handkerchief on which her scent lingered still.

I knelt before the shrine for long periods. I read no textbooks. Poured no oil on the doorstep. Took no milk in my tea. No tea. No dusty sandals. No laundry. No letters. No toothbrush. No prayers. No songs. No memories. No soft sisters. No tough sisters. No purpose. No me. For days and days I faded away. I began to sleep late and hold classes in the afternoon. I organized my thoughts into lesson plans in order to give the other teachers everything I knew before I went away. I wanted to empty myself out—to express the role of a teacher in such depth and with such detail that if somehow I vanished, nothing would be lost. I began to keep a notebook in which I wrote about every woman I had known who had been burned, or buried, shot, or silenced, paralyzed, or damaged in any way that made her less able to move, less able to speak, to think, to find peace, less able. I forced myself to write at least a page about each one, and I usually wrote more. Then, for every page of victims, I wrote a page of victors. I wrote about every woman I had known who had run away, faced down, healed, spoken out, or outsmarted those who would make her less able, every woman who not only survived, but lived a life, her own life. On the day I finished the last entry in the notebook, I knew it was time to leave Sindh. It did not take long to pack all that I needed—the shrine, the notebook, the gun.

I longed for the waters of Punjab. I would follow the vein of the Indus River through the heartland one more time. On the night train to Lahore I took a seat in the women's compartment away from the chatter of other passengers. I made sure that the seat across from me was empty this time. I read and I slept. One word rolled over and over on my tongue: Jacobabad, Taslima's hometown. The word was a drumbeat in my brain. *Tek-Dum- tek-tek. Tek-Dum-tek-tek.* I could time its syllables to the rhythm of the rails. *Ja-cob-a-bad. Ja-cob-a-bad.* Where Jacob abides. Jacob—the twin who stole the blessing that was intended for his brother—the brother who married against his father's wishes. *Ja-cob-a-bad.* Where once lotuses rose in their singular way from the mud of rice fields. *Ja-cob-a-bad.* Where the ones who ordered the death of Taslima, the ones who wounded Jina, now live without bullets in their brains.

When the train crossed the transfer station for Jacobabad, I was asleep. I dreamed of ancient peacocks with wild plumage and snow lions that no one could capture. When I woke in the morning I saw that someone had placed my mother's folded handkerchief between my cheek and the dusty window.

Two hours later I scanned the crowd at the Lahore train station in search of the tall gray-bearded Sikh with the erect posture and the immaculate turban. He stood in the morning mist behind the others. For a moment I thought I saw Ammi standing beside him. She held a lotus in her hand.

3

Malakwal, 1958

Thirty-eight years earlier

Nafeesa Ahmed was born deep in the orange groves of Punjab—in the haveli, her family's compound on the banks of the Indus. Her great-great-grandfather had equipped the British with a steady supply of horses, and, in exchange, he was paid whatever land he wanted. Take your pick, they said, as far as the eye can see. Over generations, the compound became, first, Malakwal, a farming village, then—through strategic marriages and resulting partnerships—one village became two, with brick factories and orchards, then three, adding sugarcane and cotton fields, until the Ahmeds became feudals whose influence fingered the flesh of the entire region.

The haveli was a multistoried brick mansion with marble floors and Persian gates. The farm workers were given a restricted section of the field for their dark huts, where string beds were stacked in the daytime and lined up wall-to-wall at night—a dozen people to a room. Their driver carried the Ahmeds down the road in a Mercedes. The farm workers loaded themselves onto a cart pulled by one thirsty donkey who carried them down the road—the road everyone was destined to share.

Inside the compound resided Nafeesa's parents, her fourteen-year-old brother, Jameel, and Ali, her older brother, and his family.

Ali's family's quarters were apart from the main house but still within the compound. Truly, Ali could live anywhere he wanted, and seemed to live everywhere. Everything was, or one day would be, his. As a daughter, Nafeesa obeyed her parents, and as a sister, she obeyed Ali. Any of them could forbid whatever she desired, even studying, and she knew that Ali would not hesitate to do so if he had the smallest excuse.

One day he flexed his authority directly. Nafeesa had returned from a week in Multan where she attended university. Ali was standing in the doorway as she approached, which was unusual. Normally a servant would open the door.

"Assalam aleikum," she said automatically, looking around. "Where is Ammi?"

Suddenly, he slapped her face, knocking her over. She fell to her knees and pressed her hand to the hot sting. He had pushed and shoved her in the past, and called her names, but never had he hit her like that.

Our father would never permit it, she thought. But this time, he caught me alone.

"Your clothes are too tight, like a whore," he yelled, bloodying the whites of his eyes. "Cover yourself before our parents see you like that."

Nafeesa was wearing a chiffon shalwar kameez that was cut low and tight across the bodice, and her dupatta swathed only her neck. She had to admit it did allow for a glance at the hollow between her breasts.

After that day she made every effort to avoid Ali.

He accused their father. "You spoil her!" He pointed to their mother. "And you neglect her! She must be trained like other women."

"Nafeesa is not spoiled. She will do what I say," Ammi said, but the uncles agreed with Ali.

"You, Ahmed," they said, turning to their father, "You are wasting your money on her education!"

"And, Yasmeen," the aunties predicted, "letting her travel to London will only assure she drifts away. She'll come back wearing blue jeans and bobby socks. You just watch." Their heads bobbed to confirm that they all shared the same opinion.

They discuss my life as if it belongs to them, thought Nafeesa, like so many kilos of oranges, so many goatskins.

She brought the teapot into the sitting room and began arranging the china cups without a clatter, without a chip. Relatives filled every seat, women wrapped in multicolored silken cloth with metallic embroidery. Since they were with family, their dupattas were relaxed across their shoulders. Exotic makeup and French twists revealed their vanity and attention to style. The men, too, mimicked the British, with their little moustaches, pocketwatches, and waistcoats.

The hypocrisy in the room was thick and, as far as Nafeesa was concerned, she was having none of it in her future. They are the perfect example of everything I want not to be, she thought, looking around the room, estimating the situation. And she realized that for now she had to be clever.

"If my future is just another crop to be bartered," she said, "I will negotiate for myself."

"Nafeesa!" Yasmeen pursued her lips at her daughter, turning to the guests with a reassuring voice. "She will marry soon and marry well, but first she must complete her education. My grandchildren must be well-spoken, and she will be their guide. Remember the old slogan: 'Educate a Pakistani woman and you educate a nation.'"

"But she has turned down every proposal made to her," Auntie Beezah continued. "We all know that the boys' parents have stopped calling." Her lips puckered to emphasize her point. Yasmeen recoiled.

"Puuh!"

"Foolish girl," her father sighed, watching Nafeesa pouring tea like a lady.

"Sugar?" she addressed Auntie Beezah.

"As you wish," she replied, looking pleased. Beezah thought she was bringing Yasmeen back to her senses.

Nafeesa slid a thin stream of milk into the cup and sprinkled the sugar with a tiny silver spoon. She took her time. She stirred the mixture without making a sound, looked her auntie in the eye, and lifted the cup and saucer onto her palm. Auntie accepted the tea, turned her head, and sipped.

"We must admit that we live in heaven," she sighed, sounding bored with heaven. "I have fifty servants. One massages me and my mother-in-law, one irons my clothes, another cooks, another cleans . . . and so on . . . and so on."

Oh, no, thought Nafeesa. Here comes the bragging.

"But nothing like they have in the U.K." Auntie said, turning to face her niece. "Right, Nafeesa?"

Nafeesa recognized the trap and glanced into her lap, not taking the bait.

"We love Pakistan, do we not, Nafeesa?" Auntie needled again.

Nafeesa could hear the unspoken demand: Look at me, girl! She raised her vacant eyes, looking at no one.

"I am too young to understand what love means, Auntie," she said. She turned to her father, "But Pakistan is my home and always will be."

Nafeesa saw the corners of her mother's mouth turn up slightly. She could feel Yasmeen's pride, watching her daughter maneuver this tight situation.

Clever girl—my clever girl, thought Yasmeen.

Yasmeen had connived so that Nafeesa could travel to London to complete her graduate studies in education, something Yasmeen had always wanted for herself. In exchange she brokered her daughter's agreement to accept whatever marriage arrangement they made when she returned from London.

"It will have to be a bargained-for exchange, Nafeesa. It's the only way," Yasmeen said. "The point is to find the best husband we can and, if possible, one that you like as well." Yasmeen was looking forward to marshalling all the parts of the marriage transaction. She sealed the deal with her husband by proposing that Nafeesa live in London with her older sister.

"She can stay with my Baji Najma," Yasmeen said. "She and her husband are strict, very devout. They will watch over Nafeesa, then she will return to us."

"Even with your Baji watching over her, if she goes to the West, Nafeesa will never be the same."

Ahmed wanted his daughter to stay in Pakistan, but he could not deny her anything she asked. Ali is right about that, he thought. She is my only daughter. I do spoil her.

"She'll study hard, Ahmed. She's a good girl," Yasmeen continued, chipping away.

"Who cares if she studies?" Ahmed replied, buttoning his cardigan and walking away from another argument. "It is as you wish, Yasmeen. But mark my words. In London, she'll forget Pakistan."

Car doors slammed as aunties, uncles and cousins filled their little Mehrans and trailed the family town car to the airport to send Nafeesa off for her year in London. Nafeesa would always remember their faces on the other side of the chain link fence at the entrance to the terminal. She stood inside the fence with her parents and her brothers and turned her back to the rest of them. She nestled against her mother's coat. Her father held a handkerchief to his nose. Nafeesa hugged Ali halfheartedly, but held Jameel's hand for as long as she could. She could tell that he was embarrassed by the nakedness of his devotion to her.

"Baji, you'll be gone a whole year. You must write to me every week," he said.

"I will," Nafeesa replied, placing her hands on the top of his head, blessing him, and knowing at the same time she was making a promise she probably would not keep. "And never forget me," she whispered in his ear.

Jameel turned suddenly and ran back to the car.

"Look for Baji in the baggage claim area," her mother said. "Oh, and remember, do not call her Auntie. She always hated that. Said it makes her feel old."

"What should I call her then?"

"Call her Baji, like I do. She'll like that. Ibrahim and their driver will be with her." Yasmeen's voice became dreamy. "Baji will stand out in the crowd—so elegant and—oh, her silver hair. She'll probably wear gold. She always liked fabrics with the sheen of precious metals—such a beauty my Baji was."

At Heathrow Nafeesa saw no one like her mother had described. A bevy of strangers crowded the gate to the baggage area. But there, hand-printed on a large cardboard, she recognized her name, written in big square letters. The sign was held in one hand by a skinny woman in a tight suit. With the other hand, she was smoking a cigarette. She had short, curly black hair and carmine fingernails and matching lipstick. She was wearing nylons and spiked heels.

"Baji?" Nafeesa asked, looking into the woman's face to see if her auntie was in there.

"Call me Najma," her auntie said. The woman's low voice sounded mysterious. "Come with me." She grabbed Nafeesa's hand and tugged her through a mass of taxi drivers. "I got us a taxi," she said in a monotone. "They are expensive, but how often does one's niece come to stay with poor Najma? Huh?"

Najma had not cracked a smile, touched Nafeesa's head, kissed her cheeks, or hugged her, the way women in the family always did. *Who is this woman?* Nafeesa wondered. And on the long drive to the London flat, she found out, as Najma listed the secrets she expected Nafeesa to keep.

"You mustn't tell anyone these things. You know how your mother is." She looked at her niece. "You understand me? Tell no one."

Nafeesa nodded.

Najma sighed, locking the back door and settling into the corner of the seat.

"But then it's not really her fault now, is it, love? It's really how everyone back there is. Ignorant. Petty. Tied to their backward ways." Nafeesa was flabbergasted.

"Why, Baji, I had no idea you felt that way." Najma became irritated.

"Don't Baji me! I am more than someone's older sister." She sat up and shot Nafeesa a look. "Call me Najma." Nafeesa felt a strange giddiness. She thought she might float away.

"You seem so different now than when you visit Punjab," she said.

"Call me Ava Gardner, then," Najma replied, turning her head to light a Chesterfield. A leafy remnant stuck to her bottom lip. "I am an actress when I am there—the Pakistani Princess Act, I call it. I use it whenever I return to Punjab. Or, if I run into anyone from back there here in London, I find a way to cover up. But they don't recognize me without the garb, anyway, you know?" She picked at the tobacco on her lip and then ran her open palm across the surface of her skirt. "And I rarely go into London's Asian ghetto anymore. So that is how I do it," Najma said, folding her bony arms over her flat chest. "I deceive them, I just lie, and if you can't go along with that, well, then you won't get along with me . . . Now we will see what this girl is made of," said Najma under her breath, as if Nafeesa were not there.

Nafeesa looked out the window at the blur of city lights in the London mist. Najma's challenge—what this girl is made of—melted into the sound of rolling tires on wet pavement. She was too tired to think about it.

The driver dropped the luggage on the sidewalk, and the taxi pulled away. Nafeesa realized there were no servants or uncles or cousins around. Najma eyed the footlocker, the suitcases, and the train case as she sucked her teeth.

"Grab hold of one end and I'll get the other. Good for a flat tummy," she said, patting her abdomen. "We'll get these things up in just a few trips, and then we can sit down to a nice pot of tea."

Later Nafeesa found the nerve to ask Najma about her husband.

"But where is Uncle Ibrahim?" She gulped the sweet and spicy tea.

"Oh, Ibrahim found a floozy and took off for America years ago," Najma said, turning to read the shock written on her niece's face. She brushed it off. "It's OK. I taught myself to type and take shorthand. Took an office job with the city. Worked my way up to office manager." Nafeesa thought she caught a whiff of pride mixed with her auntie's sadness. "I do all right. It's how I live my life now, so I'm glad we've set things right, straightaway."

"I don't know what to say," Nafeesa said, laughing with delight.

"Don't laugh at me, girl! Why are you here in London if you, too, don't want to get away? Hmm?" She pressed her lips together.

"Well, my studies . . ."

"Oh, that's just your cover story. I know. I have mine and you have yours," Najma said with certainty. "It has to be that way." She let go Nafeesa's gaze, got up and walked toward the kitchen. She turned to face Nafeesa. "I was young once, you know. You can go deeper than that with me."

She stood by the dining table with her fists on her hips. An autographed photo of Frank Sinatra hung on the wall above the pile of 78 LPs she had slipped into their flimsy covers. "Najma, come fly with me," Sinatra had written. "Love, Frankie."

Nafeesa could not believe her good luck.

"No no no, Baj—Najma, you misunderstand. I am not laughing at you. I am simply amazed that you have pulled this off." Najma's face relaxed and her voice became musical. She smiled.

"Just don't go getting yourself into any trouble while you're here, or it'll be trouble for me, too. You're a grown woman now and don't need me questioning you like Scotland Yard. Just be home for dinner so I won't worry about mashers getting you. And stay out of those rock-and-roll joints. Stick with the college crowd—the Arabs, the Indians, the Pakis, too. If their families ask about me, just say that I don't get out much—bad back or some such. And not a word to anyone back home," she said.

Nafeesa could not stop grinning.

What a gift fate has given me in Baji Najma! If only Ammi knew!

"Not a word," Nafeesa promised, extending her palms to heaven. "I will tell no one."

And don't lovers seal their fates by following the lure of what is forbidden?

Many years later, after Nafeesa's death, when he thought back to 1958, Kulraj Singh gave thanks to the forces that had brought them to London, where their eyes had been allowed to fall on each other's faces. When he saw Nafeesa for the very first time, Kulraj Singh knew her bones like they were his own. He wondered then if he had seen her before in a dream. It was a familiarity that he could not penetrate.

It happened at a dinner party at the home of Dean Albion from the engineering school, a fashionable bungalow not far from the tube station. He felt her presence at once when she entered the room, the way one feels the wind when a door opens somewhere. He glanced into an ornately framed mirror that reflected the light of Nafeesa in the background and his own face in the foreground. Her skin was dark and her eyes were shining. When she smiled, he saw a dimple in one cheek and a little gap between her front teeth. Over her head was a magenta dupatta trimmed in gold. He moved toward her.

She stood by the coat closet struggling to remove a wet trench coat while at the same time she managed her dupatta and a shopping bag.

"May I help you?" he asked in Urdu.

"Shukriah, but I do not need your help," she said with a measure of gruffness he did not expect. No matter, thought Kulraj Singh, It gives me something to work with.

"Of course you do not *need* my help, but may I offer it nevertheless?" Without waiting for her response he took the edge of the coat she was removing and pulled it away from her, allowing her to fold the dupatta with confidence and grace. "Like all my Pakistani sisters, you rearrange cloth with no apparent effort."

Nafeesa wanted to give a prompt retort to this Sikh. Where was he from anyway? she wondered. His Urdu did have a Punjabi edge to it. But she'd have to hear more to know for sure. To have a Sikh actually approach and speak to her was new, as were so many experiences in England. She couldn't help but notice how slowly his fingers moved and how fine they were—long, lean, and graceful. And she was relieved to hear Urdu spoken again, the language of the educated, the modern, the up-and-coming class of South Asians. She was beginning to feel more herself, more at home. She turned to him.

"If my brother were here, he would walk me away from you," she said in a relaxed, friendly way.

"You are flirting with me," he blurted out. "I hadn't expected that." His wide smile opened.

"I certainly am *not* flirting with you," she replied, again in Urdu. "What an insult."

"Not an insult," he said. "You are a grown woman, are you

not? You can choose if you want to talk, or walk away, or flirt, or—perhaps—come over to this corner and have a cup of tea with me?"

Nafeesa was completely disarmed. She knew where she was and who she was and why she had come—Dean Albion was her advisor. At the same time, she longed for a conversation with an adult male, away from the hovering men of her country. But meeting with a Sikh—well, that was twice the trouble since he was both male and forbidden. She looked around to discover that there was no one watching. No one cared. She turned her body toward Kulraj Singh, surprised to feel a warmth in her bloodstream, an undeniable surge in his direction.

"A small cup of tea?" she replied. "Perhaps so."

Kulraj Singh loved Nafeesa as if she were a newborn baby and he the mother being handed an inexpressible gift. He thought she glowed from within, entirely luminous, and he imagined sitting in that light. His eyes ran like fingers through her dark hair. Later, when they were lovers, she would argue with him about her beauty.

"No, it is only my exposure to the flare of you that caused my phosphorescence," she would say. This was their game—each insisted that the other was more deserving of the love they shared. "I am not a crystal chandelier, you dear man. I'm just an old gooseneck study lamp."

"You are incandescent. On that first night your dress was gossamer and translucent," he volleyed. She lobbed the comment back.

"It was navy blue, my darling," she said, hissing the next word, "serge."

At first Nafeesa was an enchanting child who wanted her own way—unpredictably stubborn about some things. Kulraj Singh recalled the fit she threw when the wedding flowers were wrong. He almost backed out of the marriage when he witnessed her rage.

"Marigolds!" she spat when she opened the box. "I ordered roses!"

But she was more than an indulged child—she was a woman

who wanted him like any man craves to be wanted—a woman with all the layers of desire. Not at first—it took a little time—but she let him know that she would show him everything she was and everything she wanted, without shame or fear.

"I will do anything you want," she would say. "Let me please you."

Even though they were married, the indecency of it was shocking, made him laugh, and sometimes it made him shiver.

Of course, his mind was much slower than hers. He could never keep up with her, but even their racing was only a game. Sometimes she would ask him to slow her down.

"Tell me something deep," she would say. "Something quiet and slow."

"The ocean out at sea," he'd say.

"But it rushes to the shore," she'd say.

"And then what does it do, my love?"

"It rests."

"Then be still for a moment. Be very still, Nafeesa."

Even in her most playful and agitated state, her breathing would slow, and it was all he could do not to get her going again by inhaling the breath that floated above her luscious lips.

And kind. Her love was so kind.

"The more I love, the more I love," she told him once. It went beyond the two of them, way beyond. More than the family, it was the neighbors, and the city. Really, as much a citizen of the world as she wanted to be, Nafeesa loved Pakistan best. She left a legacy of schools and programs. Her love was bricks and mortar.

Once he asked her: "What *were* you in your previous lives?"

"What previous lives?" she deadpanned, mimicking Najma's baritone. "I am a Muslim. Unlike you Sikhs, we only get one chance. So I have to give it all I've got."

Nafeesa was his loyal and willing partner—like a brother or a sister—as if they had been born to each other, reunited twins. If something needed to be done and he could not do it alone, she was by his side. She asked him about progress on his architectural projects and had ideas for new business. And although she had her friends and the children, she wanted to play, first and foremost, with him. They reveled in their word games, their nicknames, their games in bed. She wanted him to know that she cared—that even if they were from Pakistan and in Pakistan, they were not of Pakistan alone.

In 1958 the air was still sour with the stench of the slaughters that had occurred eleven years earlier when the British ran like dogs and India cracked. The blade that slashed the map also partitioned the bodies of the people, etching fear in their bellies and revenge in their hearts. Everyone—Muslims, Sikhs, Hindus—they all lost someone among the million who died. Ten million people migrated. Lines and lines of Hindus from the Indus River Valley, in what would later be designated "Pakistan," packed their lorries, rode bullocks, and walked, to cross the border into India. Lines and lines of Muslims from India carried all that they owned to be part of the new Islamic nation. Rioting occurred first in Calcutta and then spread to Punjab. The refugees scouted the routes to avoid one another in the passing. If a trainful of Hindus was murdered by Muslims from Lahore (and they were), then a trainful of Muslims would be murdered by Sikhs and Hindus from Amritsar (and they were). Entire families were butchered and their body parts were delivered by horseback to their villages. The people emptied baskets of breasts and pails of penises onto the ground—even the stubs of baby penises with scrotums like tiny figs. The soil was soaked with all the lost futures, and when it was done, when the trauma finally subsided to abide in the bodies of the people, they had to plant seeds in and eat the fruit of that same earth. Sikhs and Muslims alike knew the taste of each other's blood well, and they kept to their own.

Kulraj and Nafeesa in London. Romeo and Juliet in Verona. A Muslim and a Sikh in Pakistan. All of history conspired against them, but no matter. They would find a new way.

One day Nafeesa and Kulraj met at a London tea shop. Its walls were lined with shelves of books, cups and saucers, metal canisters of tea. His knees could not fit under the tiny tables.

"I have to admit, before I met you, I'd only seen Sikhs from a distance," Nafeesa said. Kulraj's teacup clattered against its saucer.

"Yes, religious minorities in Pakistan, or in London, for that matter, have little opportunity for social interaction," he said.

"I've offended you?"

"No. It is my choice whether to take offense or not. But it is not easy to be a Sikh in an Islamic country."

Then she tested him.

"Yes. It must be something like being a woman in a man's world?"

"Yes, it must be," he said, relieved.

Their desire was kindled by her flirtations and his restraint. Finally everything enlarged to the promise of a lifetime together. But they could not marry in Pakistan, a Muslim and Sikh, unless one of them converted to the other's religion.

"I am a sloppy Muslim," Nafeesa said. "I forget to pray four of the five times. I give to the poor when I can and have never made the Hajj. But I will be a Muslim until the day I die."

"You want me to convert to Islam?" He had not expected this from her.

"Is it always the woman who must give up her faith?" she asked.

"Are you testing me again, Nafeesa? Because if so, it is a test I can pass." He put his lips close to her ear and whispered, "You are my path to God." She began a girlish swoon, which he interrupted with a severe glance.

"No, I am not being clear enough," he said. "Let me explain. This is not a romantic notion. It is the day-in-day-out truth. What I believe: by loving you until our souls collide, I will know the Divine."

She was filled with love and confusion.

"I think I know what you are trying to tell me, Kulraj. But honestly I can only grasp maybe two percent of that idea."

"Two percent is enough. More than most. It's a good start." He laughed.

"What about your family?" she asked. He swallowed.

"I am not sure. My family is open-minded. I know they would accept our marriage if you converted, or maybe as a mixed marriage, but for me to convert to Islam—that is something else."

Betraying his loyalty to the Sikh order, something he had sworn he would never do, mirrored the risks Nafeesa would be taking if she converted to Sikhism. The battle left him wondering if they were doing something like trying to walk on the moon.

"Nafeesa, you do not know what you are asking. I wake early. I bathe. I chant." The more he talked, the more ridiculous he sounded.

"Yes, I thought you probably were devout. I can see it in the clearness of your eyes and the pink of your skin. All that breathing, all that oxygen." Then she squinted. "But as a Muslim, you could continue these prayers. Why not, if it is the same God?"

He wrestled with himself. Is religious conversion a thing of the spiritual dimension or only a thing of human history? If I am the same person, what is converted after all? Finally he understood the nature of this battle.

"You are asking me to put my head on the line," he said.

"Whatever are you talking about, my sweet guru?" she asked.

"It is a Sikh tale I heard first as a child. I remember the nights we lay, curled in our mother's bed. She would read to us from the 'Guru Gobind Storybook.' I can still see its drawing of the crowd of eighty thousand people. Each head was a tiny brush stroke on paper. The Guru's sword flashed high above his head in the yellow sunlight, demanding a sacrifice.

"It both frightened me and thrilled me to hear my mother bellow out: 'Who will give me his head? Who will give me his head?' And the Guru craned his neck looking for a man of courage. But people looked away or slipped out of the crowd, fearful that they might be selected as the one to give his head.'"

"'Would you give him yours?' my mother asked us lightly. 'They must have wondered about a guru who would make such a request,' she said and returned to the book.

"Gobind kept asking for heads. And each time, a person would step forward to answer his call. 'And from these first five'—I still know this part by heart—'Gobind created the Khalsa, a new order of extraordinary people who would cultivate in themselves profound qualities of both grace and valor.'

"The final picture in the book was full of lions. 'Each one equivalent to 125,000 ordinary persons,' my mother read, closing the book."

The story made Nafeesa want to cry. She cleared her throat.

"So is it your head on the line, or on the lion?" she asked, tears streaming down her face. He laughed.

"Then it is decided," he said, reading her tears. "We will have a civil marriage ceremony here. And when we return to Pakistan, I will become a Muslim. You will have all of me—body and soul." She blushed.

"And where shall we live?" she asked. "Even if you convert, my parents won't stomach a Sikh in the family, even an ex-Sikh. Which city do you prefer—Karachi or Lahore?"

"As you wish," he replied, knowing she would say Karachi.

The forbidden wedding was small and simple, held in Najma's flat, with a local judge officiating. Nafeesa wore a red chiffon gown trimmed in gold, like a traditional Pakistani bride. But she left her head uncovered, as is traditional for a Sikh. Kulraj wore a gold silk shalwar kameez with a crimson sash draped over one shoulder, and a turban, a bracelet, and the kirpan—the sacred knife. He entered the room from the kitchen, and she from the bedroom. They greeted each other in the language of the other's faith.

"Waheguru ji ka Khalsa, Waheguru ji ki Fateh," she said in Punjabi. The Khalsa belongs to God and to God alone belongs the Victory.

"Assalam Aleikum," he replied in Arabic. Peace be unto you.

Najma wore her gold and silver rings and bangles, and as the bride's "mother," she placed Nafeesa's hand on the end of Kulraj's sash. Then Kulraj led their procession around the room, with his bride following, grasping the sash. They circled four times while guests sang sacred songs. After each circling they bowed to one another, their foreheads touching the floor, until at last they sat face to face. When the harmonium stopped, they each read the poetry of Rumi. Nafeesa spoke first.

> *a handful of earth*
> *cries aloud*

I used to be hair or
I used to be bones

and just the moment
when you are all confused
leaps forth a voice
hold me close
I'm love and
I'm always yours

Kulraj Singh wrapped his lanky arms around Nafeesa and lifted her off the floor, reciting.

I would love to kiss you.
The price of kissing is your life.

"What you have done is dangerous," Najma said after the guests left. "A matter of honor, so risky indeed. The most you can hope is that they leave you alone."

"Even if I con—"

"Yes, even if you convert. I know how they are, and nothing is as irreplaceable to them as the family's izzat, its honor. To marry without their permission, in a foreign country, and outside of the religion! Never. You would always be an infidel to them."

"Would they harm Nafeesa?" he asked.

"My father would never allow anyone to harm me," Nafeesa said, "but I worry about what he might do to you."

"I think you both are in trouble if you return to Pakistan," said Najma. "You should make up some story and stay here. I hate to say this, but better you hear it now." She cleared her throat. "You know about honor crimes, of course."

"Of course," said Nafeesa. She had read about a woman whose ears and fingers were hacked off before her family then hanged her. Her crime had been being seen in public, alone with a male cousin. "I think it happens in Sindh. But I cannot think of a single case in Malakwal."

"But can you recall any other girl who violated her father's choice of husband?" Najma asked. Nafeesa was silent.

"Nafeesa, you must tell no one of our marriage," Kulraj said. "No one."

"So you are giving me orders already, Mr. Modern Man?"

"Yours are double sins—female impurity and religious infidelity," said Najma. "But your husband could be in the gravest danger of all. Who hates Sikhs more than the Ahmeds? You know the family history."

"But Kulraj's family had nothing to do with that," she said, rushing to defend her husband. But for the first time, when he looked into her eyes, he saw fear looking back at him. He realized with panic that Nafeesa understood that their marriage would be the ultimate humiliation for her family.

Kulraj agreed. "Your family will consider it their right and obligation to kill both of us for having a love marriage."

"I agree. We will tell no one," Nafeesa said simply. "But I want to go back. Pakistan is my home. Don't you want to go back?" She looked into his eyes.

He nodded.

"And I can't leave Jameel," Nafeesa whined.

"Wake up, Nafeesa!" Najma shouted, suddenly standing. She pulled back each of her fingers one by one as her hands became fists whipping the air. "You want your Sikh. You want your family. You want your life. You want Pakistan. You cannot have everything you want. Life has consequences. It's a trade-off. Jameel is fourteen years old. If you tell him about this marriage, you can bet he will tell everyone else. Now tell me, what do you want to keep and what do you want to lose?"

Nafeesa sighed. She, too, could hear the truth in Najma's rant.

"That's my problem," Nafeesa said. "I am greedy, always asking for too much." She touched the spot on her face where Kulraj had kissed her during the wedding. "I know what I want," she finally said to him. "I want you. And I want to say good-bye to Jameel."

Nafeesa returned to Punjab during the winter harvest of oranges, sugar, and oil. The drive from the airport was slow, as lumbering, long-legged camels caused traffic delays. They pulled wagons overstuffed with green sugarcane, covered with cloth and tied down with ropes. The driver was expert at slipping between the farm wagons and the oncoming trucks, but the closer they got to the refinery, more and more trucks appeared, each one stacked crosswise with cane and tilting under the weight. Children tagged behind the trucks to pull off a stalk, bite it, break it open, strip the bark, and suck out the sweetness inside.

Winter in Pakistan is also the season of harvesting women. Weddings occur between the two Eids, the end of Ramadan and the feast weeks later that commemorates God's saving Ishmael from Abraham's knife. By day, girls decorate their hands with henna designs—saffron flowers, peacocks, and the curved geometry of Persia. By night, random gunfire into the sky proclaims wedding celebrations.

For the rest of her life Nafeesa would remember the *tap tap tap* of rain on the roof on the day she returned to Malakwal. It was difficult to sleep, and she awoke on the first morning still tired from traveling. She spread herself across the chaise on the verandah and draped a woolen blanket over her legs. The air was a cold, thick soup.

Her parents began their prosecution again: "You are the oldest unwed girl in the district. People are gossiping. It brings shame on the family that you have no husband, no babies, nothing. We cannot tolerate it any longer."

Before London, their words had gnawed at Nafeesa's insides, but now, she spit them onto the floor. She lay there, more than the insolent virgin she had been when she left them. She had learned well from Najma. She appeared to brood, looking as if she were making an effort to be accepting and dutiful, but imposed upon at the same time. She ignored her mother's nervous prattle and inhaled her secret deep into her body.

She spent every day planning her escape, marshalling her resources to keep the effort simple and effective. Kulraj had remained in London to finish his examinations, and they planned to meet in Lahore in two weeks.

"Eloping after the wedding. What an idea!" he had chuckled

stroking his dark beard. She remembered how his thick eyebrows twitched below his head cloth when he laughed. It was hard to bring details of him to mind, how his voice sounded, how lightly he had touched her. She focused instead on the superficial parts of him—the turban of this Sikh who was now her husband, the beard he had never trimmed.

As promised, her mother had chosen her husband—Mohmar Khaliq, a local power broker whose tire factories provided the only employment in the district. The marriage of the two families would bring to each one the control over the votes they needed to maintain their positions in local politics. Her father planned to run for Parliament.

Khaliq was an old man, well into his forties, with one wife already. She had borne four daughters and no sons.

"Not Khaliq, Ammi! I remember how he used to stare at my breasts," Nafeesa complained, even though she knew Khaliq would never see her naked nipples. "Now he can't keep his eyes off my hips." She had to make some complaints, just to convince them she was still their whining Nafeesa, and not the calm married woman she had become.

"He wants sons, Nafeesa," Yasmeen said. "He needs sons to pass his land to. When land passes to daughters, it leaves the family." She sighed. "And with Khaliq, you will not be far away from us."

"I know, Ammi. I understand," Nafeesa said compliantly.

Two weeks seemed like forever, so she paced herself, moving through preparations for both the wedding and the escape. The rain was her sole confidante in those days, the girlfriend to whom she could speak the truth and who answered with her unrelenting, friendly chatter.

"We will meet in Lahore at sunset during Mela Chiraghan, the Festival of Lamps," Kulraj had said weeks earlier in London. "You will have to find me without the dastar turban. I will be a Muslim by then."

She worried about the sacrifice he was making—to put his head on the line for her.

"Kulraj, are you sure?" she asked him for the hundredth time.

"—as if it were already done," he replied. "Let's meet at Shalimar Garden, the perfect place for lovers."

"Shalimar," she savored the word. Shalimar—the purest of human pleasures—fifty acres of marble terraces, pools, waterfalls, and fountains. The sixteenth-century Moghul royals built the summer residence in what then had been the countryside. But now Lahore crept over the walls of the old fort that had once enclosed it, and the city spread in every direction, clamoring to the gates of Shalimar Garden, only twelve miles west of the Indian border.

"Let's meet at the fountain of lights, the Sawan Bhadon," Kulraj said, referring to the famous pool—the one edged by covered walkways where the Moghul princesses had promenaded on drizzly days. At sunset hundreds of alcoves embedded in the walls were filled with oil lamps and lit by tapers. The glim created multiple rainbows across the cascading water.

"That's my romantic husband," she replied. "And a clever idea as well. The family rarely visits Lahore, and never on a holiday. Too much traffic. Too much bother. My father will say that the trip is too costly, and I know Ammi will be too tired."

"My knees, Feesi. I can't go to Lahore," Yasmeen whined. "Take Fatimah with you. Find a nice scarlet brocade." They were in the women's quarter where Nafeesa was sewing a traditional undergarment for her wedding day.

"I am going with you!" Jameel announced as he pushed open the door. Nafeesa ignored him, continuing to weave a needle into the pile of fine cotton. Who will ever wear this shirt? she wondered. I'll leave it with a note for Jameel.

"Baji, please take me with you to Lahore. Please," Jameel begged, squeezing in beside her in the rosewood chair and draping his arm over her shoulder.

"No, my sweet Jameel, you can't come this time," she said. "I am sorry, but I have too much to do to be able to take care of you too."

"You don't have to take care of me." Jameel stood up. "Do not insult me. It is my duty to protect you." Glowering, he stormed out of the room.

Jameel had become testy while she was away. Sometimes he would order her around like a field boss, and at other times he would be as timid as a kitten. Jameel was a late arrival in her parents' marriage, and he was Nafeesa's favorite person in the world, the one she would miss the most when she left the family.

Although she was leaving forever, she packed only one bag. She could hear her mother singing when she returned to her room.

"I'm taking samples of the shoes and trimmings with me, Ammi, so I can match what I buy with what we already have." Nafeesa tried to speak brightly, as she watched her mother's wrapped figure moving about, searching for something. When will I ever see you again, Ammi? she wondered and winced. I'll always remember Ammi, she thought, as though she were speaking from the future. Her heart broke a little and she had to cup her hand over her mouth when Yasmeen disappeared through the door.

Nafeesa recalled the almond scent of her mother's body oil, the line of her perfect nose, the arch of her perfect brow. When she was a little girl she would watch her mother bathe. Afterward Ammi would press the big powder puff into the box of talc and flap it into her arm pits, reaching over to tickle Nafeesa, getting it up her nose, both of them sneezing, laughing. She would fluff between her legs and Nafeesa could see the powder fill the crack of Ammi's backside. Little pimples festered on her inner thighs.

"Feesi, just pray that you're skinny or bowlegged when you grow up," she recalled her mother's words.

Nafeesa conjured up the mother of her youth for the last time. She imagined offering a sprig of orange blossom to her. She recalled the touch of the hand that would pet her head when she rested a cheek against her mother's hip. Then she straightened her back. Something roared inside her, a frightened trapped animal, determined to escape.

Ammi does not need me, she reasoned. Ali and Jameel will take care of her. And as for my father, let him feel shame. He chose Khaliq for my husband, when everyone knows what an old lecher Khaliq is.

Suddenly Nafeesa realized that she felt nothing inside. Oh, but I do, I do feel something, she argued with herself. She looked inside for the old grief and could not find it. Her emotional weather had changed.

"Fatimah will meet me at the bus station," she lied to Yasmeen. "Her brother will take us to their auntie's home in Lahore. We'll visit the shops tomorrow and return by Thursday."

Nafeesa knew that Fatimah was in Multan. Ammi will never find out that I will be traveling to Lahore alone, she thought. Besides, she is so self-absorbed. She never pays attention to the details of what I do. When the driver drops me at the Malakwal station, she thought, I will wave him off and take the bus to Lahore and then to Shalimar Garden, and to my husband, Kulraj Singh.

She left the shadowed courtyard in the afternoon air, bidding good-bye to the ground of her childhood. The spacious rooms and verandahs of the enclave seemed narrow to her now, and her past as colorless as the life that would be hers if she stayed. She gloried in the uncertainty of what lay ahead.

Yes, she thought, it is time to go. I am glad for it. I am ready for anything.

On the bus Nafeesa piled her suitcase and coat on the seat next to her so that no one else would sit there. She had heard stories of women being accosted on buses. She wore large sunglasses and a common black dupatta, which she drew across her face, hoping to avoid village surveillance.

Someone on the bus might recognize me, she thought, start a conversation, and report in the village that I had been traveling alone. Then my parents will get word of it and send Ali after me.

She shuddered to think what Ali would do to her then. She retreated into her dupatta as she watched women at work across the road from the depot. Gathered around the head pump of a tube well, they rubbed big cakes of white soap back and forth across cloth. They twisted the cloth into a hard wad and slapped it again and again against a slab. The washing stone was smooth and slippery from wear. Some women threw themselves fully into the ritual, the closest they would ever come to public dancing. A snaggletoothed smile spread across the face of one woman who seemed triumphant in her results. Resting for a moment with her hands on her hips, she faced the sky while the soaked edges of her shalwar cooled her hot feet.

The village women's constant labor was the foundation of whatever small wealth their families could accumulate. They birthed children, nursed and cooked, cleaned, and cared for them, made their clothes, farmed or bartered for their food. The women married young, promised even before they menstruated, and when the day arrived, they left their mothers to live forever as servants to their husband's family. Some did not even know their own birthdays or names. They never looked at a man from outside of their immediate family, and men ignored them, too. They were as vulnerable as sparrows and as common as crows. All they could hope for was that after they died, their children would remember them for a while.

Punjabi families, whether rich or poor—for there were few who were not one or the other—guarded their reputations as fiercely as a jealous husband would clutch his wife. For the rich, the family name was the tissue that connected the fabric of the body politic. For the rest, a good name was all the wealth a man had to pass on to his children.

At five o'clock the bus entered Lahore. The old city was tarnished in the evening glow. The sandstone mosque was cinnabar, and next to it, the golden Sikh temple gleamed. For an instant the last few rays of the sun flared on the domes and turrets.

"Wait with my bags," Nafeesa told a porter, handing him a few rupees as she searched for the toilet.

"Across the street," he said, pointing at the hotel. Once there, Nafeesa removed the cotton suit she had worn and slipped her arms into a golden shalwar kameez. Without a mirror she traced a line of kohl around her eyes, and smoothed on red lipstick. She combed her fingers through her hair, and hurried back to the depot. She crossed the street, scanning the crowd for the porter.

Then she saw them! Jameel stood in front of her bag with one hand on his hip, the other one outstretched to stop her. With such hatred in his eyes, to her he did not seem like Jameel. Behind him Ali was thrashing through Nafeesa's bag like a wild animal. He stopped to read her journal where she had recorded everything. All was unspoken and completely clear: they had raced the bus in Ali's sports car. They had come for her.

I should run, she thought. But I could never outrun them.

Then she saw a man get out of a taxi and leave the back door open. As she ran toward it, she screamed at her brothers.

"Thieves! Thieves! Stop them!"

She leapt into the taxi, slammed the door, and sped away. Through the rear window she watched Ali's eyes and his monster hands coming after her. But he was helpless. Jameel was running, and falling behind. A policeman was blowing his whistle at them.

"Having trouble, Madam?" the driver asked without turning around.

"No problem," she said. "Shalimar Garden, please. I have to be there by sunset."

Nafeesa removed from her wrist the bangle her father had given her when she had come of age. The bracelet felt like a handcuff now. She would pay the driver for this taxi ride with it. If the bracelet is not enough, she thought, I will give him my silks, my shoes, even the hair on my head. Whatever he wants—because he is taking me to freedom.

Everything Ali had read in her bag condemned them, and she had seen in Jameel's eyes that he and Ali were a team. Ali was capable of anything, and now he knew where she was going and why. She had to warn Kulraj!

"Shalimar," Kulraj Singh said to the driver on the afternoon of his rendezvous with Nafeesa. The taxi maneuvered the Grand Trunk Road, the ancient route from Kabul to Calcutta. The driver's horn spoke the language of the road. A two-second honk was a warning to goatherds ahead. A light pip was a greeting to a familiar face in the bazaar.

It was a typical holiday. Men filled open stalls along the road— repairing and trading stacks of shoes, tires, cloth, and cheap bags, toys, toiletries. Some sold vegetables spread out on colorful dhurries—small oranges, a mound of bruised cauliflower, translucent long-stemmed onions. Barefoot children dawdled nearby. A young man stood with his legs apart and his elbows to his sides, peeing against a brick wall. Shopkeepers were closing early to gather at Shalimar for the evening spectacle when the oil lamps would be lit just before sunset.

Kulraj Singh's life was in order. His family understood that they would be Nafeesa's only family now. He was itching to get out of Punjab. In Karachi they could find an apartment, or live with his family, whatever Nafeesa wanted. He had bought open plane tickets so they could fly to Delhi, or to Karachi, or to Malaysia, or anywhere she desired. He did not have to return to his architectural firm for two weeks. He reserved a room at the Lahore Hilton so that their honeymoon would not to be delayed.

Shalimar Gate was a wide arch through which elephants had once paraded. Outside, vendors hawked samosas, roasted corn on the cob, and stirred their curries. Hundreds of people were packed together, moving under the arch as if one body.

All day Kulraj waited for Nafeesa at Shalimar Garden. However will she manage to get away from Malakwal on this exact day and at this exact time? he wondered. He passed the time studying the history of the fragile, heavenly place. He ran his finger along the entwined stems and faded flowers painted on the peeling walls. He rested under the apple trees and shared walnuts with fern squirrels that begged as persistently as street children. Two swans in a pond glided into a bed of tall reeds.

As shadows fell beneath the mango trees and jasmine scented the air, a small regiment of men in long, white kurtas appeared with tapers to light the famous oil lamps. They stretched their bodies across the pools to reach the farthest wicks. The lamps threw shadows that dappled the terraces, and the crowds slowed and quieted. This was their appointed hour, so he scanned the garden for Nafeesa. As darkness fell, light reversed directions, departing from earth into the endless sky. He passed a large marble throne, and turning, saw her.

She stood ten meters away, watching him approach. She glowed like a candle as she inched toward him. The gold flecks in her hazel eyes seemed to burn from a fire at a great distance. He had thought so often of this moment that he expected he might cry at the sight of her. But not a tear formed in his eye, and no tension gripped his throat. She moved in a casual way, but she was not smiling. She crooked her finger to signal him to follow her underneath the bougainvillea.

"My brothers followed me to the station," she said, and then recounted her escape from Malakwal. Kulraj Singh's mind was clear as he divided his attention between listening to her and planning their escape. He recalled garden exits he had passed during the day. Which ones were open, which ones would be the safest way out?

"I have no doubt Ali is coming for us," Nafeesa said.

He took her hand and pulled her deeper into the darkness next to the walls where the air was warmer. A musician playing his flute leaned against the bricks, and the bells of the ghungroo signaled the start of dancing. As families spread out cloths for picnics, Nafeesa and Kulraj skirted the lengthy wall.

The first gate they came to was locked. At the second gate, a guard pointed past the purple hedge to an open archway across the lawn. They promenaded with other couples, crossing the open park together, sidestepping the picnics, dancers, and poets. All the while, Nafeesa eyed the crowd for Ali's wide frame. Twice she thought she saw him, and each time she pulled Kulraj into the shadows, peering out until she was sure the person was not her brother.

Suddenly she screamed, "Jameel!" and she fell to Kulraj's feet. There she curled up and covered her head with her arms.

A boy stood over her, gripping the haft of a sword with both hands.

He panted, looking terrified.

Blood dripped from the tip of the blade. Nafeesa's blood.

A large man stood next to him with a poised dagger in his hand. This must be Ali, Kulraj thought. This one is mine!

His rage overwhelmed him. A crowd was gathering. A police

whistle blew, but he dared not turn away. If Nafeesa had survived the one blow, he thought, she would never survive a second.

"Again," Ali shouted to Jameel. "Strike her again. Do it now."

Jameel looked halfhearted as he swung the blade over his head. Kulraj unsheathed the sacred kirpan under his shirt. Growling like an animal and waving the dagger at Ali, Kulraj forced him to move in closer to Jameel. "Come here, you son-of-a-bitch. Come on!" Kulraj danced around them, threatening Ali, distracting Jameel.

Nafeesa groaned. She rolled her eyes upward to face the threatening sword.

"No! Jameel!" she begged. "Don't! I am Baji!"

But the blade began its descent as Jameel screamed.

"Bajiiiiii!"

Ali lunged at Kulraj, and Kulraj slashed his face, taking part of his nostril. Kulraj reached for Nafeesa, lifted her over his head, and they disappeared through the Lahori Gate. The crowd closed in behind them.

Kulraj Singh could hear Jameel's sword clatter onto the ground. He could not help himself. He turned back to look.

Ali writhed in pain, blood smeared on his face and hands. He yelled at the boy. Jameel stood there, stunned, as if he had been the one struck down.

4

Adiala Prison, 1996

The chilis in Rahima Mai's masala burned the edges of Ujala's mouth. Am I eating too much? she thought. Or talking too much?

"Why so quiet all of a sudden?" asked Rahima Mai, greedy for the story in a way that Ujala had come to recognize. Rahima Mai wanted to consume whatever she loved, and her expression of that urgency amounted to a demand.

Ujala had pieced together a collage of information about Rahima Mai. She seemed to have no impediments to working late. She never spoke of children. When she mentioned her husband, it was always in the past. Her gruff exterior melted when they were alone.

Rahima Mai stood over the hot pot, spooning out the spinach and cheese. Then she plopped back down into the plastic chair, which heaved a bit from the movement. With each fragment of chapati she scooped up spinach, chickpeas, and cheese from the plate and placed each bite into her mouth whole.

Ujala had no appetite for the food, so she put down her plate and continued with the story.

◆ ◆ ◆

On the day I heard the crack of gunfire that killed Taslima, something in me cracked a little, too. I carried the gunman's pistol in my pocket everywhere, even at home in Nankana Sahib. Through the kitchen window I again saw the vision of Ammi out in the field with a lotus in her hand.

The Q'ran says that angels fall with every drop of rain. In Punjab it rained for many days. Peacocks called to their harems, mewing like warring cats. The slender herbs that Abbu had planted lay flattened in little pools—their tendrils extended like arms of swimmers stretching to shore. The sunflowers bowed down until their heads hung and their spines snapped. The soaked rhododendrons glowed in the backlight of the rain. Their leaves were thick as toenails and their blossoms swelled beyond capacity. Those that bloomed beneath the foliage were protected from downpour, but, in the end, all the blossoms collapsed; flower-by-flower, each one became a dirty, drooping knob.

I took my knife out into the garden to slice the disturbing ugliness away. My woolen shawl was soaked, and the rain fell hard, forcing me back inside. But by midday the drizzle softened, and I went out again, the only human in sight. I wept in the rain at the five hours: in the morning, at midday, late afternoon, early evening, and before bedtime.

"You really have to stop this, Baji. You'll catch your death of cold," said Meena. "And the neighbors are beginning to wonder."

I snapped at her. "I'll let you know when I've had enough."

Reshma and Mohammad had written to Meena that they would not be attending her wedding.

We cannot condone marriage to someone who comforts an infidel. Ahmadis are kafir—they hold themselves out to be Muslims when they are not. They have diluted the teachings so that millions have lost their true faith. Meena, you are making a mistake, not only for this life, but also for your soul's eternity. The Islam of your husband's grandfather is not true Islam. We must keep pure the words of the Prophet. We cannot do this and attend your wedding also. I pray that Allah will forgive you and the entire family for this grievous sin.

"It will be an insult to Zeshan if they do not attend," said Meena when she read Reshma's words. Her words were angry, but her voice sounded bereft.

"I will telephone Reshma," I said, "I will make her understand."

I would not let them intimidate her, and I prayed for wisdom. I lit incense in the shrine room, where Abbu had welcomed the addition of Ammi's photograph to the altar. I placed my worries in my mother's lap. I realized that as the family's mother now, I could demand Reshma's obedience.

"Something good will come of this marriage, whatever the outcome of my conversation with Reshma," I prayed to Ammi. "What is the worst that can happen? Reshma's family will not attend, I will make excuses for them, and the couple will be honored in a loving, accepting environment. Their decision would be unfortunate, but not fatal to Meena's happiness. Ammi, please help me to remember it is the marriage, and not this power struggle with Reshma, that is the heart of the matter."

"Waleikum salaam," Reshma responded to my voice with formality. We exchanged questions about family members. Finally, I took a breath and spoke.

"Baji, Meena is crushed that you may not be able to attend her wedding." I heard mumbling on the other end of the line.

"Mohammad will join us for this discussion," said Reshma. I heard the click of the telephone extension.

"Assalam aleikum," said Mohammad. "We were sorry to hear that you have arranged this marriage for our dear sister. We pray day and night that you will come to your senses."

"Meena loves this man. She wants to marry him."

"What Meena wants is irrelevant," Mohammad said. "One must denounce the infidel. Has Zeshan denounced this relative of his?"

"It is his great-grandfather, Mohammad. Please be reasonable," I begged. "How can he do such a thing? The old man is dear to them, like our father is to us."

"Our father is also an infidel," said Reshma.

I was speechless.

"It falls to you to follow the Q'ran in this situation," Reshma continued. "You must do it for the sake of her soul, Ujala . . . Let me help you."

"What could you do?" I asked. Reshma's self-righteousness was never more irritating than it was now.

"I could speak with Zeshan myself. If he is a believer and truly loves Meena—as you say he does—he will let her go for the sake of the family, if for nothing else. Or he will denounce his great-grandfather, as he should. I could explain it to him. Someone should."

"Abbu asked me to handle this," I said.

"Abbu is part of the problem." Reshma sounded like she was speaking a shameful secret out loud. "I know he means well and has done the best he can. He is a good man, and I respect him as my father, as I have been taught. But he is not a believer—he has always been a mystic and a dreamer. Remember how Ammi used to say to him, 'Mr. Singh, if a mosquito landed on a rose, you would swear that insect was God Himself?'

"Abbu avoids making hard judgments. He allows the children to do whatever they want—and look at the result. Five adult children and only one is married. Why? Because Ammi arranged it, that's why. She understood her responsibilities as a Muslim parent. I know you and Abbu do your best . . . but, Ujala, what do you know of being a parent? You have never labored in childbirth. What could you know about what makes a good husband? You have never known a man."

My mind was spinning. I squeezed my eyes, trying to revive the wisdom I had known during prayers in the morning rain. What was it that was most important about this phone call? What was the heart of the matter? I could not recall. Dry anger expanded inside of me. I could feel my face flushing with blood, but I refused to react to Reshma's comments.

"I am listening," I said. Then Mohammad spoke.

"With all respect, my sister, your father is a product of the liberalism of modern life, and unfortunately he contributes to it. We Muslims must change all that and return to the traditions of the Q'ran. The way we live must reflect the sacred teachings. God has given women the responsibility to shape human character through the family. Do not set God's design for you aside. You must surrender to His holy will."

"What if this marriage is God's will?" I asked.

"It is not," Reshma said with authority. Then I spoke with a higher authority.

"Reshma, you should attend your sister's wedding. Ammi would expect it. And you are obligated to obey the mother of this family."

"You mean I should obey you!"

"I demand it!"

There was silence on the line for several seconds before Reshma replied.

"As a Sikh, Abbu had no authority to designate you as the family's mother. I have simply accepted it to avoid creating discord. But I cannot accept Meena's marriage to this man. And I will never obey you."

"Nor will I permit it," Mohammad said, his voice trembling. "This is the problem with inferior religions. Islam is more than a wedding ceremony; it is the supreme way of life. Look at Turkey and Jordan. Secularists like you are exterminating Islam as a basic creed and replacing it with half-baked Western ideas."

"Me? Exterminate Islam?" I said, flabbergasted. "Reshma, please?"

"Islam is under assault," Reshma said. "It is not you, really, but modern forces as well as old inside forces, such as the Ahmadis— the Christians and the Zionists, too. This is why Mohammad and I have joined the vanguard that will resurrect the caliphate and take Islam to the entire world again."

Now Reshma sounded like a fanatic—just as Faisah had warned. Suddenly, I became very calm.

"I understand better now. But I am still the mother of this family. And Meena will have her wedding to Zeshan. If you feel you can't attend, I deeply regret that."

"As the eldest male Muslim in the family I forbid this marriage," said Mohammad.

"Forbid it?"

"Think clearly, Ujala," Reshma said, pacing her words. "It is a matter of honor."

On the evening before the full moon—the first night of the four-day wedding celebration—the two families dined at their separate homes, Meena in Nankana Sahib with us, and Zeshan in Lahore with his parents. Amir and Abbu strung twinkling white lights around the exterior of the house and the courtyard, in the trees and shrubbery. They rented a generator in case the power system fizzled.

The family ate our last meal with Meena as a single woman, and I insisted on preparing it. I wanted to give her the dishes of our childhood—creamed lentils, mattar paneer, spiced chapati and milk tea. The entire family dressed in yellow, bright and fresh under the lights in the neem tree. Abbu wore his saffron turban and sat next to Meena at the bamboo table. Amir and Faisah piled carpets and pillows in the courtyard so that we could rest for the evening in the open air.

"I wish Ammi were here," said Meena.

"Oh, but she is here," said Abbu.

On the second night of celebration, during mendhi, the henna painting, Faisah, Amir, and I delivered Zeshan's wedding clothes. We stayed to decorate his hands and feet with henna. Faisah brought bags of the triple-sifted powder, bottles of eucalyptus, clove, and lemon oil, and several tipped cones. She mixed the paste with a spatula and applied it thickly.

"These designs are good luck and will last a long time—as will the luck," Faisah said to Zeshan.

Soon Amir was painting intricate geometric patterns on Zeshan's hands, from his fingertips to his forearm just above his wrist. When they finished, they sprayed his hands with latex and worked on his feet. Abida fed her son sweetmeats while Faisah and Ujala designed the patterns.

"Animal, vegetable, or mineral?" Faisah asked.

"Animal," Zeshan said suggestively, and Faisah traced matching lions on his feet.

"I had an interesting guest in my class this week," said Abida, who taught sociology at Lahore University.

"Faisah looks like she is painting with her nose," I said, trying to keep the conversation moving. "And who was it that spoke to your class?"

"Kazzaz," she said, "Jabril Kazzaz, the one they call the Gandhi of Lahore. I believe he can become the role model for Muslims in the next century. He talks of humanitarian jihad—struggle with the modern world, engagement, not opposition to it.

"Kazzaz . . . of course, we know his work, but I never heard him speak," said Faisah.

"Let me assure you that he is as brilliant as he is kind," said Abida. "His is the largest welfare organization in Pakistan, funded entirely by private donations. He has shown what people can achieve through perseverance."

Faisah stopped painting, interested now in what Abida was saying.

"It is as if the man has no ego. On principle he will not use his male privilege, he says, because it creates such misunderstandings between men and women—and you know," Abida said, jabbing her elbow into my upper arm, "he is single."

I blushed. Abida was blind to the discomfort she was causing.

"I mean he's almost as old as your father, but he is quite attractive. And now that we are relatives, I could arrange an introduction. Perhaps at our home? Perhaps next week?"

I had always wanted to meet the famous Jabril Kazzaz. Why not? I thought.

"Perhaps both Faisah and I could come?" I winked at Faisah, who rolled her eyes.

"As you wish," said Abida. "I'll call Jabril tomorrow."

When Abida wasn't looking, Faisah wagged her tongue at me.

In the morning of the third day, Meena's wedding dress arrived. A gift from Zeshan, it was carmine silk patterned with gold thread and seed pearls. When the dupatta fell around her face and over her shoulders, its metallic lining caused the flecks in Meena's eyes to sparkle like topaz. We dressed Meena like a doll. We wrapped six strands of pearls around her neck, creating a high collar. Between the necklace and the neckline, we hung two more strands of gold and pearls. We threaded the hole in her left nostril with a thin golden hoop and strung pearls across her cheek on a filament, fastening one end to the hoop and the other into her hair. Clipped to the center part in Meena's hair was a ruby the size and shape of a fig. It was the mahr, the groom's gift to the bride that would be the beginning of her separate resources as his wife. Then we took every ring that had belonged to Ammi and placed all of them on Meena's fingers.

The house became our shrine to Meena. The scent of gardenias and spices filled the garden. Amir served a fruit punch imported from Ceylon. Abbu greeted a few dozen guests and then retreated to play the harmonium as background music. Zeshan and Meena exchanged wedding vows in the courtyard and signed official papers. Meena stood with Zeshan's family while the imam held the Holy Q'ran over their heads.

On the fourth and final day, the two families dined at Zeshan and Meena's home, where they hosted their first dinner party. When we finally had to say good-bye to her, Meena was aglow in happiness and tears.

Back in Nankana Sahib, as I readied for bed that night, I recalled Mohammad's attitude in our telephone conversation. I remembered how Reshma had said that it was a matter of honor. Their absence had not ruined the wedding, and nothing bad had occurred. I removed the pistol from under my shalwar kameez, where I had carried it throughout the previous four days. I laid it on the handkerchief marked "Nafeesa." I sighed, thinking of Ammi.

"At last one of my tasks as a mother is accomplished," I told her. "Now Meena is in your hands."

5

Adiala Prison, 1996

I heard your letter on the radio yesterday," Rahima Mai said. "How did you ever get it past the censor?"

"What letter?"

"The one your sister read."

Rahima Mai's voice was friendly, but Ujala would not risk telling her that Yusuf had smuggled her letter out of Adiala. Telling Rahima Mai about her past was one thing, but she would not implicate anyone else.

"Perhaps someone wrote a letter and said it was from me."

"It was that Yusuf Salman, wasn't it?" Ujala stood still. "I let him interview some of the girls."

"Hmm," said Ujala, eager to change the subject. "What did you think of the program?" She had not heard a radio since entering Adiala.

"Well, the program was favorable—at least about conditions in the Women's Section. I liked that. And one has to admire these girls for forming their own radio station. That is quite an accomplishment in a man's world."

"It really is," Ujala said, plugging in the electric teakettle and unwrapping the box of Lipton's. "Call it a U.S.–Pakistani Friendship Project."

"A women's radio station!" repeated Rahima Mai. "Tell me how they pulled it off. I'll bet you know."

◆   ◆   ◆

It began with an American journalist I met in the Northwest Frontier Province. Lia Chee. It was her idea to develop a women's radio station in Pakistan. I remember listening to Lia and Faisah hatch their plan over hamburgers at the McDonald's across from the Lahore High Court.

"Maybe a few thousand readers see a story I write," Lia said, "So few people are literate here, but everyone can listen to the radio. It would be a great way to reach women, to educate—to—"

"To resist," said Faisah, completing Lia's thought. I could tell Faisah liked Lia's fast-talking ways. Lia pursed her lips.

"Resistance," Lia said, hissing in a friendly way. "Now that's a word you never hear in Pakistan." She bit into her Big Mac. Faisah was defensive.

"Oh, you are wrong. We have quite a history of resistance in this country." Faisah hissed. "Long before the women's movement." She emphasized the *T*. "Tuh."

We laughed.

Faisah told Lia about organizations that had defended political prisoners during General Zia's regime. "Zia promised that his Islamist policies would stop the harassment of women, but just the opposite occurred," she continued. "Then one day a woman was sentenced to death by stoning for adultery, when her partner was given one hundred lashes. Protests erupted all over the country."

Faisah turned to me.

"Remember? Ammi told us about the protest marches she and her friends were part of in Karachi—the bar associations, political activists, poets? She said everyone went."

I nodded.

"No more handouts. No more patronizing, that's what she told us were their slogans," I recalled. "The liberation of women was no longer simply a matter of charity; it became a matter of justice."

We gave Lia Pakistani resistance in nutshell, and she was impressed.

"Good Lord, you girls are tough," she said. But she kept coming back to the idea of a radio program. She had a lot of time on her hands now that her magazine editor was showing less and less interest in her stream of articles about women's lives in Pakistan.

"We're not a feminist magazine," the editor had e-mailed her. "The work is good, but not really suitable for us—we're more environmental, travel, cultural—not political." Lia knew that the editor was right. She began to research the idea of women's radio in Pakistan and to look for foundation funding. She wanted to sell Faisah on the idea.

"Radio is low-tech and cheap," said Lia.

"And where would poor women get radios?" Faisah questioned in Faisah fashion.

"I don't know. Maybe we buy them cheap and hand them out. Let me work on that one," said Lia. She was so full of energy and optimism. Then Faisah's opposition turned.

"Well," she said, "We would need our own station. Or maybe the Pak pop station would give us a slot on its schedule."

"Hell, let's just buy a radio station!" said Lia. "It may not be as difficult as you think."

"Maybe it's time to meet with Jabril Kazzaz," Faisah said to me. "Lia's research sounds promising, but this is Pakistan, after all. We need connections."

"I interviewed Kazzaz once," Lia said. "I swear he knows everyone in Pakistan. I am sure he would know about media funding. Or if he doesn't, he will know who does know."

"Maybe Abida could arrange a meeting for us," said Faisah. "Remember when she offered to do that? Huh, Baji?" She winked at me.

"Actually, I agree," I said, sidestepping the innuendo. "He might be a great source of information for us. I'll call Abida."

Kazzaz was to Lahore what Mother Teresa was to Calcutta. They say that as a young man he drove through the city and picked up corpses from the streets to bury them. Later, as people began to recognize his truck, they turned to him for medical transportation. Soon volunteers and donations piled up on his doorstep. After five years, his organization operated medical clinics throughout Punjab. After ten years, he had fifty clinics and blood banks, maternity centers, orphanages, and emergency services—an entire network of institutions to serve the poor.

Kazzaz's spiritual devotion was personal, and he was something of a mystery. No one knew exactly where he came from. He spoke and behaved like a Punjabi, but his name was Arabic—Iraqi—and he claimed no particular town as his home. And—most unusual—he remained unmarried. They said he spent Fridays in the orphanages, bathing and feeding the children, or taking them out for picnics. A living saint.

When we arrived at the Kazzaz Foundation, children were launching kites in the courtyard entrance, where a man was sweeping with a stick broom.

"Would you direct us to Mr. Kazzaz's office, please?" Faisah asked the sweeper. He pointed up the staircase and followed us to the door.

"This is it, Madam," he said, opening the door. Seeing that the room was empty, Lia turned back to the janitor.

"I know you," she said, smiling and pointing to him, and he laughed out loud.

"Please forgive me, my friends. I am Jabril Kazzaz. How can I help you?"

I liked him right away—both for sweeping the floor and for playing a trick on us. Kazzaz was not a handsome man, but he was attractive in his simple cotton robe. His eyes were narrow—one was slightly bloodshot. He had a trimmed moustache and beard, dark gray hair, thinning on top, and his skin was the color of pecans.

We entered an office with adjoining rooms visible through glass windows on both walls. A row of corpses lay on the floor in one room. Some were wrapped in white cloths with ropes, and others were being washed and wrapped by workers. There was a strong odor of camphor and a pervading silence. On the other side of his office was a small kitchen. Kazzaz gestured toward a screened portion of the central room where several chairs circled a brass table. On the other side of the screen I could see his sleeping and dressing area, a rolled up prayer rug and a large desk.

A barefoot young man handed a plastic tray to Kazzaz, who carried cups and saucers to us himself. He spoke as he poured the tea.

"I am fascinated by your idea of a women's radio station. How wonderful! So likely to encourage self-sufficiency."

"We are uncompromising in our position that ending violence against women is our purpose, not charity," Faisah said—too directly, too quickly. It was her way of stating for the record that she did not want the project to be watered down into mere social work. To her this radio project was about educating people to bring about fundamental social and political change.

"Good. Then you have a clear focus," Kazzaz said. "Strong vision is so important to success." Lia jumped into the conversation.

"We agree. And we hoped that with your experience and contacts, you would point us in the right direction."

"And give us some idea of pitfalls to avoid," said Faisah.

"There are so many wonderful women's organizations doing important work already—like Pakfem, and the Women's Legal Aid, and WASP. You don't need my advice."

"You know WASP?" asked Faisah. "Our mother was one of the founders." She looked at me. "And Ujala has worked for the organization for many years."

"So you follow in your mother's footsteps by establishing this radio station?"

"Something like that," Faisah said.

Kazzaz put his teacup aside, sat back in his chair and reached for a file folder of papers.

"I did a little research to prepare for our meeting. I've collected some documents. The names of people who may be able to help you." He handed Faisah a sheet of paper with a short list. "I know of several South Asians interested in media projects, and they might like to fund something innovative that would have staying power—an institution like a radio station, for example."

"Shukriah," Faisah thanked him, accepting the paper he offered to her.

"I strongly urge that you not become dependent on government money; even U.N. money is subject to political manipulation, so I'd avoid that too. And you would need someone like Lia, who has experience with the media, and local Pakistanis also, who know radio and who understand Pakistan. We forget how confusing our country is to outsiders. I've included people I know at several TV and radio stations. I believe they would share your point of view on the issues."

Then Kazzaz turned to me.

"I missed the opportunity of an introduction to you and your family through Abida," he said. "But I have met your other sister, Meena. She used to work in our Grand Trunk Road orphanage."

"Then you must meet our father and our brother, too," Faisah said. "We bring an invitation from him to you for dinner next week at our home in Nankana Sahib. What shall we tell him?"

"I would be delighted," Kazzaz said, rising from his chair. "Now you must excuse me. I hear the call to prayer."

Kazzaz came to Nankana Sahib during the lamp festival of Mela Chiraghan, in honor of holy man, Shah Hussain, the poet of love. Traditional music and poetry have given way now to boom boxes and radios. Nonetheless, devotees still burned lamps at the shrine. Garlands of marigolds were sold on every corner. We all waited for Kazzaz at the depot. He waved to Faisah through the bus window.

"May I introduce you to our father, Kulraj Singh," Faisah said. The men nodded to one another. Kazzaz realized by our father's name, Singh, that he was a Sikh.

When Jabril Kazzaz looked at me, I had to turn my face away. Silly woman, I thought. What is this? Your wear your nicest pastel pink. You dress up for him, and when he looks your way, you dissolve. Frankly, what I had seen in his eyes was that I took his breath away. Faisah and Abbu saw it, too. Later, following dinner under the neem tree, we found ourselves alone at the table while the others busied themselves in the kitchen.

"Enjoy the kheer," Meena said, as she placed two bowls of rice pudding before us and removed the last dishes from the table. "I am getting too fat in this new marriage of mine, so I am dieting." She left a pot of tea on the table.

A spring chill was setting in, so I added a few sticks to the heating stove beneath the neem tree. Jabril poured the jasmine tea. Then he took a spoonful of sugar from the bowl, soaked it in the tea, and placed it directly in his mouth.

"An old treat," he said, chuckling. "When I was a child, our mother was strict and did not allow candy. So my sister and I would prepare tea as an excuse to devour the sugar."

I leaned back against a stack of pillows and asked about his sister.

"Oh, Baji died many years ago," he said, "Actually, were it not for her, I probably would not have chosen my life's work."

"Go on," I said.

"I don't usually discuss it, but because of the way she died, I could not bury her properly, and I grieved and grieved. Then one day I came across the corpse of a woman in the gutter on Lindh Road. My mind must have been mixing with God's at that moment. I thought, 'Bury her. This could be Baji.' So I did, and God gave me fresh eyes to see the world. I want never to forget that each person I meet could be Baji. That is why I sleep in a room next to corpses."

I felt I knew exactly what he was describing, wanting to be with people who are suffering because you need to be. I told him how my mother inspired me in a similar way—to be a teacher. I was drawn to this man and felt at ease in his presence. I wanted to say something comforting and waited for an opening.

"It has been many months since I have made time for the simple pleasure of dining with friends in a country home," he said. "The bus ride stirred memories of my childhood. The shifting winds rippling the wheat and blowing orange blossoms in the groves. The petals spread all over the ground." He sucked on a long splinter he had dug from the tree. "My energy has been renewed by you three young women with your big hearts and big ideas."

The darkening sky was moonless. Sparrows finished their chorus and crickets were warming up for a song. I interrupted the din with a whisper.

"I believe that for every soul there is a watcher, don't you?" He looked in my eyes. "Perhaps your Baji watches your soul still, the way Ammi watches mine."

He nodded and we relaxed until it was time for Amir to drive him to the bus station. The two bowls of kheer remained untouched through the night. The flies must have relished our rich dessert.

6

Lahore, 1996

Meena was weary. She had hosted another three-hour radio program—this one about women jailed under Hudood and Zina Ordinances, laws that cause women who file police complaints about rape to be imprisoned for adultery or fornication. Meena pushed her chair away from the microphone and rubbed a fist into the small of her back.

"It is too much to take," she said. "I can't stay for the meeting tonight. This job is exhausting."

"Maybe we should give you an earlier shift," said Faisah.

"Maybe so. I have to go now. Want to catch the early bus." She chewed on a small piece of chapati she had brought from home. This folding chair is not enough support, she thought. I'll have to remember to bring a pillow from home. She slurped the last of her Pepsi Cola from a paper cup and tossed it in the plastic trash basket.

"Talking nonstop takes everything out of me," she said, picking up her shoulder bag. "I'm basically an introvert, you know." She was glad to have a job where she could spend time with Faisah. Since her marriage to Zeshan, she and Faisah rarely had time for each other, and she missed her other sisters. After her wedding she never heard from Reshma, and visits to Ujala in prison were limited. Faisah and the legal team had priority.

"You may be able to work around the clock," she said, "but I just want to get home and crawl into bed with my husband."

"I'll walk with you," said Faisah. "You really do look shaky."

"But I have to leave *now*," Meena said. "I want to catch the early bus." Faisah had a way of making everything take twice as long as it should, until *she* was ready to move, and then there was no keeping up with her. Meena's voice communicated clearly that she was not tolerating any delays today.

"No, no, I'm ready," said Faisah. "Let's go."

Outside, the city baked. Meena's eyes stung and nausea rose in her throat. She swallowed the stomach acid back down and pulled the dupatta over her head. Faisah began her fast-paced walk. Meena no longer hurried to keep up with Faisah, as she had as a little girl. She had become familiar with the shape of Faisah from behind, the angle of her body and her long-legged pacing, as if she had something heavy in her pockets. Sometimes Faisah walked with her head down, sometimes in a book, while she nonetheless advanced at a fearless pace, regardless of traffic, potholes, other people.

I might not be able to recognize Faisah's face in a lineup, but I sure would know her from behind, chuckled Meena to herself. Ten paces ahead, Faisah stopped and glanced back, waiting.

I just can't keep up with her, thought Meena. She sighed. If I miss the early bus, I'll just take the next one.

Her mind was trying to shake off some of the violent images it had created during the radio show. Meena imagined the women's bodies as if they were sketches in an art book or an anatomy text. She pictured a dull blade sawing through tendons and muscles at the back of a knee, and the whetting stone that had been passed over in favor of a rustier cruelty. She imagined chubby fingers probing the wound. She shook her head to change the movie in her mind.

"Sorry," Faisah said, as Meena caught up with her.

"I thank God I have my life," Meena said, "and not the ones we report about on the radio."

"Yeah. We are lucky."

They crossed the bazaar and entered a shady, walled alley where pedestrians walked in single file to and from the buses parked at the depot up ahead. The stencils and tin fringes of the buses were coated with dust. It was hard to imagine how they could gleam after a rain shower—when the faces of women imprinted on the sides of buses and praise for Allah in Arabic script would flash in the headlamps of passing cars. Every inch of every bus was decorated to death.

"Extreme decor," said Faisah. "If only these men treated women as well as they treat their buses!"

"Or their trucks," said Meena.

"Or their cars."

"Or their Vespas."

"Or their bicycles."

Meena snickered. "OK, you win. What else is there?"

Faisah stepped into the mud-packed street to let a woman with three children in tow pass by. Two men with their faces hidden inside shawls walked from the opposite direction. They did not step off the sidewalk, as expected, but passed close to Faisah and Meena, closer than men were supposed to walk by women. The larger man's shoulder brushed Faisah's, as he refused to yield the sidewalk. Feeling the insult, Meena turned her head automatically away to the inside edge of her dupatta.

Then she heard Faisah scream. It was an unearthly sound, a high and piercing wail. At the same time she felt herself pulled backward, pushed into the wall. She lost her balance and fell to one knee. She saw the two wrapped figures running away.

Faisah's voice rose hysterically. She was on the ground, leaning on both elbows with her face turned toward the dirt. Around her, a circle of people gathered, shrieking at the sight. Meena limped, pushing them aside and kneeling next to her sister. She saw a wet, blackening wound creeping down the side of Faisah's head, eating away at her neck and her cheek, moving toward her eye. It seemed to devour everything in its path and its edges thickened like leather. Acid masked the side of Faisah's face, burning its way into her body, mutilating and devouring as it seeped into the layers of skin.

"My face, my face!" Faisah cried in agony. "OOOOh!"

Bystanders watched, immobilized, fascinated. Meena panicked.

"Help!" she shouted at no one in particular. How to stop the pain? How to get rid of the acid? Should she touch Faisah's face or not? She ripped her dupatta from her head.

"Here, wipe it off with this," she said. "Or let me do it."

Faisah groaned as the fibers floated onto her skin. The contact was unbearable.

"Get some water," Meena shouted. "For the love of Allah, somebody get some water."

In response a man ran toward the bus depot. A child handed her a bottle of Pepsi and Meena poured it slowly over the raw, black and red, widening wound.

Faisah's moaning stopped, and Meena feared she was dead. Then suddenly Faisah sat up, leaning on her elbows. She turned her charred, disfigured face to the crowd and glared at them with her one good eye.

"Chase them," she demanded. "They are getting away! For the love of justice, catch them!"

But no one moved.

A little girl pressed more deeply into the folds of her mother's shalwar. Her eyes widened as she peeked out. She could not resist looking. An old man shook his cane in the direction that the assailants had fled. An old woman, meaning to offer her condolences, began the familiar "tsk, tsk, tsk," an expression on hearing a tragic story. Two men in Levis and kurtas turned away from the sight of acid searing through the flesh of a young woman, a woman whom, only moments before, they would have tried to catch a glimpse of, a glance of her ankle, a peek of her wrists, a momentary view of her face. The two stood motionless, unable to look at Faisah, unable to look at each other.

"Go!" the old man urged them, stirring the air with his cane again. "Go!"

The two men nodded simultaneously at his order and raced in the direction the old man pointed, their elbows pumping like boys used to competing. But they also realized that by this time the men who had burned Faisah would be lost in the crowd on the boulevard. To chase after them was one thing. For that, they could be heroic. But to catch up with them was another. That might

mean to face a fist, or a knife, or the acid bottle, to know the throb
and devastation that continued to corrode Faisah's face.

Rahima Mai thought that Ujala must have been crying all night
long. Where she had been gaunt but shining before, now Ujala
looked dull and thin. Sore eyes and swollen nose. Absolutely red-
faced, Rahima Mai thought. Awful.

"I heard about the attack on Faisah, uh—your sister," she said,
feeling her throat tighten. She, too, felt grieved. From Ujala's
stories, she felt as if she knew Faisah personally. "I am so sorry. If
you need to take the day off, you may."

"Shukriah, Madam," said Ujala, "but all that I want is to go to
the hospital to visit Faisah." She looked hopefully at Rahima
Mai. "If you please, Madam." Ujala reverted to formalities
whenever she was under emotional pressure. She found comfort
in the childhood habits she had acquired in her Christian convent
school.

She could not let herself imagine Faisah right now. She tried
not to recall the face of Bilqis, the face that haunted her still.
She tried not to picture Faisah. She refused to imagine her as a
victim. But she could not stop seeing Faisah laughing, Faisah
ranting, Faisah being Faisah, and the clear, plain, girlish face
that was hers. The mind has to picture something. It demands an
image, regardless.

"I'll look into it," Rahima Mai said. "I can ask Central Security.
However, I know that they already have categorized you as high
risk. That was a result of your little 'Letter from Prison' incident."

Ujala recoiled, and at once Rahima Mai regretted her words. It
would have been enough just to say she would look into it. Ujala
had no idea how much headquarters hated the attention that her
presence had brought to the prison system.

"Are you losing control down there, Rahima Mai?" the warden
had asked when he heard about the radio program. Rahima Mai
knew better than to point out to him that the broadcast had said
good things about Adiala's Women's Section.

"No, Sir," she had said.

"Then get a handle on the situation! Radio shows! Protesters at the gate! Next thing you know there will be petitions to take our jobs away!"

The terror of losing her job was a worn groove in an old record for Rahima Mai. Without this job, what am I? she thought. Just another lonely woman.

"Have a cup of tea," she said to Ujala. "I brought some biscuits."

Talking to Rahima Mai about my life will only bring Faisah to mind again, thought Ujala. "Actually, I would like to work today," she said. It was the first time she had not complied with anything that Rahima Mai asked. Work was the ticket. It would keep her mind off things. She looked at Rahima Mai for permission not to tell her story today.

"As you wish."

Ujala began sorting papers into piles on the table. Budgets. Correspondence. Incidents. Invoices. Personnel. Programs. Reports. The last folder contained one thin sheet of carbonized paper for each woman—the police order that authorized holding them. Nothing else here is relevant, Ujala thought. She felt a sharp pain in her rib. Here is a letter from the warden about security precautions. A slight weakening of her eyesight. Letters out of focus. And here is a bill for trash removal. Where do they dispose of the youths of the women in this place? she wondered. And a bill for the truck's battery acid. Acid. Corrosion. Burn. Bilqis—Ooh.

"Faisah," she cried out. Her voice squeaked like a puppy waiting outside the door.

Rahima Mai heard the peep but guarded her eyes for the sake of Ujala's privacy. It had been uncomfortable for her to have her request for a story denied. She could not allow insubordination, even from Ujala. Especially from someone like Ujala—a dangerous prisoner, indeed. Rahima Mai knew her superiors' eyes were on her. And Ujala has friends in high places. Her knot of worry tightened.

"Madam," Ujala said, sniffling, getting Rahima Mai's attention. "—unless you would like to hear about my travels in the Northwest Frontier Province?" Now she was appealing to Rahima Mai's curiosity. Ujala was desperate to shut out the present, even if it meant returning to the terrible events that occurred in the Northwest Frontier Province, the events of the past year that led her to Adiala.

"Oh, yes," Rahima Mai said. "Yes." Ujala's offer cancelled any concerns about insubordination and put the two of them back in their proper relationship. "I would like that." She put her papers aside and lifted the receiver on her telephone. "I do not want to be disturbed," she told the sergeant-guard. Then Rahima Mai stood and rolled her shoulders back to release the tension that gripped them. She went directly to the office door and locked it.

"Now sit down," she said.

The two women scooted the plastic chairs over to the table with the hot water pot. Rahima Mai unwrapped a yellow tag Lipton tea bag while Ujala turned over their teacups.

◆ ◆ ◆

When I left Nankana Sahib last year for my assignment in the NWFP, it was September, the end of monsoon. For once, I was not traveling alone. With me was Chanda, a fifteen-year-old girl whom Faisah had found in the Lahore women's shelter. When Faisah heard the girl's story, she asked me to take her with me.

Chanda's family lived in Lahore near the red-light district, and, as a child, she was forbidden to go into the Shahi Mohalla. But to Chanda and her brother, Sadiq, the mohalla was irresistible. They often wandered through the bazaar while their parents were at work or shopping. Buildings there lined streets so narrow that only motor scooters and donkeys could pass. Lines of laundry—bright cloths and striped towels—flapped above the buying and selling. Men in turbans pushed handcarts with mangoes, oranges, and potatoes. In the outdoor kitchens of the street cafés, they cooked samosas, cauliflower, and curried lamb in shallow pans the size of bus tires. The aromas of spices and oil mixed in the air. And, positioned above the shops, as if on pedestals, were sitting rooms with open windows and doors. At night the rooms were lit to attract customers. People meandered through the area, filling their senses.

Chanda had a friend named Lila, who was teaching her classical dance. For many generations Lila's family had operated well-established businesses in the district. They entertained male patrons with music, dancing, and, sometimes, sex. At fourteen, Lila's virginity had been purchased by a tourist for a high price. She was the rising star of her family's fortune. Her little cousins were next in line.

Lila's family gathered during the day to practice music—the tabla, the harmonium, the sitar—and the girls danced and sang, groomed themselves, and prepared for evening. At night, the room became a kotha, a performing room for entertaining guests.

Chanda adored all the jewelry and bright colors. She imagined ankle bells of her own that would ring out when she moved her body around the room. She wanted to be a movie star like the Lollywood women who towered over the neighborhood in street posters. She dreamed of bangles on her arms and the personal attention of Chanda's ustad, a famous music teacher in the district. A family would quiet with respect whenever the ustad appeared.

Sadiq, too, had found friends in the Shahi Mohalla. Lila's brothers always had extra money, rupees they earned by running errands—getting customers small change or marigold garlands for the dancers. "Coca-Cola?" the boys would ask, and seeing a nodding reply, they raced in their tee shirts and jeans to bring back the worn out bottles with plastic straws bouncing. They extended their palms. "Two rupees, please, thank you very much, thank you very much."

Time changes everything for girls, and for Chanda the confinements of womanhood came early. By the time she was ten, she was covered in a dupatta and stayed inside with her mother. While the flesh on her chest plumped up under layers of cloth, her brother continued to run freely. Once Sadiq helped her to dress like a boy so she could go with him. He tucked her hair into a cap and held open his extra pants so that she could step into them. But two aunties saw them on the street and sent Chanda home in tears.

"A whore, that one will be," one shouted. The other's black-clothed head nodded in agreement.

When she turned twelve, Chanda no longer attended school.

Instead she cooked whatever food Sadiq and her father purchased in the bazaar. After awhile Sadiq changed, too. He stopped bringing her news of Lila and her family.

"Women who sing and dance in public are whores," he said. "Lila is a whore!"

The taller he got, the bossier he became, ordering Chanda to bring him a towel or a cup of tea. He would push her down or glower if she refused. No longer did they splash in puddles together. Instead, she became her brother's servant. But every day, whenever she was alone in the house, without ankle bells or chiffon, Chanda practiced the steps Lila had taught her.

One day when she was fifteen, Chanda covered herself with her mother's old burqa and walked to the Shahi Mohalla again. The sun appeared between the lines of laundry on the rooftops. People seemed happy, and the city looked prosperous. The metal gate to Lila's compound was locked when she arrived. The buzzer was broken, so she made a fist and pounded, rattling the iron fence.

Lila's brother called out—"Who is there?"

"Chanda," she replied, but her voice was so soft he could not hear her.

"Who?" he shouted, pulling the gate open fast. He saw the short girl wrapped in a burqa. He looked around for a wali, a guardian, a brother, a father, an uncle. No one.

"Chanda," the girl said. "I want to see Lila."

She spent the day indoors with Lila, repeating the dances her body had memorized. She could still bend her knee at the proper angle and spread her fingers across her face, to hide, then to expose her dark eyes. The music was familiar and her moves were bold. By midafternoon, she wrapped up again in the burqa and prepared to leave.

"Come again soon," Lila said, kissing Chanda's cheeks.

"I'll try."

Chanda stepped onto the dirt road. As Lila closed the door, someone grabbed Chanda and dragged her away. In a vacant pile of rubble, Sadiq roughly pulled the burqa up over her head.

"Stop!" she shouted at him.

"Whore!" he yelled back, forcing her body against a crumbling wall. At that moment a man approached, holding a scalpel in the folds of his robe.

"Baba, stop him!" Chanda begged. Her father stepped in front of her, and as Sadiq held her head back into the wall, her father sliced off half of Chanda's nose and fled before a crowd could gather or the police could be called. Blood dripped through Chanda's fingers and collected in a cement bowl of construction debris. Chanda screamed until Lila's brothers came and brought her in.

In the hospital Chanda was all alone, unlike the other patients who had families to hover over them. When she became terrified that her father and brother would return to finish what they'd started, a nurse told her about the women's shelter. Chanda stayed in the shelter for several weeks, but everyone knew that she had to get out of Lahore and out of Punjab. Someone told Faisah, who told me, and I agreed to take Chanda to Chitral where she might start a new life.

Faisah brought her to me at the bus station. Chanda was light-skinned and slender. She covered the bandage on her face with a heavy veil, fastened so that only her frightened hazel eyes showed. She spoke Pashto, a language that I did not know but would have to learn in the Northwest. She knew a little Urdu.

On the first day of our three-day journey, we rode on the bus in a comfortable silence, as strangers sometimes do when their bodies are committed to being together for a limited time in close quarters. On the way to Peshawar we passed through the suburbs of Lahore, the large apartment buildings, the impoverished mud of Rawalpindi, and the flat roofs of the Afghan refugee camps where the Taliban were growing in numbers. The government hired them to guard the convoys heading west to Central Asia.

Chanda twisted her head to watch schoolchildren wave from the street—the boys in their navy blue school pants, V-neck sweaters, white shirts, and ties. The girls in their white shalwars with light blue kameezes, red cardigans, and white cotton dupattas—those who had schools nearby and families that wanted their girls to be educated. I watched the sky fill with crows and floating kites. From a distance it was hard to tell which were which.

The bus crossed the mighty Indus, the river that severs the

length of Pakistan. We stopped at the river where a security checkpoint marked the entrance to the Northwest Frontier Province. As the soldier waved the buses through a stone archway, the driver switched off his radio. In the NWFP, Shariah law is strict now and in some places enforced by both religious and government officials. Movies and radios are forbidden. Men's beards must to be worn at least a fist-length below the chin, and women and girls are being expelled from schools and are required to observe purdah or to suffer a public beating—or worse.

In the morning I learned that rain north of Peshawar had caused landslides. One bus went over the side of a mountain, killing everyone onboard. We rode in a Japanese bus that seated twenty people, a new model, but already worn from constant use. Chanda and I were the last to board it, and every seat was taken, except two that were separate. Chanda sat in the back row of the bus, between two other women. I sat across from the side door, next to a woman dressed in brown pants and a khaki shirt. She had a red cotton scarf tied around her neck. She wore sunglasses and held a backpack between her legs. She looked like she might be Chinese.

"Have you been traveling for a long time?" I asked in English. She nodded.

"I come from Lahore," I said, trying to make conversation. "And you?"

"Singapore," she said, waking from her traveler's stupor. She reached for my hand. "My name is Lia Chee." She had an American accent.

"Ujala Ehtisham," I said.

"Ujala?" Lia looked quizzical. "I've not heard that name before."

"It means light," I said. "Shining light. And Lia?"

"Means nothing. We go more by the sound of a name than the meaning, I think." She paused. "Going all the way to Chitral?"

I nodded.

"Good. Then we'll be friends by the time we get there," she said, as if the matter had been in controversy and now it was settled.

As we went on, the world became greener, nature became denser, and everything became wetter. By the time we stopped for gas, the air was the color of graphite and enveloped everything. It was as if the mountains were not there at all. The bus wound around the steepness, groaning as the gears shifted. Asphalt became dirt, which became rock, as we rose into a misty world. Dozens of waterfalls spouted from the wall of rock across the river. Water fell into light, and earth blew into water. The world became dreamy, as the elements dissolved into each other.

"It looks like we may end up drinking the Indus instead of crossing it," said Lia. She pointed to a bulging escarpment that had collapsed into the riverbed.

"They say that one who drinks from the Indus becomes as heroic as a lion," I said, quoting Abbu.

"Yeah," Lia said, with a smirk. "And sick as a dog."

The locals were trying to shore up the road. They dug up and moved the earth. They packed rocks and sand to divert the runoff. Families divided the work. Men and boys waded into the rushing river to dislodge the rocks and to carry them to the riverbank. They hefted and hugged them and left them at the feet of the women, who sat wrapped in shawls, with boulders between their knees, hammering. Children carried the broken pieces to piles close to the road, according to the size of each fragment.

Despite their exertions, the humans were powerless when compared to mountains, river, and rain. Eventually landslides spread debris, and the road was impassable. Other buses backed up on the road as people got off to collect their luggage and walk. The driver's helper climbed onto the bus roof to retrieve the baggage. He would place his hands on a bag and a passenger would shout up, "Mine, mine!" and he would hand it down. Coming from the other direction was a line of passengers from buses parked on the far side of a blanket of scree, walking toward our bus. One woman carried a small child on one hip and a pair of yak horns on the other.

Our bodies were stiff from hours of sitting. I envied anything that moved—the dogs in their muddy socks, the shrouded figure pushing a cart with oversized wheels, even the blinking signal on Lia's mobile phone. Perhaps it was the altitude getting to my brain, but I became transfixed by that blinking signal, a blip of a heartbeat, a cry in the wilderness. I realized that the ground beneath us was unstable where we were parked on the cliff's edge. The inside wheels were on the road, but I wondered if one of the outside wheels was spinning over the edge. I kept my eye on the blinking light to keep from panicking. I could hear the engine and wheels spinning, when, all at once, the bus lurched from air onto rock, and began to creep along a narrow passage.

Suddenly another bus appeared around a curve from the opposite direction. It tried to back up to let our bus pass, but a large truck blocked it from behind. The two buses were head to head, and ours was on the outside edge, above the river that narrowed into rapids a hundred feet below.

Our driver backed up as far as he could to give the oncoming bus as much room as possible. Underneath the tires, some rocks were smooth as bone, others were encrusted like scabs, or protruded like decay in a charnel ground. The oncoming bus rocked forward, inching along the inside passage. Through the window I could see anxiety on the driver's face reflected in the side mirror. I watched him throw his entire weight against the steering wheel. He turned momentarily away from what was ahead and glanced over his shoulder to the far side, where his helper, who stepped off of the bus, called out the conditions from the rear.

"Stupid driver," Lia said. "No need for us to risk staying on this bus. He should let us off."

I looked around at the other passengers. The ones who sat along the outside edge were not looking out the window, but no one was panicking. Chanda stared calmly ahead. Her feet wiggled. I fingered my prayer beads. How would it be to fall to death with strangers? There was nothing to be done about it.

The oncoming bus rocked slightly side to side as it squeezed past my window.

"Can't we get off this thing?" Lia shouted out in English.

No one replied.

Our driver was concentrating on the movement of the inside bus. The front wheels of the oncoming bus were now at our bus's midpoint. From where Lia sat by the window she was just inches from the driver of the other bus. If the wheels of the passing bus slid the least bit, its weight would coax us over the cliff.

Lia began to stand, but I pulled her back down on the seat. Her trying to get off the bus could be just the movement to shift the balance and take us over the edge, which she, too, realized as soon as she stood.

A small group of men on the road examined the situation and offered their opinions on maneuvering the passage. Their whistles pierced the moment, signaling the driver whether to stop or go. River sounds pounded all around. At last the tail of the inside bus passed by. We rejoiced without a move, without a sound, proud of our home team, but not daring to disrupt anything. Then our bus ambled squarely onto the road, and everyone applauded.

Lia saw the tears of relief in my eyes. I didn't know what to say. She chucked the palm of her hand into my shoulder.

"It was nothing," she said. "I wasn't worried. Were you?"

As it turned out, Lia was neither Chinese nor from Singapore, as she preferred that people believe. She was an American of Chinese descent who had been raised in Greenville County, South Carolina, she said—a freelance writer on assignment for *Nature and Nurture*, an adventure travel magazine. She was their first correspondent to travel the mountains of Central Asia.

"I do actually live in Singapore now," she said. "I worked in New York for many years, but I've spent the past three in Central Asia—in the "Stans"—Afghani, Paki, Uzbeki." She counted them out on her fingers. "I prefer not to tell people I am American, so I let my face lead them to believe I am Chinese and I give them an address in Singapore. It works. You know what I mean?"

I recognized the *you know what I mean?* question that Americans use, prompting a courtesy that requires concurrence with whatever they say. Where do these women come from? I wondered. More than once I have come upon an English-speaking woman who has introduced herself and begun a conversation like this.

"It fooled me to see you traveling alone," Lia said. "I rarely see a woman alone on a bus in Pakistan—except me, of course." She smiled.

I told her I was not alone and pointed to Chanda. They waved to each other.

"Your sister?"

"You might say that," I said. I was careful what I told a stranger, especially a reporter, so I changed the subject and told her I was a teacher. I was surprised to learn that she knew about WASP. She became excited and asked me for an interview. I did not want to be rude, so I said we'd see. She rifled through her file folders and pulled out the one she wanted. I was surprised see a dozen articles she had published about women in Pakistan.

"Maybe I can visit your school in Chitral? I plan to use the Hilton as a home base. I'm going to try to get to the Kalash Valley, but this isn't the best season to get there. You know what I mean?"

I was no longer listening. I just nodded and continued reading her work. Lia's writing was as much poetry as journalism. It was rich in detail, both geographic and historic, and yet it was also informal and intimate, like an old-fashioned British travel letter. She had published articles on women's education, an interview with Jabril Kazzaz, another on slavery in the brick factories, and a piece on karo-kari, honor crimes in Sindh.

She explained how she had been conducting research on women in Pakistan for a long time. A reporter friend in New York first talked to her about the problems—a friend from Karachi. I was astonished to hear the next words come out of her mouth.

"Yusuf Salman," she said. "Maybe you know his work?"

What are the chances that, high in the Hindu Kush, a Pakistani teacher and an American journalist would know the same man who lived halfway around the world?

"Yusuf and I attended university together," I said. "He was studying journalism then. I heard he left for the U.S. many years ago."

"Was he gorgeous then, too?" she asked, smiling. I knew then that Lia was playing me. She was a skilled interviewer, intuitive, and she was reading beneath my surface. Maybe she could hear my racing heart.

"Very," I said and cracked a smile. I tried to relax with her. I could own up to an old attraction. After all, we almost died together on that bus. Lia prattled on about Yusuf.

"He's a master of the new journalism—and has quite a few Middle Eastern fans in the States, and South Asians."

But hearing news of Yusuf shocked me. Right away I recalled his still eyes. Before jealousy or regret could arise, I placed my mind on those steady spots. Then I dared to play Lia's own game to find out what I wanted to know.

"How well do you know Yusuf?" I asked.

"As well as journalists know each other when they are on assignment in different parts of the world," she said. "But we ran in the same social circle in New York."

Then she launched into this lengthy description of how she and Yusuf had met when Queen Noor was lobbying Congress over Jordanian support for Iraq during the Kuwait invasion.

"It was springtime in Washington," she said, "the dogwood was in bloom, and the Shoreham Hotel was white and gleaming. Noor, so elegant in her simple tunic—"

Finally I had to interrupt her.

"Tell me about Yusuf," I said, knowing that my impatience betrayed me.

"Oh," said Lia. The tone of our conversation shifted, and Lia jumped to what she guessed I wanted to know. "No, he's not married. He said there is no one in the U.S. to arrange it for him. And that he'd have to come back to Pakistan someday to be married."

Lia and I talked off and on all night long in the capsule of that bus. At every turn, it tossed us against its sides and against each other. I practiced a kind of lightness in my body that allowed me to float with the motion, rather than be bruised by gravity. By morning, the views became vaster, each mountain more massive than the one before, each valley wider and longer. From the strip of valley highway, distant villages looked like sesame seeds scattered at the feet of giants.

We joined Chanda and the other women at the back of the bus for meals and for tea. From time to time we switched places. Hearing Chanda's story, Lia wanted to interview her. I insisted that there be no real names or places in her story, and Lia agreed. She settled in next to Chanda while I translated from Urdu to English.

"In Chitral, she wants to be a dancer," I said, repeating what Chanda told me. In English I told Lia that dancing was most unlikely since the entire area is Pathan and the vast majority of women observe extreme purdah. "Dancing is completely forbidden . . . But let her dream."

Then Chanda tugged on my sleeve. She had understood at least some of what I had said to Lia.

"Pathan," she said, pointing to her heart. "Chanda. Pathan. Purdah," she said, pulling at the veil that covered her nose and mouth.

"You are Pathan?" Lia asked, and Chanda nodded.

"Balochi . . . Pathan . . . Chanda Khan," she said again, pointing to herself, sitting up straighter.

"Ah," said Lia, "the proud Khans."

The Khans were the kings—Genghis Khan, Lord of the Earth. Kubla Khan of Xanadu, where nothing is forgotten. Aga Khan, the great benefactor, the jet-setter, the playboy. The King, whose proud legacy touched this injured bird of a woman, Chanda Khan, who wanted to dance.

"Maybe she will become a dancer, even in Chitral," Lia said. "Isn't anything possible for a Khan?"

The bus took us north into Pathan country, where landlords, warlords, and gun dealers ruled. The men's hands smelled of meat and gunpowder, smoke and poppies. Many dyed their beards red with henna, as was the fashion. The Pathans, called Pashtuns elsewhere, were blue-blooded and tall, with light skin and angular features. In their culture, blood and land were paramount. Outsiders could buy land to build houses, but only Pathans were allowed to buy land to herd goats or raise horses, or to sow crops in the rain-fed fields. A Pathan would never let his daughter marry a pretender, because he knew the authentic bloodline. Life in the Northwest Frontier had more in common with Afghan and Baloch cultures than it had with Punjab or Sindh. Tribal customs and feudal law ruled, and a woman's transgression was taken up with her father, brother, or son. Family honor was paramount, encased in the bodies of the women, treasures protected in cloth and hidden away. A man outside the family, no matter how friendly he might be to a

Pathan male, was never allowed in the inner chambers. If a woman left the home, she covered in the shuttlecock burqa with only its mesh window through which to view the world.

Lia said she intended to wear a dupatta while in the Northwest Frontier.

"Good idea," I agreed.

"I have been to the Frontier before," she said. "I filed a story on the Friendship Highway into China. The people over there were laid-back, but the way things are going with the Taliban, I think I'd better cover my head."

"And your breasts . . ." I said. Lia bent her neck, pointing her chin toward her flat chest.

"Oh, those . . ."

September in the Hindu Kush.

Our breath clung to the bus windows like whispers of conversations left behind. We stepped into the frosty air of Chitral, a remote town of twenty thousand souls, located deep in Pathan country. I tasted an unfamiliar tang hanging in the air that I later learned was gunpowder. Any excuse—a wedding, a birthday— and gunfire rang through the mountains. The area was notorious for arms dealing, supplying guns and missiles to their cousins fighting the Russians in Afghanistan. Everyone wanted automatic rifles stamped MADE IN THE U.S.A. Pistols and Kalashnikovs lay spread across the counters of the open bazaar, with boxes of shells stacked shoulder high behind the men in their long woolen vests and flat hats. A young boy with an AK-47 stood like a guard next to an open stall. Unnecessary security, I assumed. The boy was just showing off. Although I carried one of my own, the idea itself of a gun sickened me. But here they were as basic as bread.

I watched the men of Chitral lay their blankets on the cold ground for prayers. The foreheads of the elderly were bruised from a lifetime of praising Allah in this way. Some bought fruit, flour, and milk to carry in plastic shoppers to their mud-brick homes, where they handed the bags to their women. The men wrapped themselves in woolen shawls and looked up to read the clouds.

Sides of raw mutton hung like curtains in the vendors' stalls. Apple trees and mulberry bushes wound around, gnarled and brambly. Fertile ground was sacred in this harsh land, where every tree was spoken for, watered, pruned, and harvested with care. Scarecrows stood at attention on the piles of stones that separated small farm plots, though they did not scare the birds. Crows and jays were everywhere.

We agreed that Chanda would stay with Lia for the time being—until I could figure out what the next step should be. They loaded their parcels and backpacks into the trunk of a taxi, and we agreed to meet at the hotel in three days. Sabira and Asma, teachers from the school, met me at the station with their old Toyota and their driver. The family's modest wealth and the women's determination had supported the school for the past three years. I would live in a teacher's suite—one room and an outhouse—in their family compound. They were eager to show me the one room with three walls where they offered classes to boys in the morning and to girls in the afternoon. They did not permit boys to attend unless their sisters could as well. When the girls began to observe purdah, they became like puppies tied up in a courtyard, waiting to be taken out. I intended to stay for a year—if I could endure this strict rural life.

The next morning Sabira and I met the other teachers and walked them to the compound. Through the open door of a makeshift madrassah I could see rows of young boys, sitting on the floor, rocking back and forth in their shawls, reciting the Q'ran.

"They used to be our students," Sabira said. "But the mullahs object to anything except education in the Q'ran." Sabira opened her arms to the sky as she mimicked the mullahs. "'Geography, history, literature—these tempt young people away from God. The Q'ran teaches us everything we need to know.'"

At noon we washed and prayed before sitting outside of my room in the sun-baked courtyard. We shared a pot of tea, a bowl of lentils, and roti.

"Everything here starts with the Q'ran," said Sabira, pulling the bread apart with her fingers and dipping into the warm lentils. "The Prophet—peace be unto him—lived a simple life, and was gentle to women," Sabira continued, sighing. "Oh, that he would return to remind these men how to treat women!"

Tahira was the youngest of the three sisters, bright-eyed and chubby. She told me about a girl whose father had forbidden her to return to the school.

"She threw herself off the roof of her house and broke her neck," Tahira recalled, speaking very fast, "—and the next week another girl did exactly the same thing—threw herself off the roof." Tahira's voice split as she spoke.

"Easy enough for grown men to criticize a young girl—such an easy target," said Asma, the oldest sister.

I recognized the burn in her voice. The conversations of women when they are alone are the same everywhere. In all the places I have taught—cities, seashores, and deserts, and in the northern mountains—it's all the same. Women's dissatisfaction is the cough that won't go away.

I saw an old man hobbling through the courtyard gate. He wore a long white coat and lungi and the Pathan hat. He had the orange henna beard of a Haji. He neither looked at us nor walked near us as he padded across the courtyard and disappeared into a mud-brick room. A scraggly red dog slipped in the door behind him.

"Our grandfather, Aga Ji," Sabira said, nodding in his direction. "He does not speak to women outside of the family, so he won't come over here as long as you are with us. Nothing personal to you. It's just his way."

"But how will that work if we take meals together?" I asked.

"We eat before or after the men, so it is no problem. We will hardly even notice him come or go. He takes care of himself. He waters and prunes a few poplars for one of the landlords, then spends the day at the mosque and the teahouse. He lives in his own world—he and his dog."

On Monday it was sunny. I pulled on my boots and walked along the muddy road to meet Lia and Chanda. I looked up to face Tirich Mir, the baby toe of the monstrous northern mountains, the twenty-five-thousand-foot wall of sheer rock and ice that stands at the gate of three ranges—the Hindu Kush, the Karakoram, and the Himalayas. It was awesome to behold, an enchanted, impossible place. It was as if the mountains were the only beings who knew the way things are and the way they always have been.

I trembled in their shadows. I knew that Tirich Mir was no protector. Soon it would be October when the mountain would offer no hospitality and the winter winds would blow whiteness around, covering the known world. Twice a week a plane flew to Chitral from Peshawar, the inaccessible city only a thought away from the lost horizon. Suddenly I was startled by the shriek of a falcon that swooped over my head in its endless search for rodents and water.

The Chitral Hilton was surrounded by a brick wall with broken shards of glass embedded along the top. Fiery red bushes framed a shallow pool where hundreds of floating candles were lit at twilight. Sparrows flew cheerily through the open lobby. Groups of businessmen, as well as trekkers and guides, formed small clusters. Embroidered wall hangings depicted local battles—against the Mongols, against the British, even a recent one against the Russians. Elephant blood ran beet red against the untouchable snow of the Khyber Pass.

I saw Lia and Chanda sitting on the terrace. Chanda was wearing a lavender shalwar kameez. Her gold necklaces gleamed in the sunlight. A string of seed pearls was attached to her hair on one side of her head under a gold-trimmed dupatta. The other end of the string of pearls was attached to a small bandage where the side of her nose used to be. I was speechless at her transformation from a wounded spot of a girl into this elegant woman. In the glow of her face and the flash of her bangles, Chanda Khan was the acclaimed Pathan beauty revealed.

I shook my head in disbelief.

"She has finally found out who she is, and she will be nothing else," said Lia, clearly enjoying my reaction. "I'm pretty brassy, but I wish I had her pluck. I mean, look at that girl."

Chanda nudged Lia with her elbow, as she gestured toward me.

"She can't wait for me to tell you," Lia announced, laughing. "Chanda got a job!"

"Dancer!" Chanda said in English. "No nose!" She pointed to her bandage. Chanda and Lia's laughter infected me, too, and we giggled like schoolgirls.

"Stop!" Lia pleaded, trying to catch her breath, "I'll wet my shalwar." And we laughed some more. When we saw the waiter bringing ice cream, we regained our composure. "It's too wonderful! And I get to tell the world her story."

"Tell me first!" I begged. And while Chanda enjoyed the attention she was attracting from the hotel guests, Lia told me about the previous three days.

"First, we did a little shopping," Lia said. "My magazine, *Nature and Nurture*, did some extra—'nurturing,' shall we say, and bought Chanda several fabulous dance costumes. Classic. Tasteful. Perfect for her audition."

"Audition?"

"Yes. We took a taxi into the backwaters of Chitral, where the artists hang out—the woodworkers, weavers, and potters. There we found—of all things, and in Chitral, of all places—Farhada's Daughters."

Farhada's Daughters was a traveling theater company, they told me, that was in need of a classical dancer. Mostly young women, and a few men, they performed skits, dances, comedy routines— even puppet shows—all about the relations between men and women—about dowries, street harassment, marriage to the Q'ran, honor killings. Some women were married, and their husbands worked with them. The other men pretended to be brothers of the single women, so that no one bothered them. They planned to stay in Chitral until spring.

"Then Chanda will be safe. She will move with them to Sargodha and on down the valley," said Lia. "She danced for them like an angel. Her movements were silkier than the clothes she is wearing. No seduction, no rupees in the belt, no razzle-dazzle. Just dancing—lonely, glorious, solemn, proud. Really, it broke my heart to watch her."

"But what about her—" I said, whispering, tapping my nose, "—you know—"

"They ate it up!" said Lia. "They presented the story of her attack, and her sliced nose, as the truth unveiled: 'This is what happens behind the veil, behind the metal gates,' they said. They encouraged Chanda to dance with her nose just as it is."

Chanda laughed when Lia stopped talking. She pulled on my arm.

"Baji," she said, adding in English, "now Chanda not too nosey!"

That evening Asma told Aga Ji he must accompany us to Chanda's performance. Aga Ji sat in front with the driver and never looked at me. The Toyota stopped at a nondescript metal gate across from the ice factory. Inside a tentlike canvas covered the courtyard where twinkling white lights had been strung. In one corner a few musicians assembled—a tamboura, tabla, and tambourines. The audience of twenty or thirty men sat cross-legged on blankets, leaving an open circle in the middle for the performers. They passed around paper bags of walnuts and dried apples.

"Assalam aleikum," said the emcee with a wide smile across his face. He wore a striped woolen shawl and bright cap. The crowd mumbled its response, "Waleikum salaam." We have a very special performance tonight," he announced, "—the debut of one of Pakistan's finest interpretive dancers—Chanda Khan."

The lights dimmed. The emcee disappeared into darkness. Then slowly the stage lights came up, focused on Chanda's still body, her white silk shalwar kameez, and her outstretched arms. The sparkles on her nose patch caught the light. Her pale eyes, lined with thick kohl, were the only things that moved. They circled the courtyard, stopping ever so briefly to match the gaze of each person. It was not a seductive move, although it drew us in. Her measured glances evoked the feeling of a witness' oath, with a surprising, powerful effect. It was over in less than a minute, and then the steady rhythm of the drum and the tambourine began. Chanda's movements were lyrical, like the strings of the tamboura, as she practiced the most basic moves of a beginner. She took small steps to each side of her central spot, always returning modestly to that point. Her glossy, stained lips opened soundlessly as the emcee returned to tell the crowd her tale as she danced.

Chanda hugged another dancer, and the friends mimed waving good-bye to each other as Chanda covered her head and face with a gossamer veil and moved into the imaginary street alone. When a male dancer entered the circle, he pulled Chanda into the shadow. The crowd gasped. Then an older dancer appeared at the edge of the circle, and Chanda recognized him—"Baba, Baba," she cried out joyously. "Help me! Rescue me!" The audience was relieved as the father approached.

"Whore!" the emcee shouted out in the voice of Chanda's father. Instantaneously, the young man bound her arms behind her back, as the father's blade glinted in the light and sliced the night in front of Chanda's face. She fell to the ground as the men ran away and the music stopped. The sparkly patch was gone. A pool of beet-red stage blood dripped into her cupped hand.

A man in the audience stood up, outraged. "Where were the four witnesses?" he shouted, cutting the air with his fist.

"Yes, the Q'ran demands that there be four pious witnesses to a charge of fornication!" said another.

"There were none," Chanda said in her own voice.

The audience was silent as again Chanda looked into each one's eyes, and they knew in their hearts the truth of her courage and the truth of her dance.

The next day Lia visited my quarters at the school. Overnight she had learned the truth about Yusuf and me. She had e-mailed him that she and I had met on the bus, and he replied, telling her how I had turned down his marriage proposal.

"You forgot to mention that you shattered his world," she said. She was hurt that I had not confided everything to her. The truth was that I liked Lia, but I did not trust her.

"Well, *shattered* is an exaggeration . . . I wanted to marry him," I said, "but Yusuf never would have been happy without his big family . . . My mother had died. I had responsibility for the children. No, I didn't break his heart. It was Pakistan that broke both our hearts."

I could see that Lia understood. Yusuf must have given her the details of our last conversation.

"He hasn't married yet, Ujala," she said. "Do you think you'd like to see him again? Just to see what feelings might still be there? Who knows what the circumstances might be with his parents now?" For once Lia was not being a matchmaker or a gossip or pumping me for information. She was being real.

"His life now is so different, so cosmopolitan," I said, "living in the world's capitals. Mine is a village life, teaching the poor. How far apart we have traveled from our university days. No, I think it best to leave the past in the past."

"But will you marry someday?"

"And who will arrange it for me, Lia? This is a different world from yours. And even for a modern woman, it is hard to meet a man to talk to, one I might trust, who might listen and understand me."

"It's true. I can feel it myself—the attraction between men and women here is pervasive," Lia said. "Don't you feel it?" No one ever had ever spoken to me so frankly about something so personal. "I see how cousins flirt with cousins. The boys take any opportunity to tell the girls they are beautiful. The girls slap them away in play. All that forbidden desire. No wonder people are killed for it."

"Fulfilled, it would tear our families apart," I said, trying to close the conversation. But Lia would not let the conversation end.

"I've watched how the men control the streets here. How they pierce the community with their eyes, craning their necks, scanning for new females—any unfamiliar shape in a shawl might be a woman, with perhaps a few inches of visible flesh. What is that staring about? Intimacy? Disapproval? Are they undressing women with their eyes, or what?"

"I'm not sure," I said. "I never look at men on the street. But I know what you are talking about. In the faces of the men I know, it looks like an unnamable longing. I think the men are trapped, too."

"Especially if they are homosexual," Lia continued, speaking a word I had read, but never heard spoken aloud. "In this culture of forbidden love, family honor, and violent revenge, I cannot help but notice that the favorite TV sport is wrestling—millions of Pakistanis gazing for hours at dominant, bare male bodies, brawny and sweating, clenching other males, small and slim."

Now I was irritated. "We are not robots, you know," I said. The conversation felt dangerous, degrading. "At heart Pakistanis are romantics," I said. "Like the entire culture of the East. More than wrestling or even football, mostly we love our weddings."

"Yes, brides dressed like dolls," Lia continued in the same critical vein. "All the elaborate wedding hoo-ha. Not that it is so different in the U.S., but here there is no sex before marriage. Not even dating. Where does all that repressed sexual energy go, anyway?"

"I have no idea," I said, gathering the teacups. I wanted to end the conversation, but Lia would not stop. She stood next to me, speaking over my shoulder.

"What happens between the red and gold gown and the first baby's birth?" she asked. "With all the bedrooms being shared with relatives, how do newlyweds get any privacy, get to know each other that way?"

"Brides get pregnant right away," I said, feeling relieved to see the teachers were returning so that this conversation would soon end. "So something must happen somehow."

"Why is it," Lia asked me, in her rhetorical way, "that the Islamists acknowledge the equality and dignity of women in the sacred texts, but then kindle the fire of every antifemale custom from Afghanistan to Yemen?" Her lips and her tongue seemed to chew on her words. I could tell that Lia wanted to argue. It seemed like her primary mode of relating.

"Originally, Pakistan had no seclusion and no veil," I said, "Just like Egypt had no genital mutilations. When Islam expanded, the religious leaders absorbed the customs they found. The Arabs had certain customs—"

"I know. I know. It's all the Arabs' fault," she interrupted. "Why is Islam so violent?"

"Tribal life can be violent," I said. "Poverty and hopelessness can provoke violence. Islam is peace. Understand the difference."

But Lia was not listening. She looked disgusted. Again she had put me in the position of seeming to defend what I did not believe in. I raised my voice and wagged my finger like an old auntie.

"Your Western biases are showing," I said. "We have heard of forced marriages in your Christian state of Utah. Was that the fault of Christianity?"

"—a sect of Christianity," she said.

"And what about that football player on trial for slashing up his wife and her boyfriend? Perhaps you should write about American girls."

"You've got a point," said Lia with a sigh. "Americans are no better."

But now I was on the offensive against her arrogance.

"Did you hear about the American Christian who came to Chitral, declared himself a Muslim, and bought a Pathan girl?"

"Yes," she said, "the girl had to be rescued by Amnesty."

"And returned to Pakistan," I said. "Was that the fault of Christianity?"

"What difference does it make if the man was Christian or not?" she asked. "What does Christianity have to do with it?"

"Exactly! And in the same way it is unfair to blame Islam. Cultural politics went hand in hand with religion in the ancient Islamic world—as it did with the Romans, the British, or with the American empire today."

"American empire?" Lia said. She did not like to hear me call her country by the term the rest of the world used. "Now you sound like a fundie."

"Just a turn of phrase," I said, "but *empire* does signify something. You know what I mean?"

In winter the pace of life in Chitral slowed like the pulse of a bear, as everything submitted to the twin fates of climate and altitude. The river froze over, and blocks of ice littered the riverbanks like boulders. Snowdrifts blocked the roads.

My life became a constant effort to stay warm. I wore homespun leggings, mittens, and shawls everywhere. All the woolen layers left me feeling heavy. I collected snowmelt for cooking, drinking, and washing. We ate oil and grains, dried fruit, peas, and beans, and I began to put on weight. Religious practices gradually became part of my daily routine. Women were not permitted inside the mosque, so I prayed at home. It was new to me, a quiet, naturally contemplative life. I decided to fast during Ramadan. I realized that for the first time I was fulfilling four of the Five Pillars—faith in God, daily prayers, fasting during Ramadan, and service to the poor. The only one left was the Hajj, the pilgrimage to Mecca I was obliged to do once, if I was able. But I was not eager to join a throng of two million and their patriarchs.

"Maybe it's the long winter," I said to Tahira, "but in this isolation, with our daily life centering on simple practices, the core of Islam means so much."

Tahira smiled.

"It's the closest we Muslims get to living in a monastery."

My brother arrived in Chitral on the day that the first impassable snowstorm began. Amir had collected donations of used computers while in the U.K. and then shipped them to us. He offered to install them at the school. I could hardly wait to see him. It was a double blessing!

"You know I wouldn't be here if Abbu had not insisted," Amir told me impatiently after we climbed into the backseat of the car. "Computers need a dry, temperate climate for their survival—and, by the way, so do I."

"You always were a bit spoiled," I teased.

The city was hushed. The only sound was the Toyota's tires crunching the snow beneath them. On the streets the loudspeakers that hawked blankets and prayers had shut down. The air was cleared of the stench of diesel. Wood smoke hovered then dissolved into the river. Day and night, the valley wore every shade of white. All of the city's sharpness had softened and rounded, except one.

"There it is, Amir—" I said, as the car crawled along the main street. I hooked my arm into his and hugged while I pointed. "—Shahi Mosque, its minaret is a needle that pierces this cottony world. On clear days its blinding light is magnetic."

"You are going to the mosque?" he asked.

"I pray at home now," I said. "But just wait. You'll see what happens to you here."

By spring, the teachers' father, Syed, had returned home from Peshawar where he had been teaching at the university. Nothing gave Sabira, Tahira, and Asma more pleasure than seeing their father happy. Syed and Amir spent the day hauling cedar logs into the compound to build a new wall for the school, while Aga Ji directed their work. The women watched, picking their teeth with poplar wood.

"Put the wall over there," Aga Ji insisted, pointing to his mud hut on the opposite side of the courtyard.

"But, Father, the school is over here. We are building a wall for the school," Syed reminded his confused father.

"Of course, the school is over there," he replied, hesitating. "I knew that. Well, put it over next to the school's other three walls, you idiots," he shouted. "Why in the world would you put it over here by my room?"

Amir laughed out loud.

"Do whatever he says, Amir," I shouted. "He's the head man."

One day Aga Ji made Amir an honorary Pathan. Amir was recovering from the hour he had spent pulling a wagon full of bricks and mud. The clouds were playing a game with their humans, drifting in front of the vanishing then reappearing face of the sun. He was chilled and putting on a puffy ski jacket when he saw Aga Ji approach. The old man moved with purpose, muttering and flapping his arms like a chicken. His red dog ran far ahead, returning to Aga Ji's side again and again.

"I must talk to you, young man," Aga Ji said with authority. Amir rose from the pile of wires that circled his knees. "Syed is away for the day, and I am too old. You are the oldest, so you must take this responsibility for the men of the family. We are Pathan. If anyone asks for our protection, we must give it—even at the cost of our lives. And it is our first duty to protect women—even those who are not of our blood."

Amir's eyes popped open as Aga Ji continued.

"In the coffeehouse they say that the mullahs are discussing Chanda Khan again. Although they have no witnesses, they say she is a fornicator, and they have issued a fatwa, a religious ruling. The mullahs say to kill her on sight."

That afternoon Amir knocked on my door.

"A fatwa." I said when he told me what had happened.

I imagined more bloodshed coming—to Chanda, maybe to all of Farhada's Daughters. Was there no end to it? At once I knew what had to be done. I prayed that my plan would work, but I no longer relied on prayer alone. I still had my gun. If necessary, I could slip my intention into the crook of my finger and watch the world explode. In all this time, I had not felt the bullet heat myself, nor its burrowing burn, but the shockwave that had rocked Taslima's body that day in her lawyer's office had shocked my own. I was determined that Chanda's name would not be added to the list of blown-apart bodies that fly in this war. Imagine a hot bullet piercing something you love, say your sister's hand—so like your mother's—or shattering your baby's belly that you pucker up to kiss and blow on lustily to make him giggle—or can you imagine your own splintered backbone? Look at yourself lying there forever, inert. There is no end to what that piece of metal can do.

Then there were no more images. No more heat. There was only a cold, loaded gun. I prayed that my life would become a power like that, one I could burrow deep in my pocket. My quiet, stupid life would be over. Instead, it would be like that gun. Now it would explode.

"I will go to town now to talk to Chanda," I told Amir. "She can leave on the morning flight to Peshawar with you. If she travels as your wife, and if she wears a full burqa, it should raise no questions."

"She can stay with my friends in Islamabad," he said.

"One thing is important, Amir—what Faisah and I call rule number 1: Tell no one. No one must know how Chanda escaped. Not your friends in Lahore. I will impress on Chanda also how dangerous it would be if our part in this is known. How it would make it more difficult for us to help others. You must understand this, Amir. Do not tell even Abbu or Meena."

He nodded like an obedient child.

"What about Lia? She knows about the fatwa."

"Especially do not tell Lia. I love her dearly, and she loves Chanda, too. But Lia is a journalist, and an American. Hers is a different world than ours. No, she will figure it out on her own after Chanda has disappeared."

"Baji," said Amir. He looked frightened.

"Remember what I said?" I asked, grabbing his upper arms. "Rule number 1?"

"Tell no one," he said, mouthing the words without a sound.

"My clever boy." I laughed and held him to me.

And, sure enough, when we met for tea, Lia demanded to know where Chanda and Amir were.

"Who?" I asked her.

"Don't be coy with me—where are they? I was up with the birds this morning, and she was gone."

I wondered if Lia was dense or only pretending to be dense. Amir said that Lia knew about the fatwa. Couldn't she figure out what happened?

"Maybe they eloped," I said. "Let's change the subject."

"Change the subject! There is a fatwa against Chanda, Ujala. Maybe some zealots kidnapped her." The hotel waiter brought us tea and sweetmeats, and we stopped talking until he finished serving. "Now I get it," she said. "Amir and Chanda took the morning flight to Peshawar—for her protection. If she were missing, you'd have your feathers all ruffled. That's it, isn't it?"

"My lips are sealed."

"You mean you will not confirm nor deny. I hate that about you," Lia said. "You always leave me out when something exciting is going on. You think I can't be trusted because I'm American, isn't it? Because I'm not a Muslim."

Lia's frustration spilled open. She sat there fuming.

"Don't be angry," I said. "And let's drop our stereotypes and be glad Chanda is nowhere around. After all, you still have her story to tell the world."

"But now I won't know how it ends," Lia said. I was so tired of her complaints.

"Create any ending you want."

"I am not Scheherazade. I'm a journalist. I have to know the truth."

"Well, you know two endings that weren't possible—her being

a dancer in Chitral, and her being murdered in a fatwa. Isn't that truth enough?"

"OK, I guess," Lia said. "I guess I can work with that . . . But next time you go on a rescue, can I please come with you? Just once?"

"I can't promise you that."

"So it's information on a need-to-know basis only, is it?"

"You can understand that, can't you, Lia?"

"But, Ujala, I have been writing stories about people like Chanda for years. Does it make any difference, really? I want to do something real for a change, take some action to help even one person."

"Do what you do best," I told her. "Keep writing about it. Keep talking about it."

"But so few in this country can even read what I write. Aren't they the ones we want to reach? The ones who ultimately will make these changes happen?"

"We'll think of something," I said, emphasizing the *we*—this is when I realized that Lia was becoming part of the family, too. "Don't leave Pakistan," I said. "Come with me to Lahore. I want you to meet my sister and her friends. If you are serious about working on these issues, they are the people for you to know."

Her smile spread from cheek to cheek.

"I can't wait to get out of here," she said. "Let's go today."

I left Lia at the hotel to walk back to the school. I bound my shawl against the wind, donned my sunglasses and work boots, and trekked along the tractor paths. I passed the bazaar and turned down the road to the school. I inhaled the crisp cerulean air, feeling happiness expand inside me. By now Amir and Chanda would be leaving Peshawar on the flight to Lahore. Amir would be home, and Chanda would dance again. It was spring, and my work in Chitral was almost done.

I passed Chitral Gol, the wildlife sanctuary where snow leopards hunt the horned goats. A sparrow and a thrush whistled on the holly oaks that grew in the cracks of cliffs. In a field of snow-covered rhubarb, a pair of partridges called back and forth in staccato, as if I were a wild cat to warn other birds about. Crows swarmed as one body, cawing their criticisms across the back fences.

Who is she? What is she doing? Where is her husband?

When I reached out to push open the gate to the enclave, I heard Aga Ji arguing with someone. He sounded distraught. I pulled back to watch through the crack between the doors. A rotund figure in a striped woolen shawl shook his walking stick at Aga Ji. I waited, then hid behind a clump of scrub oak as the Jeep slid through the gate and turned toward town.

"Baji, Baji," Aga Ji cried out when he saw me slip in through the gate. I was shocked to hear his voice. He had never spoken to me in all the months I had lived there. A sheet of tears spread down his cheeks. I ran to him while he knelt by the lean-to, holding a cloth to the head of his shivering dog.

"Who was that?" I asked. Aga Ji just shook his head.

"From the tea house. They are looking for Chanda Khan." His voice cracked. "And you." He lifted the bloodstained cloth and howled like a child.

"Look what he did." The red dog's ears were gouged with V-shaped marks. "But," he said. "It is no worse than what I have done." He buried his head in his hands. "I told them Chanda was with you."

I had to find a way to leave the school compound without being seen. I telephoned Lia.

"Want to come on a rescue?" I asked.

"So soon? Of course I do, Baji, but who are we rescuing and when?"

"Me," I answered. "Now."

"Well, damn, girl. You are letting me into the club."

Soon Lia arrived at the school by taxi. She instructed the driver to collect a special package from Tahira—a large tamboura case wrapped in thick blankets.

"No! Don't touch it! My musician friend is very particular about who handles this instrument," Lia told the driver. The three sisters and their father lifted the case up, and the driver tied it to the roof of his taxi. "Drive very slowly," Lia instructed as they pulled out of the gate. "I wouldn't want to damage the merchandise."

Inside, I closed my eyes and breathed through a metal tube Aga Ji had bored into the tamboura case. For the next three days—until the Saturday flight left for Peshawar, I remained in hiding at the Hilton. Lia did not let waiters or housekeepers into her room. She ordered room service, or large portions for meals in the dining room and brought the leftovers to me. We passed the days playing cards, watching TV, checking the Internet, and watching the activity on the street.

By Saturday, I wore a boyish European-style haircut and heavy makeup. I borrowed a pants suit from Lia, dark glasses, and a stylish floppy hat purchased in the gift shop. I no longer looked like the Pakistani schoolteacher in work boots and a shalwar kameez. I passed by the police station easily on our way to the airport.

Deep in one pocket, I carried the handgun, and in the other, the Q'ran.

7

Clifton, 1985

Eleven years earlier

The polyphonic discord of Karachi broke the dawn. First, there was a screech of loudspeakers from the Clifton mosque, then the chanting of a tone-deaf muezzin, followed by a distant electronic shriek. Then another, and another. Kulraj Singh prayed.

"Can't you please help them to harmonize, just once?" he asked, opening his palms to heaven. How he missed the breathing melodies of the harmonium, the light strings of the tamboura. I'm beginning God's day entertaining this annoyance, he thought, and turned to kiss Nafeesa's smooth cheek.

"You are my beloved," he whispered in Punjabi, as he did each morning. "You are my path to God." Her eyelids fluttered under a mass of black hair, and her breathing was even and noiseless.

The room where they slept together spoke of order and devotion. The mahogany dresser and bureau stood like totems topped with lace scarves. The Iranian carpet was so clean it had not a stray hair on it.

The prayer Kulraj Singh slipped into Nafeesa's ear was his first whisper of gratitude. The bath was his second, the enactment of his intention to remain clean, body and soul. In the ambrosial hours he had transformed these habits of Sikh practice by facing Mecca on his knees. Allahu akbar! God is great!

His conversion to Islam had been a way to protect the family.

"For you, I can be anything on the outside," he had told Nafeesa when they began their life together. "God knows who I am on the inside."

The most difficult part had been telling his father that he had decided to become a Muslim. But even though his father's heart had quickened with grief at the news, the man had not flinched.

"We did not fight only for our right to live and believe as Sikhs," he told Kulraj. They sat in the temple compound under a neem tree, where the kites of young boys flew above them. The boys' identically wrapped topknots bobbed as the kites responded to the slightest crook of their fingers. His father watched the paper battle as he continued. "We fought for the rights of all to worship as whatever befits them. And here, where ninety-seven out of one hundred Pakistanis are Muslims, where the government is useless and the mullahs rule, your family needs the protections that being Muslims will bring to them. Do not worry about conversion. The hand of God is on your head."

Sikhs in Pakistan understood the compromises their choice to remain in the country required. Kulraj Singh had retained whole what his father had taught him—the core of the Guru's teachings. But publicly he carried an Arabic name, Ehtisham Mohammad. Now he studied the Q'ran and the Islamic holy men with interest, but, in his mind, he was still his own priest.

He opened the window to feel the cool air on his face and turned the faucet for the bath. Amber water trickled out.

"Allah, tsk-tsk-tsk! Be merciful!" he prayed. "Nine million people in this hot, imploding city by the sea, and eight-and-half million are thirsty!"

Nafeesa had been fearful during the night. Her private demons returned again and again. She had never been able tell their five children the tragedy of her family's injustice to them.

"Shall I tell them now?" she asked Kulraj for the millionth time, and he replied, "They are old enough now to know the truth."

"I can't do it. I just can't," she said, turning her head to the pillow. "They might become curious and go looking for my family. It could be so dangerous. Telling them will create all kinds of questions that I cannot answer. They have only known kindness and protection. I'm afraid, Kulraj. I'm afraid."

It was a conversation they had been having for twenty-seven years.

"It is your decision if and when to tell the children. We'll talk about it in the morning, Nafeesa," he had said the night before. "We also have to talk about whether to let Ujala and Faisah visit Karachi Central Prison."

"Remember dinner last night, God?" Kulraj prayed. "What is it you want today? You want our daughters' heads, too?"

He fastened an undergarment around his waist and tied the knot. He was almost dressed, working with precision, as his father had taught him. Then he returned to the bedroom, and was surprised to see Nafeesa drinking tea.

"You are awake!" Their servant, Masood, had lain the copper tray next to her in the bed. She held a teacup to her lips with one hand and smoothed her hair with the other. "The water is bad again," he reported. "Please ask Uji to wait for the water man."

Nafeesa was not listening. She sighed.

"I feel torn, Kulraj—between wanting our girls to be safe and wanting them to be brave."

"I know."

"But to be brave, they have to practice. Should we let them go into that jail? What do you think, Mr. Singh?" Nafeesa called her husband Mr. Singh either when she was teasing him or when they were deliberating a serious point. "Ujala would be good at legal aid work," she said. "She's a good listener."

"She is the listener," he agreed. "People like to tell her their stories." He laughed. "And Faisah is the doer, never sitting still."

Nafeesa curled her legs under her and leaned back against the headboard.

"How could we ever have known which child would be the listener, which the doer, or the talker—"

"Reshma, of course," he continued, recalling how, at an early age, she knew all ninety-nine names of Allah. And how, when she began to speak English, she could not pronounce the *F* sound. "Remember how Allah, God of the Orphans became Allah, God of the Orpans?"

"Allah, the Prend of Everyone." Nafeesa chuckled.

"The Alpa and the Omega." They laughed hard until the air was empty. Then they both felt that something was missing. "I miss our Reshma," he said quietly. "I miss those days." But before his melancholy could grow, Nafeesa lobbed another idea to him.

"What about the watcher?"

"That would be Meena. I always find her hiding somewhere near where I am working. And what about our boy?"

"Amir. He may have been born only ten minutes after Meena, but he'll always be the baby to me. He doesn't have to do or be anything."

"So," Kulraj Singh said, "do we let our girls go or not?" He waited for her reply without looking at her, without imposing. But when Nafeesa did not respond, he went to her side. "Their intentions are good," he said. "The professor will go with them. And they are not babies—or little girls—anymore. I think it's the right thing, don't you?"

"Of course it's all right. I don't know what I am so afraid of. When I was their age I traveled all the way to London alone. I just worry, that's all."

"And you worry about Uji not being married yet," he said, raising a subject that was on both of their minds. As the mother, it was Nafeesa's job to find the husbands. "The pressure is building. She's almost twenty-two. She should be next, you know."

"I know," Nafeesa said, irritated, defensive. "There is a young man she knows from the university. But I don't know much about him."

"I think we should wait for Uji to tell us about him," said Kulraj, laughing. "Then we can begin our detective work."

8

Adiala Prison, 1996

Rahima Mai entered the office and headed directly to her desk. Not looking up from her work, Ujala heard the swivel chair squeaking. The supervisor groaned, and Ujala could hear plastic bags rustling.

"Here, you can have this," Rahima Mai said. She held out a few yards of orange polished cotton. "Make a new suit for yourself, but—" Ujala stood across the office, opening another file drawer, putting papers away. She reached out her hand.

"Shukri—" she began to say thank you.

"—it is not a gift," Rahima Mai interrupted. She had seen pleasure cross Ujala's face at the sight of the cloth. "That would be a violation of the rules. Think of it as an office uniform. The Women's Supervisor cannot have a smelly coolie working in her office." She smiled. "So I have a question for you."

Ujala looked up from her work.

"Where was this Yusuf, back then?" Rahima Mai said, as if their conversation had been only briefly interrupted. Ujala could read the change in Rahima Mai's tone of voice. She pushed lightly on the file drawer, and it closed with a click. "Could your parents not find a suitable husband for you when you were—marriageable?"

Ujala laughed.

"Marriageable? Yes, the family tried to get me married ten years ago—way back in Clifton. They tried, in their way. But you have to understand about my family."

◆ ◆ ◆

It was one of those days when the water went bad. I twisted the kitchen faucet to fill the teakettle. Nothing but a few drops of yellow and the stench of sewer gas. I slammed open the window and grabbed two plastic jugs. Normally the family would boil both tap water and bottled water, and we had plenty, but Abbu had arranged for an extra delivery on brackish days such as that one. I waited on the verandah for the rumble of the water truck. I could hear the scratching of brooms outside the walls where the sweepers were whisking the street. On the telephone wires, crows broadcast their morning reports. In the courtyard, light washed the cuffs of the calla lilies that Masood had planted.

"Calla lilies with toast," Ammi had said the previous evening. "That's what lilies look like in your hand."

"Sounds like the title of a French painting," I said.

"Uji, you are as beautiful as a French painting. If only you could see it."

My flamboyant mother had a way of naming colors and letting them know the work she expected them to do. Once she handed me a skein of cotton, announcing, "Now this is Sunrise Titian. Wear it when you feel lonely." Then she draped a few yards of chiffon over her knees. "And this," she said, opening her hand underneath and spreading the cloth, "this is Silver Ebony. It will attract true love."

Husbands, marriages, and weddings, I thought. Is there nothing else to talk about? I wanted to challenge the aunties when they started in on it, but Ammi protected me when they talked about how soon the bloom would be off the rose, the cow's milk would run dry, and all the carrots would go soft. They prattled on, as if I were deaf.

"It is in God's good hands," Ammi told them, "which have plenty to do without picking this little mango from its branch too soon." She would pass a plate of pastel sweetmeats to Auntie Tara, who would stuff one into her mouth and begin licking her fingers. "Kulraj and I will not choose husbands for our daughters. You know we are not like that."

Privately she told me, "I am sure we will have our views of various prospects, of course. But you must choose wisely for yourself in all the important decisions of your life. Which means, first, find wisdom. Then find a husband."

And just where does one find wisdom? I wondered. I scratched my shoulder blade against the porch post. *Where is that water truck?* I could hear Faisah's hair dryer making a racket. Meena was bellowing, "Where is Mithu? Give him back!" Amir must have hidden her parrot again.

I watched the neighborhood's morning rituals and routines. The horn of the milkman's motorcycle sounded its two tones. Masood exited the door under the bougainvillea. His immaculate shalwar kameez and turban caught the brilliance of the sun. He had a ladle in one hand and the milk can in the other. Round containers hung on either side of the motorcycle's back wheel, where sunlight flashed on their copper bellies. Masood dipped into one, then he meticulously poured fresh milk into the can.

I don't want just to be married, I argued with myself. I want love. I want to see the kind of look on my husband's face that I can see on Abbu's when he wants Ammi. And they think we're not watching!

I began dreaming of Yusuf.

My stomach was jumpy on the day I had ridden on the back of his Vespa, sitting sideways, tucking my clothes to avoid the wheels and wrapping my dupatta around my neck, tucking in the ends. I held the inside of the seat with my right hand and balanced my left on his shoulder. His muscles tightened as the Vespa picked up speed.

I have touched him, I thought, and felt a gush of blood rush through my body.

Respectable women are provided introductions through their

families and otherwise do not socialize with young men. But Yusuf and I met, instead, in a literature course at the university. I knew that seeing him apart from my family was not forbidden, but it was new to me. I knew others who went much farther than we did—who dressed like Europeans, dated, and favored the music and customs of Americans. Yusuf considered himself a modern Muslim, educated and egalitarian, but observant of certain rituals. If I looked in his pack, I knew I would find a prayer mat tucked inside.

We approached Clifton Beach, the city's public playground. It ran parallel to Zamzama Boulevard, across the avenues and modern buildings of Karachi's Defence area. On the khaki-colored beach, families dined on roasted corn and almonds, curries and ice cream. Two old men led their camels across the littered sand. Children waited in line to straddle the molting hides of the raggedy beasts. It was low tide. One by one each wave kissed the sand, creating a long streak of surf.

As the Vespa slowed, I cupped Yusuf's back firmly. He parked by an old hotel that had become a hangout for drug dealers. We joined a few college friends—Bilal, Sabah, and others whose names I did not know. They sat at a wooden picnic table by the edge of the sand, near the street, enjoying fruit drinks. This group liked to think of themselves as the New Yorkers in their favorite TV show, *Friends*. An ice cream cart tinkled a childhood tune.

"It's entirely off-key," Yusuf said.

"Could it *be* any more off-key?" mimicked Bilal in Joey Tribbiani's singsong rhythm. Bilal sipped coconut milk through a paper straw as we all laughed. He had wrapped his head with Sabah's dupatta. He was entertaining the others with his impressions of political characters. Benazir Bhutto and General Zia were his favorites.

"I've seen this show too often," Yusuf whispered. "We're going for a walk," he announced.

"Ooh. A walk!" Bilal said, lifting his eyebrows. "Want to be alone?"

Yusuf carried my shoes. As my toes felt the chilly surf, I scanned the horizon.

"I've always been afraid of the sea," I said, shuddering.

"Would you rather not go?"

"No. I can do it. It scares me a little, but in a way I like that."

What also scared me on that day was the vastness of what Yusuf was not saying. Although we had discussed marriage, he had not talked to our parents about it.

I let the wind play with my dupatta. Yusuf would catch one end and return it to my shoulder, and I would let it fly away again, until at last we grabbed its corners and spread it out on the sand, before the wind could grab it again. We sat together, not touching—never touching—but close, squeezing sand between our toes.

"I have something for you," he said. I watched the way his eyes moved slowly as if they were finding satisfaction wherever they looked. They followed his hand into his pocket and back to my face. Then he lifted his palm to offer me a short, leafy branch on which three pearl-sized lemons were perched.

I remember my reactions to this gesture, like a movie, frame by frame.

Grateful. It was a gift.

Trapped somehow. Did I have to please him in the way I responded to his gift?

Disappointed. Had I expected an engagement ring?

Confused. Could finding love be this hard?

I laughed in order to keep myself from revealing so much.

"Ammi always says that lemons are oranges God created for those whose sweetness is a lie," I said. He looked pleased.

"Then I'll have to take these back and get you oranges instead." My body felt a new and undeniable heat, and slowly I relaxed.

Weeks before he had said that we might wed after he completed his journalism program.

"I'll present the idea to my father," he said, but in the intervening time, he said nothing more.

"He won't approve," I had predicted. Although I was Muslim, and my father was a converted Muslim, I had to admit, he was not a very convincing Muslim. Yusuf's family's approval was unlikely.

"If my father doesn't approve, then we will leave the country," Yusuf said. "The world is much larger than Karachi, and I want to see all of it."

Suddenly, he jumped up and raced to the ice-candy man. "Here," he said when he returned, panting, handing me an iced orange. It had been sliced open and dipped in coarse sugar. "For one whose sweetness is the truth."

I took the thawing fruit into my mouth. The crunch of sugar and the bursts of juice could not interrupt my questioning mind. Had he spoken with his parents or hadn't he? I wondered if he would bring up the subject. He seemed dreamy, more interested in communicating with his eyes than with words.

When we walked back to rejoin our friends, I pushed into the chill.

"How did your parents respond when you discussed our marriage?" Yusuf squinted at the sea.

"I haven't asked them yet, Uji. I'm waiting for the right moment. Father has been irritable lately, but I will bring up the subject soon." To me he sounded like a pathetic little boy, apologizing to his mother.

"Of course, Yusuf," I said. "I don't mean to rush you." Finding the right time is important, I thought, or is he putting me off? "I am so eager to plan our future, and without knowing what your parents will say, it is hard to know if we will have a future together." I thought I sounded whiny, like I wanted him to do something, anything, just to have it done and over with.

"I wish I could kiss you right here, right now," he said.

"The sooner we get on with our lives," I said, "the sooner we can get on with the kissing, too." We both were excited that we had said the word: *kiss*. But I fretted. *What if I never marry? I can't see myself married, or unmarried, either. Live with my parents for the rest of my life? Would it be worse than being someone's wife? But women always get married. What else can I do?* I was a woman who could not imagine her own future.

From the verandah, I could cast my sight out into the sea and again think of Yusuf. *His intensity frightens me. It is like the sea—a vast, blue thing that grabs the limbs and the lives of the young, the careless,*

*and the unlucky like a wild woman who has lost her mind, and I do not
know how to swim.*

The cranking of the water truck's gears shifted me out of worrying.
I glanced down to the gate. INDUS WATER COMPANY, the sign read.
The words were encased in the company's oval logo—two lions
drinking peacefully from the royal river. I grabbed the two water
jugs and headed for the stairs. I wondered if Abbu and Ammi had
decided to let Faisah and me visit Karachi Central Prison today.

The previous evening, the family had gathered around the old
bamboo table. The armchairs were stuffed with big pillows
embroidered with mirrors and beads. Reshma had always sat
between our parents. But now she was married and living with her
husband, so Amir and Meena sat to Ammi's right, and Faisah and
I sat to Abbu's left. Meena's parrot perched above us, squawking.

"Shall we set a place for Mithu?" Amir asked. He cupped a
handful of apples and monkey nuts for the bird.

Masood carried in a tray with dal, rice, chicken curry, lamb
masala, chutney, sliced cucumbers, carrots, and yogurt. We passed
the dishes around the large table.

Our father loved to tell our guests about that grand table. It
came from the fire wreckage at the library of the Architectural
Institute in Lahore. He had selected that particular table, he used
to say, because its roundness made impossible the dining hierarchy
of traditional families, where the parents sat at either end like a
king and a queen. Then he would glance at Ammi, as he built the
legend of their love. "But I don't need a queen," he would say,
"and I don't want to be that far away from my beloved."

Ammi knew it was a staged glance, and she would shake her
head with embarrassment. "Such nonsense!"

We would roll our eyes at our father, but truly we would have
been disappointed had he not taken yet another opportunity to
praise our mother and proclaim his devotion to her.

"The girl I interviewed is only fourteen," interrupted Faisah,
who was eager to share her experience from that afternoon, when
her university seminar visited the prison for the first time. "She

has been in Central Prison for eight months. It was crowded, and hard to find a corner to talk privately. So hot and smelly in there." Faisah wrinkled her nose.

"What are the charges against her?" Abbu asked.

"Prostitution," Faisah replied. I could see she was embarrassed to speak this word in front of Abbu and Amir, but she had to overcome that shyness if she was going to become a lawyer. "However, she's not a prostitute," Faisah said, repeating the word, it seemed to me, as a kind of practice. "It's much more complicated than that."

She took a breath and made eye contact with each of us. Her eyes sparkled through her wire-rimmed glasses as she waited for our complete attention.

"The girl comes from Jacobabad," she said. "She was a nanny for the landlord's grandson. Last year the landlord asked her mother to allow the girl to accompany his daughter-in-law with the baby on a trip to Bangladesh, where his daughter-in-law's family lives. The mother trusted the family, since she had worked for them for many years. And the girl wanted to go, thinking she would be back in Sindh within a few weeks.

"Well, weeks became many months. Finally, the girl's mother went to the landlord and asked when her daughter would be back."

"Why didn't the mother just telephone her daughter?" asked Amir. He stuffed his mouth with chapati as he spoke.

"Poor people don't have telephones," Abbu said, and placed his hand over Amir's forearm to prevent him from cramming more bread into his mouth. "And even if they can find a public phone, and even if they have the rupees to use it, the phone may be broken, or they may not be able to get through to the other end. Especially to Bangladesh." He turned to Faisah. "Go on with the story." He passed the yogurt and cucumbers to Ammi.

"After we heard the girl's story, we had a hard time reaching her mother, but finally we contacted her through a family friend in Karachi." Faisah paused, lifting her head and tucking a loose strand of hair behind her ear. To make a long story short," she said, taking a breath, "each time she asked him, the landlord said that her daughter would be returning soon. Eventually, the mother became angry about the delays. 'You should be glad we are taking care of her,' the landlord told her. 'One less stomach for you to feed.' Then she became furious."

"He wasn't being fair to her," Meena said. There were nods of agreement around the table, supporting the mother's indignation.

"At last she told him that she insisted he send her daughter back."

"I imagine her making such a demand was an insult to the landlord," said Ammi. "A feudal would never allow that!" Faisah nodded and waved her arms as she continued her story.

"So instead of sending the daughter home, the landlord gave the girl to a friend of his—someone connected to organized crime."

I could tell that Faisah was enjoying telling the dark turn the tale was taking.

"This friend then brought the girl to Karachi, leading her to believe he was taking her back to her mother. Instead he put her in a brothel—"

Meena inhaled sharply. She was still in elementary school. Could she know what a brothel was? I wondered.

"—where the police picked her up eight months ago," Faisah said, completing her story.

"So what happens to her now?" I asked.

"I'll learn more when we return to the jail tomorrow. The lawyers say it won't take long to get her out of jail because she's being held illegally. But will her family take her back? Now that she is no longer a virgin, who will marry her?"

"It's outrageous how those girls are treated," Ammi said. I thought she was hoping her comment would bring the chapter to a close. I could tell she was uncomfortable with this discussion, especially in front of Meena and Amir. But Faisah continued.

"And this is just one of the stories," she said as if she were ready to tell another one. "The legal aid lawyers really need more students to interview these girls."

"Perhaps one of our neighbors could take the girl in as a nanny until her mother gets here," Ammi said to us, but I could read her mind: They might think such a girl too risky to have in their homes. Too tempting to their husbands and sons.

I interrupted.

"I want to go with you to the jail," I said, touching Faisah's arm and turning to Ammi. "Can we both go?"

We knew they would let us go. After dinner Faisah and I had talked about it. When have our parents denied us anything? Someone tapped on the door to our room. When I opened it, I saw Abbu's face, solemn, as I knew it would be.

Here it comes, I thought.

Abbu handed a pile of old clothes to Faisah.

"Your mother and I have discussed the matter," he said, "and we think that since you two have such good intentions, and will be in a group, and with each other, you should have our permission to go to Central Prison. Your mother collected these clothes for you to take to the women there."

"Thank you, Abbu," we said and pulled him into the room to give him a hug.

"Tell Ammi not to worry. I'll take care of my little sister."

After Abbu left, Faisah rustled through the plastic bags that covered the floor of our closet.

"I wish I could wear my new Levis," she said.

"Ever since you bobbed your hair, you certainly pay more attention to fashion."

"I like the casual look," she said.

"If you wear Levis, Ammi will never let you leave the house." Ammi did not want her daughters becoming, as she put it, "all European all the time."

"I'm just kidding, Ujala. Honestly, sometimes you are so serious! Professor Daniel told us to dress like lawyers, and as chair of the Legal Advocacy Committee, I do have to look the part." Faisah flaunted her title and the navy blue suit that Anna, our housekeeper, had made for her. "How do I look?"

"Very proper, Madam Attorney."

I wore a black muslin shalwar kameez and carried a cloth bag over my shoulder. In the mirror we approved of the modern women we saw. Then we clapped our hands three times over our heads and shook our ankles like dancing girls, as we had done many times as children. We were happy to be playing together again.

Karachi Central was notorious. Built in the 1890s to hold one thousand prisoners, the jail's population then was close to five thousand. Fewer than five hundred prisoners were female, twelve of whom were on death row, ten for killing their husbands.

We met the professor and three law students at the office of the jail matron. I remember it as a hot, humid day. The lady jailer, wrapped entirely in green cloth, peered at us from behind her big, round sunglasses. She moved as little as possible; only her lips had any life in them. As she spoke, they seemed to thicken and inch forward like two slugs. Seated at a metal desk, her body appeared to tower over it, her girth marking her as a lifelong seated functionary.

"You can take those clothes inside. Give them to these girls to carry." She lifted one shoulder and cast her glance like a fishhook that landed on two women standing by the office door. The women did not look up.

"Could we speak with them, please?" Faisah asked rather boldly, I thought.

"As you wish. Ask them anything. Just ask them how they are treated." The lady jailer's confidence spread across her face. "We have nothing to hide."

"How is it for you here in the prison?" Faisah lowered her voice to question them. "Do you have enough to eat? Do they treat you well?"

The women nodded in unison.

"Answer them," the lady jailer ordered, without looking up from her paperwork. She leaned onto her elbows, her arms hidden in the folds of green.

"Yes, Madam," one woman said. "They treat us well. It's just like home here."

Suddenly, the lady jailer pushed her chair backward, scraping the concrete floor. She strained to lift her body, signaling that the meeting was over.

"The gentlemen will have to wait here. Only ladies inside."

The male student, the professor, and a policeman with a belt full of keys headed for the men's side of Central Prison. Faisah and I, and two other students—Rani and Laila—trailed the two inmates down a covered corridor to the women's section. The key turned noisily in the lock, and the metal doors creaked. I cringed a little.

The doors opened to a large yard packed with women and children. The space was roofless, framed by mudbrick walls. On one side of the courtyard was a line of small rooms without furniture, a larger dormitory with a few string cots, and several stalls for toilets at the far end. Next to the dormitory was the outdoor kitchen where women were chopping mustard greens and boiling rice. Others washed clothes at the hand pump and hung them on a line, or they clustered under the only available shade—a thatched verandah outside the row of sleeping rooms. Women sat cross-legged on the bare ground, eating with cupped fingers from plastic bowls and feeding their children in the same way, or laying their babies across their laps underneath their shawls, where the babies sucked until they slept. Quite a few women were pregnant.

"It's a kind of village," I whispered to Faisah.

"A village of the damned!" she said.

"Call me Sita," said the Kholi girl who carried Ammi's clothes. "Will you help us, too?" She squeezed my elbow, keeping hold of the soft spots by my tendons.

"I'll try," I said, pulling my arm away. The girl was hurting me.

"Follow me," Sita said. Then she grabbed my forearm and led me to the area where laundry was stretched across a wall to dry. Children squealed, playing tag between rows of wet clothes.

Sita wore a chiffon sari that was spring green in color and embroidered with cheap red and white thread. The scooped neckline of her blouse rested in the pockets of her collarbones. Her veil was clipped to her head and hung freely down her back, as if it were an extension of her hair. White plastic bangles circled her wrists. The girl looked different now than when she had mumbled her replies to our questions in the lady jailer's office.

When she spoke, she placed her fists on her hips. Her tiny body was as unmoving as a mountain.

"We shouldn't be in here," she said. Her voice rose in anger. "It is injustice! We don't belong here at all." I motioned for her to sit down next me on the ground, and I opened my notebook.

"What is your full name?" I asked.

"Sita Chengur. My two sisters are here with me—Hanan and Manya." She stopped talking and looked at my pad of paper, unable to read it, but waiting for me to include her sisters' names in my report. "My people were in debt bondage near Hyderabad. When I was ten my family was released by a court action, but we had nowhere to go."

A small child walked toward us, trying to balance two cups of tea on a piece of wood. A bright orange and blue print sari caressed her frame. Her right cheek dimpled.

"You didn't spill a drop," Sita said, grinning at the child, as she spread a clean cloth in front of me and reached for a cup. She rested her cup on her bent knee.

"Hanan," she said, shooing the child away. "My family walked from interior Sindh to Karachi looking for work, anything at all— just to stay alive. Our mother worked a weaving machine in the cotton mill, but she got asthma and an eye infection that made her blind. Our father earned money in the villages along the way with his two dancing monkeys and by playing his drums. But he says that people aren't interested in monkeys and music anymore, now that they can watch TV and play video games. But he told us that Karachi is by the sea and the sea is rich, so we would be rich too. So we came here."

Ammi had told us about the Kholis, Hindus who originally inhabited Sindh and the western desert of India. Many became nomads or workers to landlords who bound generations of them with debts, and who hired thugs to make certain they never ran away. I remembered Ammi saying, "Sometimes they only have bread soaked in chili and buttermilk. And children are forced to pick cotton or carry mustard flowers, make bricks—and the landlord's men use the girls as they wish."

"But isn't bonded labor illegal?" I had asked Ammi.

"Of course, but anyone who complains is thrown in the private jail. Thousands live in virtual slavery. It is self-perpetuating, all part of the feudal economy and Sindhi and Punjabi social structures."

Sita continued her story.

"In Karachi somebody beat up my father and stole his monkeys. Now he can't walk at all."

"Where are your parents?" I asked.

"We don't know," Sita said, matter-of-factly. She paused and her voice saddened. "Probably in jail."

"Tell me about your case. Why are you and your sisters here?"

Hanan returned with Manya and stood by Sita's side. Manya looked to be eight years old and had a dimple similar to her sister's. When she laughed her lips parted easily, displaying large teeth yellow as corn. Her sari was a magenta print with gold leaves, and it framed her face. All three girls were barefoot. As serious and determined as Sita seemed to be, her two sisters seemed carefree and playful.

"They called us whores," Sita said, without a bit of embarrassment. "But we are not whores. It's all a mistake. We made our living as garbage pickers in the landfills on the edges of Karachi."

I had heard of the dangerous squatter settlements where tens of thousands of people lived in shanties and tents.

"At night we would burn whatever fuel we collected during the day—chewing gum wrappers, cardboard, anything like that," Sita added, nodding. "We cooked whatever our family scrounged to eat that day. Or we would sell the paper to rag dealers. But we didn't get much for it. It was better just to burn it."

I could not imagine such a life and had no time to conjure what it would be like because then Sita's story worsened. She cleared her throat.

"Our father was beaten up, so now our youngest brother sits with him on street corners, tugging the sleeves of passersby, begging for coins, while father plays the drums."

Hanan and Manya listened to Sita tell their tale. When she signaled to them, they sat cross-legged in our circle.

"We have to be careful of the men in our shantytown, Madam," she continued. "They will snatch and hurt young girls." The younger ones nodded. "There was an old man there who had a bicycle and a few tools. He would ride through the neighborhoods, calling to the women to let him sharpen their knives. You know. You've seen him, or others like him."

The girls nodded.

"Well, one day when it was getting dark, he was riding by." Hanan and Manya covered their mouths at the memory. "He reached out and grabbed me, touching me here," Sita said, gesturing with the fingers of both hands turned to her breasts.

"What did you do?" I asked, immediately annoyed at myself, worried that the way I framed the question made it sound like I was blaming her.

"I slapped his hand away. That's what I did." She paused to register my reaction.

I showed none.

"My sisters were the only ones who saw what he had done. We told my mother, but she said not to tell our father. Then the next thing we knew, the police took all of us, including my parents, and brought us to this jail. They said that the tinker reported he had seen my sisters and me alone with three older boys, which wasn't true. He was just mad because I slapped him, so he lied and said we were whores."

I looked up from my notetaking.

"That's all there is. Can you get us out of here? We have to get out of here."

"But I like it here," Manya protested, leaning her elbow into my leg and grinning up at me. "The food is good and there is lots of it. We have a clean bed."

"I miss my mother and father," said Hanan. "Madam, can you find out where they are?"

"I don't know, little one. I don't know, but we'll try," I said, careful not to make promises I might not fulfill. I wrote down the girls' ages, their parents' and family names, the name of their village, the tinker, and the shantytown.

"We have to go," Faisah said, shouting from a distance and pointing to her wristwatch. Sita grabbed my sore elbow again.

"And the jail lady?" she said. "We told you she treats us well because she was sitting right there. But she doesn't. When we first got here she used to beat us. She beats most of the new girls. Behind her back we all call her Jallad—*the Executioner.* That's the perfect job for her."

Once outside, we waited for the others to emerge from the men's side of Central Prison. I leaned against the mudbrick wall, stunned by what I had learned.

"Their stories break my heart," I told Faisah, "but the girls themselves are so vibrant, so full of life."

Faisah nodded. She kept her thoughts to herself.

Soon the professor walked us to a nearby Internet café where we made notes about our meetings. For once the freedom to choose even the tea we would drink seemed luxurious, unreal.

"I only managed to get information on one case," I said to Faisah. "You were able to do two."

"Pipe down," Faisah said. "It was your first time."

But I did have three clients in my case, I thought, pleased to have "clients." I scribbled everything I could remember into my notebook.

"No problem getting the girls released through the civil courts," Rani said. She was a first-year law student. "Arbitrarily jailed by the Shariah Court, it is just a matter of having jurisdiction transferred. They can be out in a matter of days—if we can find some relative to release them to. We checked the jail roster, and their parents were not there."

I imagined the girls on the street wearing cotton gloves and dragging plastic sacks as they walked, like common garbage-pickers.

"But what will happen to them then?"

"Without parents, they will go to the streets, or return to the shantytown to try to find their parents," Rani said. "Fortunately, it's not our problem. We get to be lawyers, not social workers."

"What will happen to these girls?" I asked Faisah afterward.

"Who knows? Rani thinks that caring what happens isn't part of legal work, but I disagree. A good lawyer is a good social worker, too. I told the girl I interviewed we'd try to find a place for her to stay until her family comes to get her."

"Let's go home," I said when the bus came into view. "Let's see if Ammi has any ideas. Maybe the Women's Aid Society can help."

As the bus carried us back to the flat-roofed mansions and high-rises of Clifton, my eyes absorbed Karachi. I realized I lived my life in a kind of tunnel from school to home, from here to there, a kind of shroud around my upper-class life. Now my vision was crystal clear, one lucid image after another.

A grandfather drove a donkey cart loaded with burlap bags, and a young boy sat beside him. I longed for a close-up view. Who are they? I wondered. I imagined the boy clambering into the back of the cart when the man could not. And the grandfather would guide the donkey through the traffic when the young boy could not. *Where are they going? And what is in the bags? Who are their people?*

The bus jolted forward and again my vision blurred. Still, I kept watching, and the clarity returned again and again.

I saw a young man in a skullcap selling cauliflower. His hair was almost completely gray, and both of his arms were wrapped in gauze. *Is he sick? How was he injured? Where did he get the cauliflower? Will he share his money, and with whom?*

When the bus stopped at the Two Swords traffic circle, I focused on a figure in a red-and-white-striped shirt—stripes wider than those on a rugby shirt. It was a boy—maybe twelve years old, standing with his back to the street. He was bent over, and his forehead was near his knees, hanging between his legs.

"His master is making him put his ears behind his legs. He is being disciplined," Faisah said. "God only knows how long he has been bent over like that."

"This is how they treat children!" I said in disgust.

"This is how hatred is born."

The boy's master, a bearded man in a tan shalwar kameez, watched the boy from inside a nearby machine shop. His hair was slick and parted down the middle. Two men inside the shop looked up from their work. I wondered how the machinists would react to the man who was torturing the boy in this fashion. *Does it make them uncomfortable? Or is this treatment accepted and common? Do they notice we are staring, disapproving?*

They smiled at the boy's master and exchanged a few words.

The master moved casually toward the boy, who tried to straighten his back but could not. His torso remained at a right angle to his legs as he leaned onto a wooden chair in front of him. When he lifted his head, I saw that he was crying, not only the slow tears of humiliation, but also the hard, uncontrollable tears of a crying child. It was the tears, not the backache, which were the purpose of the torture.

Finally, the boy inched away from the road. The master spoke to him and then wandered back to the neighbor's shop. The boy watched the master out of the corner of his eye. His back now was stooped as he tried to recover from the ordeal. His eye remained always on his master. The master would always be there, the enemy who would wake him in the morning.

By the time we reached Clifton it was late afternoon, when women are expected to be home. We walked the winding path, eager to tell Ammi all that had happened. The purple bougainvillea petals at the entrance glowed like thousands of small paper lanterns. My back ached as I pushed the door open.

Abbu was sitting in the front hall.

"Come in, girls," he said, wrapping his arms around us. "Your mother is sick. The doctors say she has had a stroke. Come upstairs. She wants to see you right away."

Life stood at its blackboard like a crazed mathematician scribbling his proofs. "See that?" he said, pounding his chalk into the slate, then turning around to look us straight in the eye. "There are no progressions, no formulas, no geometry. God is the only constant."

Everyone in the family suffered. Nafeesa's losses were only the most obvious. The first stroke took her mobility, so Kulraj Singh carried her to the bamboo table for meals or onto the verandah for tea. The next strokes robbed, first, her concentration, then her speech, and finally, they seized her massive energy, and her life.

He purchased two wheelchairs, one for upstairs and one for down. Until the electric lift could be installed, he took her up and down the stairs in his arms. He would come home from the office to do it if necessary.

"Iqbal can carry me," she said. "You need not leave work to do it."

"It has always been my pleasure to touch you, Nafeesa. I won't share that honor with the gardener."

On summer nights they slept on the roof under Karachi's blanket. He placed her chair at the roof's edge, where they had a clear view of the Arabian Sea.

"I'm afraid, Kulraj," she whispered. "Just look into the blackness of the ocean. Look at it out there, waiting for me. It sounds like the rattle in my grandmother's throat."

He dragged over the two string beds that Ujala had prepared with pillows and dhurries. The beds' guts were dried and prolapsed, in need of mending. He bent toward her and Nafeesa took his hand.

"Let me help you lie down," he urged, but her shadow remained stiff and still. She would not turn away from her view.

"Where will I go?" she asked. The question circled in the midnight, and he let it be. "Will God go with me?" Then she turned to him with a force he did not know she still retained. "You are the priest," she said. "I am just a woman. You tell me, my guru, my imam, what next?"

"You are always with you," he said, "and you are divine—what I have worshipped all these years."

She did not respond.

"And in the dark you must not forget that when it is daylight the sea is calm and blue," he said cautiously. "And don't we love what comes to us out of the blue?"

Then she laughed, dropping his hand.

"You are a crazy old man, Kulraj Singh!" Then she became quiet. "Will you miss me when I am gone?"

She wanted something from him. He stared at her question. Miss her? If he thought about missing her, he would never be able to harden his voice to encourage her. So instead, he argued.

"First, you are not going anywhere soon," he said, clearing his throat. "You have had a stroke, not a death sentence. Second," he continued with his list, like a lawyer arguing the losing side of a case, "dying is something we all must do alone." He said the word, *dying*, then hurried to add, "but we will never abandon you."

He knew it annoyed her when he numbered his arguments, but she was listening. He picked up her hand again.

"And, third," he said, "death does not want to separate old lovers like us. It is the lovers who abandon each other—the mind of the one who is going moves too quickly into the future. The mind of the one who remains lives forever in the past. Isn't that how we humans are?"

"I love the way you say *we* and *us*," she sighed, her eyes filling with tears.

"And, God willing, I won't be far behind," he whispered. "I will meet you out there."

She looked at him, suddenly stark and dry-eyed. She went directly to the heart of the matter.

"No—oh, no. You must stay here with the children. What about Meena and Amir? They still need my attention. Who will be their mother now?" She took her hand away and held it against her mouth to keep from crying out loud.

"You decide," he replied immediately, knowing she would say Ujala. She was the obvious choice, and he had already spoken to Uji about it. He felt guilty, having usurped what was a mother's decision.

"Uji," Nafeesa said, squeezing the sound through her throat.

"Yes," he agreed. "Uji."

"Uji listens," Nafeesa said. "She has a big heart, and learns quickly. Reshma has her own family, and she is so rigid. Faisah is self-absorbed, and too young anyway. Ujala must be their mother now."

Later Kulraj Singh laid his arm across Nafeesa's body, gently over her abdomen. His hand rested on the edge of her pelvis, weightlessly, as it had for almost three decades. He inhaled her body's fragrances—both the sweetness of jasmine and the sting of rubbing alcohol. She never failed to delight him.

9

Lahore, 1996

On the day of Ujala's trial a breeze coaxed a few stray clouds across Lahore's sky. The air was spiced with the sharpness of marigolds. Hyacinth beans twisted their purple leaves around a chain link fence. Plump pods littered the street. Hundreds of supporters gathered outside the courthouse with placards and chants.

Women's Rights Are Human Rights! Free Ujala! Free Baji! There is no honor in honor crimes!

In the holding cell Hasaan Behrani, Faisah's bodyguard, was at her side, as he had been since the day of the acid attack. Jabril Kazzaz had sent his muscle man to the hospital with a note for Faisah: *Hasaan is your bodyguard now. He will watch over you as he has watched over me. And if you will permit, I will pay for his services.*

"Permit it? Bring on the bodyguards!" she shouted, laughing. "Bring on the army! Bring on the nukes!" Faisah longed to feel safe again.

Hasaan controlled the cell door while they waited for the bailiff to announce the opening of court.

"Are you ready for this?" Ujala asked Faisah. She wondered if she was ready herself.

163

"Am I ready?" Faisah beamed. "Baji, I have been preparing for this my entire life."

It had been four weeks since the acid attack on Faisah, and Ujala wondered if Faisah actually felt the confidence she was projecting. She knew that this was not the time to ask. She leaned her cheek into the curve of her sister's neck, avoiding the gauze taped to Faisah's cheek and eye. Underneath the bandage, the scab had taken the shape of the nitric splash. Faisah's right eye was burned shut in one corner. She would probably lose its vision.

"It's physical vision you might lose, my lily," Kulraj Singh said to her the night before the trial. "You will never lose the greater vision you carry in your heart."

But the words he hoped would inspire Faisah clanged like a hollow pipe on concrete. At first, and for many days, Faisah had hidden in her room with the blinds closed. She ached for the consolation of her mother's body. She wanted to roll up in a fleece with Nafeesa and lean into her collarbone, where she had often fallen asleep beside a book of children's stories. For days following the attack, when they let the morphine flow freely into her, Faisah became that child again. She recalled that the fleece was soothing, dark brown and musty; her mother's scent was both acrid and sweet. She thought she could hear Mithu squawking. Had he escaped his cage again? Meena and Amir were arguing in the next room, and Ujala was running an iron back and forth over cloth. Faisah could smell scorched cotton as Baji pressed it into a towel. Reshma brought a tray of tea and cake rusks into the women's quarter, and all was peaceful. Once they took the drugs away, pain became her only sister, whom she shared with no one else. When at last her suffering subsided and her bouts of crying were exhausted, she remembered who she was. She invoked the discipline of her profession to prepare for her baji's trial.

"We call the docket in five minutes," the bailiff announced. The courtroom could barely contain the raw emotions of Ujala's supporters. Reporters and photographers gathered in the rear. Entering behind Hasaan and Faisah, Ujala scanned the cavernous room. She panicked for a moment, until she caught sight of her father's turban, Amir's mop of black hair, Meena's green dupatta, and Yusuf's prayer cap. She dared not look around.

All these people, she thought. A wave of nausea rose from her belly.

Faisah straightened her posture in her white linen suit, and she focused her good eye on the space several feet in front of her nose. Then a door slammed back against a wall, a gavel pounded, shoes rustled, and the gallery rose as the judge entered. The people murmured, straining to hear. They leaned forward as if they were one body, putting the room off-keel. They would need each other to return to balance.

Seated at the table adjacent to Faisah and Ujala was the provincial prosecutor. He strode to the podium, and the judge nodded for him to start the government's case.

"My Lord," he said, "a most unusual set of circumstances has occurred in the past twenty-four hours—circumstances that have caused the province to reevaluate this matter."

What is this? wondered Faisah.

"Due to the diligence of Mr. Khan Shazad, father of Chanda Khan, who is now released on bail, new witnesses have come forward who will provide credible evidence that this defendant has been engaging in a deliberate, nationwide pattern of criminal behavior. She has torn asunder a number of marriages held sacred under Shariah. Therefore, the Province moves to dismiss this case and to transfer jurisdiction to the Federal Shariah Court in Islamabad for further proceedings by the judges and the Shariah scholars, the ulemas."

Faisah was on her feet at once. Her voice was strong and dramatic. She hoped that the weight of her rhetoric would add heft to the weakness of her legal position.

"My Lord, the defense graciously accepts the confession of dismissal made by the prosecutor," she said, smiling at her opponent. "But we object strenuously, I repeat, stren-u-ous-ly, to any transfer. As this Honorable Court knows better than we"—she gave her most serious expression to the judge—"without further evidence, this court's jurisdiction ends when the case is dismissed.

If further proceedings are warranted in Islamabad, let the Shariah Court decide—*not*"—she turned to the prosecutor for emphasis—"a provincial functionary."

She glared down at the prosecutor with her one good eye, and he rose to respond.

"Oh, but we can have an evidentiary hearing right now, My Lord," he said, sweeping his arm away from his chest. His hand led viewers to a row of chairs against the far wall. "The Court can hear not only from Mr. Khan of Lahore, the father of Chanda Khan, but also from Mr. Wazir from Rakhni, the husband of Khanum Wazir."

Dread filled Ujala's heart. How had Chanda's father located Khanum's husband in Balochistan? What had Aga Ji told him?

"This snake woman," said the prosecutor, "deliberately hid their wives and daughters away from them in defiance of their lawful authority as husbands and fathers."

The mumbling in the courtroom required the judge to use his gavel. One strike was enough.

"Silence!"

"By what lawful authority," Faisah's voice boomed, "may a woman not take steps to protect herself from physical abuse? To protect her body in which a child may someday dwell?"

The prosecutor stood again.

"This court is no place to discuss such personal matters, My Lord. The wife owes a duty of obedience to her father, first, and then to her husband. Neither man gave their consent to the actions of his wife or daughter. Not having authority to make these decisions for themselves, the women were legally incompetent to give the defendant their consent, and thus she kidnapped them unlawfully."

"If you will indulge me, Your Honor," said Faisah.

"Objection. She is out of order."

The judge was a patient man, known both for his fairness in following procedures and for his harshness in punishing offenders. His reading glasses were balanced on the front wedge of his nose, causing his gaze to cross the horizon of his cheeks. He waited until the room was perfectly quiet before he said a word.

"Be seated, Madam," he said to Faisah, almost in a whisper.

Here it comes. He's ready to rule, she thought.

"I will not indulge either of you any further," he said. "The prosecution's last-minute request has inconvenienced many people today, and unnecessarily burdened this court's workload. And you are right, Sir, this court is no place to discuss such personal matters. But, the Shariah Court is. Thus, in light of the issue you have raised—the meaning of proper obedience of a wife or daughter to a husband or father, this Court hereby dismisses the current charges and, upon the completion of documents, transfers jurisdiction to the Federal Shariah Court. However," the judge added, "whether or not the defendant remains in custody is a determination to be made by that august body, not by me. The defendant will be released without bond at once. This court is adjourned."

He slammed the gavel one last time, and the courtroom erupted. Faisah herded Ujala into the holding cell area, and the family followed. In the courtroom Hasaan's eyes scanned the crowd, and Rahima Mai, her arms folded across her chest, stood next to him like a rock.

A man with wild eyes and a thick moustache pushed his way through the crowd.

"Get the infidels!" he shouted, grabbing Kulraj Singh's neck. Kulraj slipped his hand inside his shirt to touch the sheathed kirpan. A melee exploded for several minutes, until the moment someone jumped up and grabbed the end piece of the turban from Kulraj Singh's head. Then, as the turban unwound, as if in slow motion, the room also spun until Kulraj Singh's naked topknot was exposed. The attackers stepped back, as if to make room for the ignominy.

Amir, Yusuf, and Zeshan, with their backs protecting Kulraj Singh, extended their arms against the attackers. Hasaan jabbed two of the offenders, and Rahima Mai lifted one of them by the hair on his head. The man bellowed. The bailiffs were shouting, "Clear the courtroom! Everyone must clear the courtroom!" Police appeared with their Kalashnikovs. Zeshan grabbed the white muslin of his father-in-law's turban and pushed open the door to the holding area, where Meena, Faisah, Ujala, Lia, and Jabril Kazzaz welcomed them inside.

The family retreated to Nankana Sahib. Hasaan was posted at the street on the edge of the lot. Neighbors delivered dishes throughout the day and into the evening—fried onions and spicy peas, Kashmiri potatoes, sweet rice with yogurt, lentils, plates piled with pistachios, pomegranates, and mangoes. Each time the bell rang, the twins went to the door. Meena greeted the neighbor and passed the dish to Amir, who served it.

Kulraj Singh left the door to the shrine room open as he began his rituals and songs of praise. He lit candles and sat cross-legged before the photo of Nafeesa—the one Ujala had placed there when she returned to the family from Sindh. Nafeesa looked directly into the lens—a vital, even shocking, effect. Her hair was pulled back, its length and fullness unseen by the camera, but clear in her husband's memory. The shadows of her eyes created the impression that she had been crying. At the same time she seemed to be annoyed about something, and strict, yet tender enough to kiss. The portrait was both straightforward and contradictory, as Nafeesa had been.

Kulraj pulled the harmonium close to him, opened the valves, and searched for his texts. He did not turn when he heard the knock at the open door.

"Yes?" he replied, still searching through the books. He was hoping it was Amir, or one of the others, wanting to join him. "Who is it?" Kulraj asked, and turned to see Jabril Kazzaz standing with his hand on the doorknob. Kulraj Singh rose at once, smiling.

"Would you like to come in, my friend?" he asked, aware of the puzzle that the moment presented. A famous Muslim like Kazzaz might not want to enter a Sikh shrine. But recognizing the common light in their hearts, Kazzaz said nothing. He just nodded and entered.

Jabril's senses were overwhelmed—the smell of incense and ripened fruit, the candlelight, the photo of Guru Nanak above them on the wall. But when Jabril's eyes fell on the photo of Nafeesa, they softened.

He fell to his knees.

"Baji," he whispered. "Baji."

At once Kulraj recognized the profile of the fourteen-year-old boy who had stood over his beloved wife with a sword in Shalimar Garden.

He sank to his knees.

"Jameel?"

Kazzaz shifted and looked into the eyes of Kulraj Singh.

"I thought I killed her," he whispered, his throat feeling as if it were filled with the length of a sword. His tears flowed easily.

"You almost did," replied Kulraj, recalling the weeks his wife spent in the hospital and the months in recovery. "But she was strong."

"I thought I killed her. After that, I wanted to die."

Then Kulraj remembered how Faisah had said that Kazzaz slept next to corpses.

"Nafeesa is the sister you went looking for in the gutters of Lahore?" he asked.

Kazzaz nodded.

"It was like a myth others spread, so it became my cover story," he said. He kept his eyes on the photograph. "After Shalimar Garden, I was a lost soul. The family honored me for what I had done, but I hated myself. I saw the sort of man my older brother was and knew I did not want to be like that. So, I decided to do what Baji had done. One day I took the bus to Lahore, let go of my past, changed my name, and never returned to Malakwal. I knew I would never find her body, but I searched anyhow. Praise Allah, she survived. Praise Allah, she was with you." Jabril's tears dropped into his hands.

"She forgave you long ago," said Kulraj. Jabril was rubbing the tears between his fingers together and leaning back on his heels. The eyes of Nafeesa stared out at them.

"And you?" Jabril asked without facing Kulraj. "Did you forgive me?"

"Me?" Kulraj laughed. "It took me longer to forgive myself than to forgive you. Remember, I was an adult and you were still a boy. I left Nafeesa alone in Pakistan for those weeks after our

marriage. Anything could have happened to her and I would not
have been there. Meeting in Shalimar Garden was a stupid idea—
and dangerous—to think we would not have been conspicuous!
Did I think we were invisible? We were young and in love. I was a
careless fool."

"That one event shaped my life—it led me to God," Jabril said.
He turned to Kulraj, relieved to tell his lifelong secret.

"Nafeesa had a way of shaping others' lives," Kulraj said. "She
was a miracle, and I adored her. I adore her still." He nodded at
the shrine, the flowers, the place that reflected his devotion. "Loving
Nafeesa was my first serious spiritual practice. She still is my path
to God."

A speck of a candlewick dissolved into itself and died.

"I don't know how to tell the others," Jabril said. "I am full of
shame for what I did. What did you and Baji tell them about
Malakwal? About Shalimar Garden?"

"Nothing," Kulraj said. He reached for a fresh candle and struck
a match. "She never wanted the children to know the truth . . .
well, that's not quite right. She wanted them to know, but was
afraid to tell them . . . we could never think of a way . . ."

"No. No. She was right!" Jabril insisted. His voice was
spontaneous and gruff. He was pleased that the rest of the family
did not know. "My family is dangerous. They were proud of me.
The only mention of Baji was on her birthday, when my auntie set
a place for her at the table and my brother spit on her dishes. The
uncles called me a hero, but I felt the chill between our parents. I
heard my mother call out Baji's name in her sleep." He folded his
legs under him and looked up.

"I had not thought of it that way," Kulraj said. "I haven't thought
about it for a long time."

"Who do the children think their mother was? Didn't they ask
questions?"

"Yes, we had to tell them something, so we invented a past for
Nafeesa. She worried that they might think less of themselves on
account of your family's rejection. She worried that if they knew,
the children might seek out the family, only to expose all of us.
She did not want to feel it or to have them see her in pain. Instead,

we enjoyed the gifts we were given—and before long the Lahori train story was told to explain her lost family, and that was that. She never spoke of them."

"The Lahori train?"

"Yes. I remember the first time it came up. I was reading the newspaper and Nafeesa was nursing one of the babies in the rocking chair. Reshma was looking at picture books spread across the floor.

"'Where are your Ammi and Abbu?' Reshma asked. I wondered what Nafeesa would say.

"'I have no memory of them,' she told our young daughter, and she began her tale. 'I lost everyone during the Partition. My family was on the train to Lahore, and all of them died, my parents, my brothers, my uncles, altogether twenty people, including eight children,' she said, embellishing her lie. She must have thought it through many times, preparing for the day when one of the children would ask her. 'I hid under my mother's body until it was over, so they thought I was dead because I had a cut on my head, by my hairline.' She pulled back her hair to reveal her scar your sword had caused. Reshma's eyes had widened at the proof. 'I remember I was hungry,' Nafeesa said. 'I was just a baby. I slept and slept.'

"'Then what happened?' Reshma asked. She must have been six or seven years old at the time.

"'I was lucky. God protected me so I could grow up and become your mother. Someone took me to a wealthy woman who sent me to a missionary school. I guess you could say I was another Muslim raised by missionaries, the Sisters of the Immaculate Heart of Mary.'

"'I have no cousins?' Reshma said. Her voice sounded disappointed, being deprived of cousins.

"'You do have cousins. You have your father's entire family,' Nafeesa laughed. 'That is our family.' She rubbed the fibrous mark, at her hairline.

"'Oh, Ammi!' Reshma said, pulling her little finger along the scar's rough edges. I remember how Nafeesa shifted the conversation's tone.

"'But it's my only flaw, Buttercup!' she said. 'And, have you ever noticed how a flaw can make a thing more beautiful?'"

"Your spirit survived us, Baji; forgive me," whispered Jabril.

He turned to Kulraj Singh, widening his smile at the memory. "When I first set eyes on Ujala, she seemed so familiar. The small gap between her front teeth—like Baji's." He hesitated. "That is why I came to you tonight—to confirm my suspicions. When I learned you were a Sikh and your wife's name was Nafeesa, I began to wonder. I had to know." Jabril Kazzaz's composure began to crack. "And now I feel not an ounce of the hatred I deserve from you. And I feel Baji has forgiven me."

Kulraj began to empty and dry the offering bowls as he listened to Jabril. He poured the water into a bucket he kept under the altar cloth.

"Shall we tell the children? They should know, now that they are grown." He posed to Jabril the same question he had posed to Nafeesa for many years. And Jabril's reply was the same.

"No. Don't do it. My brother Ali's only regret was that he did not kill you! And he vowed he would do so someday. It is a wonder to me that you have survived. No, it is best that the family not know. He could still be out there, looking for you. And for them!"

Kulraj thought about the decision as he wiped each empty bowl, inside and out, until the glass squeaked. Then he passed each one to Jabril, who replaced them slowly, overturning them in front of Nafeesa's photo. When they finished, they extinguished the candles. Kulraj turned to Jabril.

"I agree," he said. "We will tell no one."

In the courtyard Ujala was seated in Nafeesa's wicker chair, her feet resting on the ottoman. She made room for Faisah to squeeze in beside her. They could hear their father singing in the shrine room. Amir arranged three pots of tea around the bamboo table.

"I like that Judge Rizvi!" said Jabril Kazzaz, entering the courtyard.

"He is a no-nonsense judge," Abida agreed.

"From an old Lahori family," said Jabril. He tore the chapati and scooped up the dal.

The phones began ringing. Supporters were calling to offer congratulations and help.

"Tell them to call WASP," Faisah shouted to Amir. "The office can give them plenty to do."

At the sound of the word *office*, Ujala thought of Adiala Prison. *I wonder what Rahima Mai is doing right now?*

Rahima Mai locked her office door behind her and marched straight to the teakettle. She untied the string from the box of sweetmeats she had bought in the bazaar on the way to work. The sweets were so orderly, each in its very own cubicle. Squares. Rectangles. Rectangles. Squares. Pink. White. Brown. Pink. White. Brown.

With the thousands of these sugared treats I have consumed in my life, sugar must be backing up in my veins, she thought, imagining each grain waiting its turn to enter her bloodstream and deposit its crystal load. She took a pink one and popped it into her mouth, whole, thinking of Ujala's day in court. *Ujala is gone. I have to admit I will miss her. . . Maybe it is just as well. We were getting too close.*

She opened the yellow tag Lipton box, poured water into a cup, and dropped the teabag in. This time she chose a brown sweet and pinched its flank. She ran her finger along the smooth side of it, patting lightly, then squeezing it.

Ujala's story of winter in Chitral reminded her of her own childhood in Muzaffabad. She recalled the freezing, starry Kashmiri nights. Nights must be like that in Chitral. She thought about Noor, the prize miniature donkey she raised as a child, the one she ran to when the earthquake hit, the donkey whose soft ears she patted and squeezed for comfort. Childhood had been a lonely time for her, like now, since Akbar's death.

But I was lucky. They married me off to a good man. Even if he was dimwitted, he was kind. A dolt and a donkey! The only ones who ever loved me! She laughed out loud.

It was a risky thing for her to spend so much time with one prisoner, but, after all, she was the Women's Supervisor and Ujala did work for her.

If anyone here found out about our little story times, I would be disciplined, have my paycheck docked. I might be demoted, or even lose my job entirely—everything I have worked for all of these years. Then where would I be? As it is, I have nothing extra—rupees are coming and rupees are going. No savings, no husband, nothing. If I lost my job I'd have to look for help from some of my girls out on the street. I could get back into Adiala through Intake and work my way up again!

She laughed to herself as she licked her fingers. She chose another sweetmeat. Its flesh seemed almost alive.

The rings and pings and pop tunes of the mobile phones kept interrupting the meal.

"Can we turn off the phones for a while so we can relax together?" Ujala asked. "Amir, please get Abbu."

Kulraj Singh sat cross-legged in the shrine room, reading scriptures about the role of a warrior in oppressive times. Amir listened to his prayer from the doorway.

"My daughters suffer imprisonment, threats, assaults. Oh, give them wisdom," he prayed, holding his head in the palm of his hands. "No hatred, no confusion, no tyranny. Give them victory. And fearlessness. Victory is Yours."

Amir reached out his hand, and his father accepted his help getting up. He rose to join the others.

Zeshan went looking for Meena and found her sitting by the front door, crying.

"I picked up Abbu's phone," she told him, between sobs. "It was a man—he seemed to recognize my voice. He said, 'Oh, you're the radio girl.' He said, 'We will ruin that pretty face of yours, too.'" She turned to her husband. "Zeshan, he called me the radio girl. He said 'It will be blood next time for all of you.'"

"We have to tell them about the threat," Zeshan said to Meena, checking to see that Hasaan was posted next to the road. He threw the bolt to lock the front door.

"But I hate to ruin this evening. Just when Baji has been released and Faisah is recovering. I hoped this would be the perfect time to give them our good news," she said, patting her belly.

"Who says this isn't a good time to tell them?" Zeshan asked. "The idea of a baby will bring more hope to the family."

"Or more fear," she said.

Zeshan took Meena's hand and led her back to the courtyard.

"Aren't they two sides of the same rupee?" he asked.

Later, Ujala locked herself in her room for the night. Before she closed the door, she pulled the pistol out of her bag and handed it to Yusuf.

"Here," she said. "Do you know how to use this?"

"Yes, Uji," he said, amazed by her yet again, that she would be carrying a gun. "But we won't need it. Don't worry." Hasaan and Yusuf took turns guarding her door, and neighbors patrolled the area around their home.

Faisah dragged two string beds from under the rooftop eaves where they had been stored upright against a wall. Lia brought a bowl of apples and sugarcane from the kitchen.

"Sugarcane!" Faisah said.

"Shh! Neighbors are sleeping all over these roofs," said Lia.

Faisah cut a piece of cane with her pocketknife and pulled down a width of green with her front teeth. Inside the pulp was spongy. She stripped the sweetness with effort, sucking and nibbling, draining the sugar from it. She spit the remnants onto the pile of green skins on the floor.

"Just like Carolina," Lia said, handing Faisah's pocketknife back to her. "Sugarcane, just like home."

When they were done, they slept together in the chilled night air.

In the morning the police arrived with a warrant from the Shariah Court, demanding that Ujala go with them at once. Neighbors gathered to witness the arrest, and Ujala took one last look at her family. Faisah looked firm. Amir's eyes glistened. She saw her father's mouth form words she knew to be his Punjabi blessing. Lia was taking notes on a small card, and Yusuf kissed the palm of his hand and blew the kiss to her.

"I will stay here with your family, Madam," said Hasaan. Ujala nodded.

"I am grateful, and I will be back soon. Inshallah." God willing.

She climbed into the back of the police car that would return her to Adiala.

"Call the press," Lia said. "Baji will be safer if the authorities know that reporters are aware she's been arrested again."

She and Yusuf grabbed their mobile phones and spread to separate rooms to call their contacts. Faisah telephoned Meena at the radio station.

"Interrupt the program to announce Baji's arrest," Faisah instructed Meena over the phone. Moments later, Amir was listening to Meena's announcement on the radio when Kulraj Singh entered the kitchen and switched it off.

Amir busied himself cooking parathas. He mixed flour and water into a firm ball of dough, then formed it into a snake, wound it into a bun, and spooned butter along the folds of the dough. Kulraj Singh watched his son pat a thick round piece. Amir tossed and twirled the mixture in the air and then laid it flat on the spitting grill.

"*Baji's arrest,*" Amir repeated Meena's words bitterly. "I just can't get used to it."

Amir fired his anger at the parathas. Each time the yeast tried to rise out of its circle, he smacked the bubble with the back of a spoon, flipped the dough with tongs, and watched it fry. He folded it in half, then spooned more butter, folded and buttered it again, until the dough was quartered and sizzling, and began to burn.

"Be careful with that," his father said, taking the tongs away. "Let me finish it." Amir looked at the scorched paratha and cracked a smile.

"I think it is laughing at me," he said.

Standing at the open back door with a mug of tea, he felt a breeze, sniffed fresh-cut hay, and emptied his questions into the sky. Why is the weather perfect when the worst things occur? he thought.

"It's God's way of letting us know that humans are part of the beauty of the world, too," Kulraj Singh replied, as if Amir had spoken his question aloud. "Perhaps the haystacks think we smell good in the morning." He smiled. "Even on a day like this one, the world remains beautiful, even the police are beautiful—"

"—but this lawyer is not beautiful," Faisah said. They had not heard her enter the kitchen. Amir turned and saw that Faisah had removed the bandages from her face. On her right cheek, a scarlet lesion lay curled like a snake. Splashes of nitric acid had caused thick, black burns, both on her cheek and down the side of her neck. Several tiny spots close to her eye were scarred from the emergency grafting. Her swollen eyelid seemed to merge into the lower scar tissue like a melting mask of wax. A tear balanced on the lower lid of her good eye.

"Can you see anything at all?" Kulraj Singh asked.

"Not really," she replied hesitantly. She covered her good eye. "Well, I do see something—it's like a black and white striped fan. I don't know. It comes and goes. I can't tell if I am seeing something with my eye or if I am imagining it. I can't control it. And it is too painful to try to move my eyelid." Lia walked up behind her.

"Don't try, Faisah," she said.

Amir was speechless. He never imagined his sisters weak in any way.

"She's got a terrific wink." She paused. "At least that's what I think!" Lia's rhyme fall flat. She shifted tones. "I'll go with her to the doctor today. We'll know more about the surgery afterward." Faisah glared at Lia.

"I hate how I look," Faisah yelled. "I hate the men who did this to me. I hate those doctors. I hate that hospital, and I don't want to go back there for any reason. Ever."

"It has been only six weeks. Let's just wait and see," said Lia.

"I think I'll pack the car," Amir said, leaving the room. He was distressed by Faisah's face, and could take no more arguing.

"Faisah," Kulraj Singh said laying his arm around her shoulders. "Let your skin breathe in the open air. Let's sit under the neem tree." He motioned to Lia. "Will you bring the fruit?"

They sat on string beds in silence, watching two squirrels chase each other and listening to the sparrows. The birds flitted up into the branches. Thick socks dried on a line strung above their heads. A pile of trash waited in the corner for someone to come with a dustpan and a broom. They passed a red plastic basket of tangerines. Each fruit still had attached to it a small stem and a few dark leaves. They peeled and broke them into clumps and fed each other with their fingers—spitting seeds, picking their teeth. Kulraj Singh kept his arm around Faisah and pressed her against his bony chest. Again he would be both mother and father.

"You must tell those hateful thoughts either to pay rent or to get out of your head," he said, grinning and kissing the crown of Faisah's head. "You think you are not beautiful, but you are beautiful. You have a wound on your face that will heal. Do not let this acid also burn into your soul."

"But I do hate them, Abbu. Look what they have done to me! Look what is happening to Baji—who will be next?"

"No one is happy without struggle. Only after death do we not struggle. You can be happy even in this, Faisah." She looked at him in disbelief. "Talk to your mind and tell it that you are a good person and it should not mistreat you this way by entertaining all these angry thoughts. Look at your mind and watch its door open. Then you can laugh at hate and anger as they run away. Peace will reappear."

Lia wondered what in the world this old man was talking about.

"How can someone be happy in the face of such injuries and such injustice?" she asked.

"Happiness is ours naturally," he said. "Look, people say, well, I am taking a trip to London because that will make me happy. Why will that make you happy? Is everyone in London happy? No, all that going to London does is relieve the desire to go to London, the tension of not having something you want. So we think that London makes us happy. It's not London. It's our mind. After London, we will want Paris, then America. You don't really have a problem."

"My face has a big problem," Faisah said.

"Yes. Your face does, my lily, but think of how the negativity you feel has arisen since this incident. I, too, have felt this way.

When your dear mother died, I became angry with God and afraid—for the family, for my own loneliness. I watched my mind for hours every day and what did I find? Fear. Over and over again I sat and relaxed and looked and there it was—as if sitting on a fence post, a big hairy bird marked *Fear*." He laughed. "My mind created this feathered thing I was keeping alive—feeding the pain, the drama, even the artistry of it. Why, I wondered, does it seem so natural for these bad feelings to arise and so unnatural for love, kindness, and gratitude to arise?"

Faisah sighed. "My mind will never be as peaceful as yours, Abbu. I am just too vain, too selfish. My mind won't give me any peace." Now Lia wanted to hear more from Abbu.

"I read somewhere that the mind is like a monkey," she said.

"A drunken money stung by a scorpion!" he laughed, hugging Faisah. "At first, anyway. But, the mind will follow orders and it can learn."

Lia looked at him quizzically.

"The mind learns in two ways—through shocks like this one—they make us stop to consider how we respond to what life places in our path. And also, the mind learns through repetition—it can develop the habit of letting the bad thoughts go. If we do not nurture them, they are like seeds that get no rain. Fear can blow away. And *then*," he repeated, "*then* love will arise naturally."

"Abbu, I cannot imagine loving the men who have done this to me. I'm just not that good."

"Loving them is not the point, Faisah. It is the not-hating that is the point, so that your own peace of mind is not destroyed. In a way, you have been offered a gift."

"A gift?" Lia asked. "But Faisah has been attacked."

"It is the gift of waking up. Play this game with your mind. First, let yourself feel the fear."

"No problem," said Faisah, sighing.

"Now look at yourself feeling that fear." He looked in his daughter's eyes. "What do you feel now?"

"Nothing," Faisah replied.

"Not even fear?"

"The fear is gone." She was amazed.

"That's it!" Kulraj Singh said. He was triumphant. "That is the quiet place—the spot where you can start."

"But now it's gone and I feel confusion returning," said Faisah.

"And it will," he said, slipping a thin metal bangle onto his daughter's wrist. "Wear this to remind you to watch the fear from a distance, as if this happened a long time ago in a faraway place," he said. "Be the landlord of your own mind. Tell those thoughts to pay rent or get out!"

10

Adiala Prison, 1996

Rahima Mai had to admit she was happy to hear that Ujala had been arrested again. *Now she will be returned to me. But, they are seeking the death penalty, those bastards! I wonder how long we will have her with us.*

The next morning when Rahima Mai looked up from her desk, there was Ujala in the doorway, ready to work.

Strange, Rahima Mai thought. She's smiling. She looks happy to see me.

Strange, Ujala thought. Once I was afraid of this woman. Now I am happy to see her.

"I'll be at a meeting in the Central Office," said Rahima Mai.

"Yes, Madam."

Ujala began organizing index cards. On each white card was printed a name, date of birth, religion, date of incarceration, judgment, and date of release for each female prisoner in Adiala. For male prisoners the same information was typed on yellow cards. Many hands had scribbled on the cards over the years. Ujala's task was to type the information on fresh cards and file them in metal boxes.

Her fingers unwrapped the bands, shuffled through the cards, and then wrapped each one back as it had been, until at last she found her own card. She slipped it down under the typewriter's platen and cranked the cylinder into place. Staring at the empty space for her release date, she thought of Yusuf.

I am not the naive, middle-class girl who wants the lush wedding, the bright children, the foreign travel, maybe a small, acceptable career that would become a hobby, she thought. How foolish to think that I would not have to choose. Once I thought I wanted a relationship that was intense and vulnerable. Now I just want what is safe and real.

Suddenly Rahima Mai's presence blew into the office.

"Those men in Central Office think they know so much," she complained. "They insist I attend all their boring staff meetings, but do they ever ask my opinion?" Rahima Mai was raising her voice. "No! They never ask. They only let me sit at their table. Then they go on and on about the next promotion they expect. It never occurs to them that I may have applied for the same position. They act like their jobs are the only ones that matter—to hell with them!" She returned to the door, banged it shut, and turned the key. She leaned her back against the door, recovering from her storm. Finally she looked over at Ujala. She paused, noticing that Ujala was moving toward the hot pot.

"Now fix us some tea," she said in her usual way.

Rahima Mai's mood shift did not fool Ujala. She noticed how Rahima Mai was beginning to bring her little treats to share while she told her stories. Rahima Mai cleared her throat.

"So you were saying that your mother had a stroke? I am sorry to hear that, but—is that what brought you to us at Adiala?"

"Madam, it is much more complicated than that."

"Go on," signaled Rahima Mai.

◆   ◆   ◆

Abbu called me into his study where we sat on the old settee.

"Ammi will need you every day now," he said. "You will take care of her and the house with Faisah's help, and you will be a mother for Meena and Amir until Ammi is better."

"I will, Abbu."

"Please understand, Uji." Tears streamed down his face and mine. He coughed a little as he spoke. "We do not know if or when God may take her. It could be weeks. It could be years. I prayed on the rooftop all night long about what to do. I asked Allah, the ancestors, the Guru, the stars. I have come to this place of understanding and peace about it."

My father spoke to me differently than he ever had before. As if I were not his daughter, but his partner.

"We must accept this terrible thing," he said, "as God's will, not only for your mother, but for all of us—especially, I think, for you, Uji. We cannot see what He can see, or where life will take us now. Our view is too small."

As he said these words, Abbu leaned in close to my face, holding the thumb of each hand to its forefinger in a gesture of confidence that I recognized.

"I will make certain that everyone gives you the respect you will deserve as the mother of this family," he said. "Everyone."

How can he understand so much so quickly? I wondered. He knows that Ammi will not recover, and that I am being called to Ammi's role. What I may have planned does not matter to him, and strangely, it does not matter to me, either.

Abbu was not asking me to change my life. He was pointing out that my life was changing, the way a flag signals to a sailor the direction of the wind. I was not resisting his idea in the least because what he said felt true and natural. I realized in a flash, in the same way my vision had cleared after visiting the jail, meeting Sita and her sisters, and riding the bus home, that now I could imagine my future.

"Actually, I like having a break from my studies," I told Ammi after my graduation ceremony. Masood brought our tea into the study. "You always said I'd have to marry someone rich since I was never good at cooking and cleaning." I smiled at her. "Since we have not found anyone rich, maybe it is just as well that I take this chance to improve my domestic skills."

"You have been a pampered hot house flower," Ammi replied,

and I felt a sting. "And now what is in store for you? Housekeeping? It is an honorable life, but I don't think it is for you." She looked around at the walls of her books—ceiling to floor. "We are alike in so many ways. I think of the life I might have had as a scholar. I have no regrets, but I treasure my dreams from so long ago. I wanted so much when I was your age."

She paused, waiting for my reply. I held my breath, steeling myself for what was coming.

"To be honest, Uji," Ammi said.

Please don't be honest, I thought. I am not you. Ammi continued, "I sometimes wonder why you seem to want so little."

Ouch! There it was. The pinch of disappointment my mother could not resist causing when she compared herself with me. Without even realizing it, she ripped the scab off the old sore again.

"I am not at all sure what I want in the long run, Ammi." I inhaled deeply. "But for now I want to take care of you and the family. I will have plenty of time for travel and study when you are feeling better."

We dropped the subject of my advanced education before Ammi could bring up the other topic that I knew was worrying her—how would she be able to find a husband for me from a wheelchair? Ammi had arranged the introduction of Reshma to her husband, and I knew she wanted to offer the same service to me. But I was not sure I wanted her help, or her anxieties about my future. What Ammi did not know was that I had already chosen and rejected a future husband. My hope of marrying Yusuf had begun to unravel at the student center weeks earlier. Then they disintegrated when Ammi took ill.

I remember the day Yusuf waited for me at the university entrance. He towered over everyone on the crowded street. I waved from the motorized rickshaw. How handsome he looked in his black silk kameez and black Levis. I noticed he had trimmed his hair and beard. He met me at the rickshaw, handing me a pink dahlia, then he ferried me through the traffic. I can still recall the pressure of his fingers against the small of my back.

We found a small table in the crowded student center, and I waited while he brought a red plastic tray with two espressos in tiny ceramic cups. Light foam clung to the surface of the coffee, a tension that bubbled at the edges.

"How is your family?" he asked. Yusuf always began with formalities. The overhead fan hummed.

"Good. Everyone is fine. Meena and Amir were arguing over video games all morning—nothing unusual." I paused, thinking what else to say. "Abbu just returned from Islamabad . . . and how are your parents?"

I intended to return the courtesy of his inquiries, but the question of his parents was pushed out of my mouth by the larger topic waiting behind it: Had he spoken to them about me yet? Was he aware of the question on my mind but searching for words to explain? Or was he avoiding the topic?

Yusuf slowed his eyes until his gaze fell on my face. He cleared his throat.

"My parents are used to arranging everything for their children, especially their marriages," he said. "They want to treat my marriage the same way they treated my older brothers' and sisters' marriages. They want my consent, of course, but they have been looking around in their circle for a good Muslim wife for me . . ."

"Oh, I can understand that," I said. But I am good and I am a Muslim, I thought to myself.

"Oh, Uji, I should just go to your father and ask him myself if I can marry you."

"My father will let me choose for myself, Yusuf," I said. "But we don't want to start our life together with dishonoring your parents . . . Perhaps if they meet me?"

Yusuf looked away, but even in profile I could see what was written on his face.

"You already talked to them about me, didn't you?"

He nodded.

"And they said no. Is that it?"

"Yes," Yusuf admitted at last. "They are firm about it, Ujala. My father is a bigot. He said he would not go to an infidel to ask for a daughter's hand."

"But my father converted!"

"I know, but my father says that if your father was once a Sikh, he is no Muslim to him. Kafir was the word he used. Infidel. But we can marry without my family's approval."

As much as he complained about his parents' narrow-mindedness, Yusuf was devoted to them and to their extended family. As a student, he was financially dependent on his father. The consequences to him of marrying me would be devastating.

"I don't think so, Yusuf. Our marriage is a Romeo and Juliet idea," I began. He looked up at me with hope. " . . . and in the end," I said, "look what happened to them."

Weeks later, when Yusuf learned of Ammi's illness, he visited our house for the first time.

"Come in," I said, smiling, opening the door wider. I felt so happy to see him. I took him into the study to meet Abbu, who was gathering papers to take to the office. The sun filtered through the voile curtains that covered the large windows. The wind cast light and shadow about the room.

"I was sorry to hear of your wife's illness," Yusuf said when I introduced them.

"Thank you for your concern. I am pleased to meet you at last," said Abbu, nodding to Yusuf as he continued on his way out the door. "Sorry I have to rush off."

Then Yusuf raised his voice. "I want permission to marry your daughter, sir."

Abbu stopped. My face was hot and my mouth dropped open. I turned to Yusuf, who was very focused on my father. Abbu returned to the settee and put his briefcase at his feet.

"I want to marry Ujala, sir."

"Then you will have to ask Ujala," Abbu said. "We do not choose husbands for our daughters. We trust they will choose wisely themselves." And then he laughed. "But I must say I do like being asked anyway, don't you, Ujala?"

"Yes, Abbu, I do like being asked." My voice was stern. "And Yusuf has asked me before."

Our marriage was a closed subject. Why had Yusuf brought it up again?

"Perhaps you two should talk some more," said Abbu. "Invite Yusuf to dinner, and we can discuss it when your mother is up. I am sure she will want to be part of that discussion." He looked me in the eye and was out the door.

"I didn't want to do it that way," said Yusuf, "but when I saw him and then he was leaving, I was afraid I wouldn't have another chance to ask, so I just blurted it out like a fool."

"Oh, Yusuf, whatever are you thinking? That we could marry when your parents feel the way they do? Yusuf, we cannot." He tried to soften my determination with a slight smile, but I would no longer let his charm work on me. "You know we cannot marry. Your parents oppose it. And now my family needs me to be here for them. There are just too many signs that marriage is not right— at least not now. Our lives are not going in the same direction. I wish it weren't so, but it is."

Yusuf's smile faded and the darkness in his eyes deepened. He had heard the certainty in my voice. At the same time I wanted him to pull me close to him. But it was time to pull away, to undo what had been done. It was time to say good-bye. Neither of us could move away from the other, could speak the last words, or offer some superficial gesture. My heart ached from being torn in two directions. I watched Yusuf's sad eyes squint into anger. He put his hand in his pocket, rattled his keys, and went to the front door. Without a word, without a backward glance, he mounted his motorscooter and disappeared under the bougainvillea.

That evening when we were alone, Abbu asked me about Yusuf.

"What a surprising question Yusuf asked this morning," he said. "I am sure your mother will want to talk to you about it when she feels better."

"You and Ammi instructed me to choose wisely, and so I have. There is no need to talk about Yusuf again."

Afterward I tried to go about my family duties with equanimity, but sometimes, when the winds from the sea stilled and the heat sent my parents to the rooftop to sleep under the stars, I could hear them up there through the windows—my father struggling to carry my mother, fussing with the blankets, the two of them giggling so much that they snorted out loud, and then whispering for a long time before falling into the cool dark of sleep. Then only the closed buds of the rooftop flowers that dangled outside my window heard my muffled crying in the night.

A month after Ammi's stroke, she had regained strength in her left arm and hand, but her right side was still weak. She was unable to walk without support for balance. She could push into a sitting position, hold a book, and eat. It was slow, but she insisted on doing it herself. Faisah and I alternated helping with her morning routine that took more than an hour. Ammi avoided her wheelchair and chose instead to sit in her room by the window, or to work at her desk where she tried to correspond with friends and to tend to family finances. She became frustrated by complex mental tasks and spent more and more time rereading historical works and novels from her library.

"Fortunately, I've read Churchill before or I'd not know a thing he was talking about," she laughed, using her chin to motion to the book lying open in her lap. We sat together on the upstairs verandah. It was obvious to everyone that Ammi was depressed. Her mood was sharp-tongued and irritable. Physical therapy taxed her strength, and she napped often.

"Would you like the newspaper or something else to read, Ammi?"

I wanted to suggest that she watch television instead of testing herself with world politics and history, but I knew that Ammi's pride would not allow her to sink into the world of soap operas and game shows. I did not want to risk insulting her by raising the subject.

Meena moved back into the bedroom with Faisah and me, so that physical therapy equipment could be set up in her room, next to our parents' bedroom. Ammi insisted that her exercises and treatments not occur on the first floor.

"I don't want it to be in anyone's way," she said.

"She doesn't want anyone to see her helpless," whispered Faisah. We had never seen Ammi wounded or weakened. Everyone rushing to help only seemed to annoy her.

"You can have my room until you are better," Meena said to Ammi. To me, Meena said, ". . . which I hope is soon, so I can move back into my own room. It is my room, you know."

The room we shared was a square space with white walls and oversized dark furniture. The wooden double-plank door was painted brown. The three of us shared a king-sized platform bed. A round plastic clock ticked high on the wall above a long florescent bulb and ceiling fan. Every surface and every container—drawers, closets, boxes—spilled over with our possessions.

Meena was moody and resentful, Faisah was quick to anger, and I was bossier than I meant to be. Because we woke and dressed at the same time, until Faisah and Meena finally left for school, the mornings were tense.

Mrs. Jamali, the physical therapist, arrived after lunch every day. As I watched Ammi struggle to walk a straight line across the room, the muscles in my hips would respond to the therapist's demands. Mrs. Jamali showed me how to help Ammi practice her bedtime exercise.

"This will retrain your nerves and strengthen your muscles," Mrs. Jamali said. "They have forgotten how to move you across this room." Standing behind us, Mrs. Jamali placed my hands on the outlines of Ammi's pelvic bones. "Hold her here," she instructed, "firmly, but not too tight, just enough to resist when she steps forward."

But Ammi tripped repeatedly while Mrs. Jamali held her back in this way. Her right foot dragged along the wood floor.

"It's no use. I can't do it. It hurts too much. Just get me a cane I can lean on like an old woman," she said, plopping into her chair, exhausted.

"None of that now," Mrs. Jamali replied with patience and conviction. "Rest a moment and we'll try again. You will do it." Were Mrs. Jamali's words a command or a prediction? She turned to me. "Show the others how to do it, so that they can help your mother in the evenings."

I tried to imitate Mrs. Jamali's professional detachment, but I failed repeatedly.

"Uji, let me stop now," Ammi would say. I felt as discouraged as she did, and I easily let her quit the exercises whenever she asked.

Then one day I pried Amir's fingers away from his Game Boy and showed him the physical therapy routine. Although only eleven, Amir, like Abbu, was tall, and he was the one person who could always make Ammi laugh. Within weeks, Ammi's attitude improved and her legs strengthened. Her right foot would drop as she walked, but she was erect and moving at least for these short periods each day.

Abbu helped with the twins' homework, but it fell to me to solve problems for them when he was not home. Meanwhile, Faisah was busy at Central Prison, where she had obtained releases for some of the inmates. I envied Faisah's freedom, and sometimes, while I cooked, or later after dinner, Faisah discussed her cases and their outcomes.

"We found Sita's parents!" she announced one afternoon, dropping her books on the kitchen counter.

"Where?" I asked, excited to hear the news. I stopped chopping greens and reached into the cupboard for two ceramic mugs.

"We went with her to the shantytown."

I was shocked.

"A policeman went with us. It's not that bad," Faisah said when she saw my distress. She lifted the tea cozy off the pot and poured. "It only took a few questions to the right people to locate the parents."

I remembered my promise to Hanan to find out where her parents were.

"Where were they?" I asked.

"They were right there, living in tents and straw shacks. Dirty floors, polluted water, runny noses, hungry babies, no plumbing. Everyone is back to garbage picking."

"That is success?" I asked.

"At least they are together, Ujala. Not everyone can live in Clifton, you know."

"What's with the attitude?"

"Nothing." Faisah said. I was surprised by her vacant response. She rarely hid her feelings.

"Nothing?" I asked.

"We did what we could. After all, they were in prison and now they are not."

"But they are on the street and vulnerable again, hungry, not in school." Faisah turned away from me.

"You wanted to get them out of prison, too." Her voice was bitter.

"Hey," I said. "We're on the same side, remember? Is it your fault their choices are so few?"

"Then why do I feel responsible for them?" she asked.

"And why do I? Why do we?"

Amir and I walked along Clifton Road, away from the market where Ammi's friend, Mrs. Shahani, had helped me shop for food. I felt happy. Rainfall seemed to be over for the day, and the steaming ground warmed us. A few small clouds with their tiny loads passed overhead. Amir rushed a few feet ahead of me, carrying two woven cloth bags loaded with food. I went directly to the kitchen where our housekeeper had nestled a pot of tea in a yellow gingham tea cozy.

"Bless Anna," I thought and began to put the purchases away.

Fruits, vegetables, bean curd, meat, butter, eggs, milk, and oil were kept in the refrigerator. Adjacent to the water pump was the pantry. A wide range of pickles, chutneys, mustards, preserves, and sauces lined the top shelf. On the next shelf, sealed containers of spices—chili powder, garlic, coriander, cardamom, cloves, ginger, cinnamon, saffron, mace, fennel, and curries of all types. The third shelf held large glass jars of wheat, rice, sugar, lentils, almonds, and pistachios. The bottom shelf was full of bags of potatoes and tin cans. Along the north wall, shelves held dishes intended either for cooking or for serving, separated according to whether they were wooden, metal, glass, or ceramic.

I heard a hum and a wooden squeak as Ammi's chair rolled into the kitchen. When she turned the chair, one knee bumped a shelf, knocking a wooden bowl onto the floor.

"Ouch!" she cried out. I hurried to help, but she brushed me away.

"Uji, you must go for condolences today or tomorrow. Samina's grandmother died." She sighed. "I can't go anymore."

"Yes, Ammi. Would you like tea?" She nodded.

I hated going for condolences—sitting with the grandmothers and married women, eating sweets, drinking tea, listening to the wailing and the complaints. But I would do it. Otherwise, the neighbors would notice no one from our family came to see them. I stirred the tea leaves into the hot water and turned up the flame until the mixture started to boil over. At once I turned it off, aware that Ammi was supervising.

"Mrs. Shahani helped me to shop this time," I told her. The last time Amir and I had shopped, we returned with little food. I had not known what to buy, what it cost, and how much to get.

"Let's see what you bought today," Ammi said.

I felt shy but proud as I placed on the chopping block three enormous stemmed onions that were so fresh their pale surfaces shone. I removed two glass jars of thick cream from the bag, six thin-skinned lemons, and bunches of gleaming greens. In the plastic bag a chicken still had a few feathers clinging to it.

"Beautiful, Uji," Ammi said, pleased. "Just beautiful. We'll make your father's favorite spiced chicken, murgh tikka haryali, and some fresh chapati. We can fix onion rings out of these," she added, holding a shining onion up in the afternoon light.

I cut up the chicken and placed it in a bowl with salt, chili powder, and lemon juice. I chopped coriander, mint, and spinach leaves, and then ground them with the mortar and pestle. Ammi sat nearby, with a contented look on her face. She was quiet while I worked. With an aluminum bowl in her lap, she mixed flour and water for the chapati we would cook right before dinner, after the chicken was grilled and the onions were fried.

"I searched a long time to find spinach leaves like these, Ammi. No bugs, no holes, no brown spots, just young and crisp. Aren't they lovely?" I said. "But you know what surprised me? The other women didn't seem to know how to choose the best ones. Some of the leaves they bought were wilted. Some were even soggy."

"That's because those leaves are not as fresh, but they are cheaper. Not everyone can afford the best, you know." She spoke without looking up from the bowl where her good fist was pressing into the mixture.

I was embarrassed that I had not thought of something so obvious. Here I was, a college student, yet I failed to see the most basic economic issues around me. Today Ammi seemed relaxed, back to her usual way of correcting her children without making them feel either stupid or naughty. She would simply speak in an unadorned fashion and let the facts and their implications dawn.

"Of course," I said, as I mixed the green paste with curd, cream, ginger, garlic, and spice mix—garam masala. I scooped my hands like spoons and rubbed the chicken pieces thoroughly. "I've made too much sauce, Ammi."

"Never too much sauce."

I ran water over my hands, wiped my fingertips on a towel, and put the chicken and spices in the refrigerator.

"No, really. I think I'll use the stored bean curd and take half to Mrs. Shahani. I want her to know how grateful I am for all she is teaching me."

The next day I waved good-bye to Ammi, who was sitting on the verandah listening to street sounds—children calling, babies crying, a puppy yelping, and motorbikes demanding more than their share of the road.

"I'll be back before noon," I shouted. In a woven bag I carried a covered dish leftover from last night's meal.

"Wait and take Amir with you," my mother shouted out, but I wanted to walk alone, so I ducked under the gated arch, pretending not to hear.

The bougainvillea dripped purple flower petals onto my white dupatta. I was pleased to be the one bringing a gift to a new friend. I could not recall making such a visit in my entire life. I had gone with my mother to a neighbor's door for this or that reason, but I had never gone inside by myself.

I walked with care on the broken sidewalks. Motorized rickshaws, taxis, donkey carts, bicycles, and mopeds whizzed by. I passed the high walls and glassed estates in Clifton Garden—Number 70 where the Bhuttos lived. Pastel buses careened wildly along Zamzama Boulevard, decorated with fringed cloth and framed photographs of saints with garlands of marigolds. Stuffed full as they passed Shaheen Boulevard, the tops of the buses brushed the stringy beards hanging from the banyan trees.

In a parking lot, a boy held a bouquet of balloons attached to stick. He wore soiled slacks and a white shirt open at the collar as he followed families with children around a parking lot, hawking his wares. Behind the parking lot, a bearded man wearing wire-rimmed glasses and a white skullcap sat reading the newspaper on a plastic lawn chair in front of a restaurant. From time to time he would look up at the boy. The restaurant owner was careful not to splash the reading man as he tossed buckets of water over the sidewalk. A limping boy with a stick broom swept the water into the street.

I was drawn to the outside of a video store where I could watch the TV screen. It showed the familiar story of forbidden love—a young man and woman sing back and forth to each other in separate scenes, a father puts his foot down, a mother tries to placate him, a son slams the door, a girl's heart breaks. A train departs. An airplane takes off. An unwanted wedding begins as the lovers are given away to others.

I tried to ignore the smacking lips of the men at the video stall, but could not. I wished I had brought Amir with me after all. Then the men would not click their tongues at me. I crossed the street and stood by the gutter.

Two barefoot girls in dirty dresses peeked from the doorway of their one-room mud house. One held a worn deck of cards, with the heads of German shepherds printed on them. All those sharp teeth, I thought, shuddering, and stepped over the gutter to let a donkey pass.

A boy in gray cotton guided the cart full of laundry bundles. His donkey twisted its neck to look at him, and the cart stopped. Another donkey, a white one with sacks of flour loaded in its cart, also stopped. The donkeys looked happy to see each other and seemed to want to visit for a while. When the boy slapped the reins, suddenly I realized I was the only female in sight.

I panicked and could not think. *What am I doing? Where is Mrs. Shahani's street? Why are there no signs?* All the side streets blurred. I stopped, and when I next inhaled, I saw it—her street, a passage so narrow that decency required you to step aside if someone else passed by. A goat was tethered to a stake at the far end of the street. As I entered the passageway, it eyed me suspiciously.

At last I found the third door on the right. The house's exterior was smooth sandstone, painted black from the ground to knee height to protect it from the dirt of passersby. The windows had wooden louvers, and the door had faded to a mottled red. Mrs. Shahani opened the door as soon as I knocked.

She was surprised to see me, but welcoming. It was afternoon, when women often visit one another unannounced.

"I brought you some tikka to show my appreciation for taking me shopping yesterday, Mrs. Shahani," I said, opening the plastic bag.

"Please call me Robina," the woman replied with an easy smile. That was when I realized for the first time that she was not much older than I, maybe twenty-nine, or thirty at the most. She had a thin body with rough skin. Her wide eyes were shadowed, and her lips were thick and expressive.

"It is a Punjabi dish—my father's favorite. And some fresh chapati, of course . . . Robina," I said.

"Oh, this was not necessary. I owe your mother so much. I am always happy to help her family. Shukriah."

I let my dupatta fall to my shoulders as I entered the house. Robina took the dish into the next room while I sat with four young children—two girls, a boy, and a baby. The boy sat cross-legged on a bed piled with blankets. He wore a Mickey Mouse sweatshirt, crossed his arms over his chest, and tucked each hand into the pit of the other arm. Something about him does resemble Mickey Mouse, I thought. The girls grinned, and one tickled the baby she held on the bed. All the children had cropped hair and big brown eyes.

In the corner of the room was a large trunk half-covered with colorful cloth. On top, a rectangular clock leaned against the wall. Next to the trunk was a shiny spittoon and a pink plastic trash can. A stack of metal milk crates served both as shelves and drawers. The house was filled with the overwhelming odors of kerosene and curry paste.

The older girl stood and approached me slowly, saying nothing. She reached to touch my hair, causing a tingling in my spine. Robina returned to the room with a round tray. On it she had placed a pot of tea, two cups, sugar water for the children, and a few cake rusks. They made room on the floor to sit more or less in a circle. Robina gave the children their treats first.

"So what is your grade in school?" I asked the boy.

He did not answer. He turned away from me, his eyes fixed on Robina.

"The children don't go to school," Robina stated. "The only schools in the area are private schools that I cannot afford, or they are religious. I fear for my son attending a madrassah. They don't teach languages other than Arabic, and I hear that sometimes they beat the boys or cuff them to their beds. I guess I am not a good Muslim, but that is not what I want. I do my best to teach them here at home, but it is difficult."

I guessed from the way Robina hesitated that she could neither read nor write.

"I've had only four grades," Robina announced defensively.

"This is good then," I said, wanting to erase this class difference between us. "We can be friends. We both have been to school."

Robina relaxed and poured more tea. The children finished their snacks and Robina sent them off into the next room. She held the baby in her lap.

"You know," Robina said, "these are my children, but they are not my children. Their mother was my sister, Mukhtara, who was killed a few months ago. So the children came to live with me, and now I am their mother."

I did not know this about Robina, and wondered why Ammi never mentioned it. I touched Robina's hand.

"Our parents live outside of Sukkur. They were too poor to give a dowry for my sister, so they gave her to a man older than our father who was already married with five children. She begged them not to do it. I told her to run away, but she said to me, 'If I refuse to marry him, they will kill me.' And I knew it was true, you know, so she was trapped. Seven years later she had four children, plus she took care of the first wife's five."

Robina said nothing as she lay the baby down on the string bed. I thought she was gathering strength to continue her story.

"One day a neighbor told her husband he saw Mukhtara talking with one of our cousins. He accused Mukhtara of adultery, and her husband filed a case against her in court. Before the court ruled, the mullahs condemned her—she is *kari*, they said, *black*. *Trash*. Five men cornered her at the well pump one day. She tried to hide in the rows of sugarcane, but they caught her. They stripped her naked and stoned her to death right there in the field."

Robina was rocking back and forth as she spoke. I reached out to touch her, but she waved my hand away, smoothing her kameez and attempting a smile.

"So now, suddenly—motherhood—my sister's four, and I'm expecting a fifth later this year," she added, patting her belly. "My husband sells cloth in the street all day and works on cars at night. We get by."

I didn't know what to say. I had never faced problems like these, or seen such fortitude. I admired it, but it also made me uncomfortable.

"I should go," I said, and Robina stood to open the door.

"Ujala, your mother is a saint, you know. Even with the problems she is having now, she has offered to let me use her sewing machine to make some extra money. Please tell her that I will accept her generosity as soon as I can find time away from the children to do some sewing."

I was surprised by this news about Ammi offering the use of her sewing machine. She was always very particular about who used her machine and how. She still would not let me spin the wheel or tap the treadle unless she was by my side, supervising.

"May Allah heal her quickly and bless your family," Robina said. "Let me walk you to the road."

"I'll be all right. I'll find a taxi at the corner," I said, kissing Robina on both cheeks.

Why didn't Ammi tell me about Robina's sister or about loaning out her sewing machine? I felt a sudden jealousy of their relationship that held secrets, and of Robina's strength. She knew what she believed, and she spoke her mind. She accepted whatever faced her, and at the same time was gracious in a natural way, not the result of convent training. I wondered what else my mother was not telling me. I wanted to know Ammi's secrets, the missing pieces of her childhood, all the things she never talked about. I realized that in wanting these things, I was violating an unwritten rule that only she could control the subjects we discussed. I had to find a way to get her to talk to me.

As I walked up Clifton Road I considered that maybe the missing details of Ammi's life were the keys to finding out where life was taking me. Turning into the family compound, I saw my father pacing next to a truck parked at the door.

"Abbu, what's going on?" I asked. "It's Ammi, isn't it?"

He squeezed my shoulder. "We're going to the hospital, Uji. She may have had another stroke. She is still breathing. Please be here for Amir and Meena when they get home."

The men pushed the wheels of a gurney over the cobblestones and lifted Ammi into the truck. Abbu climbed in next to her.

"I'll call you when we know more."

Then he stretched his arm out to grasp my hand. He spoke in Punjabi, "'Jau tau prem khelan ka chao, sir dhar tali gali meri aao.' Say it many times," he instructed. "It will calm your fears." I knew my father's old Sikh prayer about preparing yourself to make the sacrifice that love requires.

But the words didn't calm me. They frightened me.

As the porters closed the back of the truck, I heard my father's voice calling to me, "We have to love God more than we love each other. We must accept the will of Allah, not our own."

I could only swallow to hold back my tears.

"Jau tau prem khelan ka chao, sir dhar tali gali meri aao," I whispered to myself. *If you want to play the game of love, come to me with your head in the palm of your hand.*

My mother used to tell us that the first thing she noticed about our father when they met was his long, smooth fingers.

As I stood at the door to their bedroom where my mother lay immobile, I watched those fingers arrange and rearrange her blankets—to warm her, to ensure that the smoothest silk edges were close to her face, to have something to hold onto, something material, physical, undeniably present. If only a blanket.

I imagined I heard her call him "Mr. Singh," as she so often had. "Mr. Singh, is that you?" she would have said. But she could not speak. She could only hear her worried children who surrounded her bed.

Meena, curious: "Is she asleep? Why doesn't she say something?"

Faisah, bossy: "Shh! She can hear everything we say."

Amir, sad, questioning: "But her eyes are closed."

Reshma, thinking of Ammi: "Everybody out of here."

Like the tax collector, Ammi's second stroke took its toll bit by bit. She could not walk, but with help she could sit for short periods. She could not talk, but she grunted in several tones. Her weak arm became the stronger one because what had been her stronger arm following her first stroke became entirely useless following the second. Her memory seemed intact, as did her hearing and vision, but she could no longer read anything but the simplest words. She had trouble swallowing.

We took turns spooning yogurt and kheer into her.

I could see the effort it took her to make her crooked smile. She wanted so much for us to think that she was holding up. She would pull herself together for dinner and try to perk up for visitors, appearing to listen, nodding and smiling. But eventually her eyelids fluttered and her consciousness drifted away.

I knew it was only a matter of time. *Allah, be merciful!* She was a tiny boat on a vast horizon.

Everyone's routine changed. Before leaving for her classes, Faisah bathed and dressed Ammi. Abbu took leave from his firm to be home when Meena and Amir returned from school. He prayed even more than usual. Often he was on his knees by the window when she woke from naps. I was determined that the twins keep their routines, dress properly, and have their books and assignments ready for school. I watched them board the school bus in the mornings. Then I would sit on the verandah and read the newspapers to my mother.

One morning I sat at Ammi's feet reading the news while she rubbed mustard oil into my hair. She dabbed the oil onto the palm of her bad hand, then dipped the fingertips of her good hand, to work it into my scalp. She pulled the oil down the strands of hair slowly as I read, until my scalp was slick.

"Whew! I smell like a lamb kabob!" I laughed and Ammi tried to cuff my head but missed her mark and batted the air like a kitten.

It was a close and peaceful time for the two of us. We kept each other's worries company.

She sat in the wheelchair with her legs propped against a flowered pillow on the string bed. She didn't look sick at all.

"You look lovely today, Ammi," I told her, which brought out her crooked smile again. "Your color is clear, even your eyes look lighter."

I placed a mirror in her good hand, and she dared to look. Her hair was beginning to gray. Faisah had woven a single braid for her that morning. When she was vertical, the braid hung down like a spine. When she slept, it rested on her shoulder and fell over her breast. I could see that Ammi found some comfort in fingering the braid during the day. At night she unloosened it slowly, and our father brushed her hair before lifting her into bed.

"The government's report on progress in Pakistani education is on the front page today," I said, placing her cup of tea on the tray between us. She took a sip.

Ammi mumbled and grinned.

"Yes, that would be a short report," I replied, realizing I had interpreted her mumbles accurately. Then I began to read the report's statistics.

"'Twenty-six percent of Pakistanis are literate, ranging from almost sixty percent among Sindhi men, to less than two percent among Balochi women.' It says that this may actually represent a decline in literacy compared to ten years ago."

Ammi groaned, knowing that as bad as the numbers were, the

statistics had been inflated. The government counted you as literate even if all you could read or write was your own name.

I folded back the page.

"Here's an interesting commentary," I said. "'Studies reveal that parents' biggest concern about sending a girl to school is the possible danger that might occur to the girl's honor.'"

Ammi snorted. *Honor*—a word I knew she despised for the cruelty it concealed.

With her index finger Ammi began making little circles on the pillow. I stopped reading and watched. Concentrating in order to control her arm, she drew a short vertical line on the cotton cover, then a horizontal line to cross the vertical one.

"You're trying to write!" I said. I was really excited. "Are you trying to write?"

Ammi relaxed back onto the pillow, nodding, forcing her face into a relieved, uneven smile.

"I'll be right back."

I rushed away and returned with a pad of paper, a pencil, and Amir's round red plastic See and Spell game. It had the entire English alphabet on it. "You can write with the pencil, Ammi, or just point to the letters," I said, placing the items by her good hand.

She pushed the pad onto the floor and took up the pencil. She stretched to point to the letter *T*.

"*T*," I said, looking at her expectantly.

Ammi nodded and put the pencil down, which confused me.

"OK, Ammi, I understand—T is the first letter, now, what else?" I asked. Again I put the pencil between her fingers, but I could see that Ammi was running out of patience. She lifted the pencil again and stretched her arm pointing to the *E*.

"OK, T . . . E . . ." I said, scrutinizing, as Ammi strained to point next to the A. "T, E, A," I said and laughed. "Oh! You want some tea?"

Ammi grunted and lay back again, nodding. *Yes, I want some tea!* I held a cup to her lips. She slurped her satisfaction, then pointed the pencil again.

"R," I said.

Ammi pointed to the *U*.

"R . . . U," I repeated, " . . . Am I what, Ammi?" I asked her.

But she jiggled her head with two lengthy grunts, demanding that I pay closer attention. She pointed the pencil at the *S*, and before she got to the *K*, I was feeding her cake rusk from her plate.

"I miss hearing your voice," I told her. "I wish we could talk back and forth. It seems so selfish for me to be in a monologue all the time."

Ammi expelled seven even grunts, rocking her head back and forth. "It is not a monologue," she expressed in her way.

"Great," I said. "Then let's keep talking—do you remember our talk about why the other women bought the stale vegetables and I bought the fresh ones?"

She nodded, listening.

"Well, since you've been sick," I told her, "I've been out by myself more—not just sending Amir. I visited Robina and her neighbors. For the first time I am seeing poverty—not in the abstract, like they write about it in reports like this one"—I snapped my fingernails into the newspaper—"but in the real details, with real people."

Ammi pulled her lips tightly across her teeth. I continued.

"Robina's sister was murdered—stoned to death—merely for talking to her cousin! You knew about it, didn't you?"

Of course she knew. Ammi closed her eyes and nodded, closing her eyes.

"Why didn't you let me know before I went there?" I asked, but then hesitated. Ammi couldn't explain herself now. "But never mind. Robina told me about it, and I saw the four children that are now hers. And did you know she is pregnant?"

Ammi kept her eyes closed and nodded again. I wanted to ask about the sewing machine.

"Robina said you told her she could borrow your sewing machine. Should I take it to her? It would really help, and we're not using it."

Ammi opened her eyes and nodded her assent. She looked pleased that I was interested in Robina and her problems.

"I'll take it to her tomorrow. Of course, she needs time away from the children to do any sewing, but the children don't go to school. None of the children around there attend any school. Robina says she tries to teach them at home, but I don't see how she can. I doubt if she can read or write herself."

Suddenly Ammi tapped the See and Spell to get my attention. She pointed to the *T*.

I reached for the teacup.

Ammi tapped the cover again, and I watched as she pointed next to the *E*, then the *A*.

"I understand. You want more tea, right?"

But Ammi ignored me and focused on what she was doing, pointing next to the *C*, and then to the *H*.

"Teach . . . ," I said, reading the word aloud, while Ammi continued pointing, spelling out the letters—*T . . . H . . . E . . . M*.

"Teach them. Teach them. You are telling me to teach Robina's children?"

At last I understood. Ammi smiled and relaxed back onto the pillow.

"Teach them," I kept repeating. "I guess I could do it in the afternoons when Abbu is home—at least for a while. It would give Robina time to work on the sewing, and it would be interesting, and I might really enjoy it. I'd have to get some supplies. Maybe I could call your friends at the Women's Aid Society for some ideas."

I was very excited.

"Yes, I can do it. It would feel good to help somebody who needs it."

As Ammi drifted into sleep I lifted the tip of her braid and draped it across her heart.

11

Adiala Prison, 1996

A persistent knock on Rahima Mai's door. Ujala's heartbeat quickened to the sound.

"Madam, Madam," the sergeant-guard's voice called through the metal door.

Rahima Mai was not responding. Her eyes were fixed on the shadowed wall. Teach them, she thought. *Teach them.*

Daylight had disappeared during the storytelling. Ujala knew it was time to return to her cell. She laid her hand on Rahima Mai's knee, and the warden jolted back to life. Rahima Mai gestured toward the door.

"Shut her up!"

Ujala rose. Could Rahima Mai understand her now—after all she had heard? She started to ask her, but then thought better of it. Instead, she unlocked the door to let the sergeant-guard into the room. The woman handed her a slip of paper and glanced at Rahima Mai, who sat by the teakettle.

The message was nothing important. Ujala locked the door behind the woman. She began to return the papers to their filing boxes, as she usually did at the end of the workday.

"And after your mother's second stroke? What happened then?" Rahima Mai tilted her head and raised her eyebrows.

Ujala realized Rahima Mai did not want her to leave.

"My eyes opened again," she said.

◆ ◆ ◆

"You go on ahead, Amir," I told my brother. "Take the butter cakes to Mrs. Shahani so she will have something to offer us when I arrive." Amir latched his fingers under the box's strings and headed for Clifton Road.

"I'll be back for you in thirty minutes, Baji," he called to me.

"No need. Wait for me there," I said. "I will bring the sewing machine in a taxi."

Under the archway the faded edges of the bougainvillea were summer crispy. I stood in its shade and tied the sewing machine to the wagon with ropes. I dragged the wagon to Clifton Road and hailed a rickshaw. The driver grunted as he lifted the machine and the wagon onboard.

"You are a seamstress, Madam?" he asked.

"No. I am a teacher," I said. I liked saying it.

"Ooh," said the driver, pretending to be impressed. "A teacher!"

My comment edged the class line between us. I withdrew from his false, sticky flattery.

Standing by her door, holding the baby, Robina watched me tug the wagon down the passage to her house.

"Amir!" she called to my brother who came from inside her house. He took hold of the wagon's handle, and I pushed from behind.

"Tsk! That driver should have brought you all the way down here," said Robina. "Those guys move too fast, always on to the next fare, cutting corners." Amir lifted the sewing machine onto a metal crate in the corner. One of the girls napped on the couch next to a spittoon. Robina and Amir disappeared into the next room.

"Where are the other children?" I said in the direction of the door. Robina peeked around the corner.

"Oh, they are out here. If you don't mind, why don't you join us?"

What I had assumed was Robina's "other room" was actually a mudbrick courtyard that her family shared with ten others. Robina's "living room" was the family's only room. Outdoors each family had its own kerosene stove. A community toilet was concealed behind corrugated tin under a thatched roof. Laundry lined one wall, where women sat cross-legged, crocheting, shelling beans, kneading dough, nursing babies. Two girls swept the packed dirt floor with tied sticks. A dog slept in the shade beside a naked toddler. Flies swarmed near them. Older children played with a pink soccer ball.

Robina offered me a metal folding chair in the shade, and tea and the butter cakes that Amir had delivered earlier. Soon the neighborhood children crowded around. I realized they were hungry.

"Run along," Robina said, shooing them. They moved a few feet apart, but kept their eyes on me, this stranger with butter cakes in her hands.

"Robina, I've been thinking about becoming a teacher," I said, "but I need experience."

"Oh?"

"I was wondering if you would help me by letting me work with your children." She broke off morsels of butter cake and gave them to the children who were back at her side. "What if I taught some lessons here for a few hours in the afternoons, while you work on your sewing?"

"Here?"

I tried not to sound insulting or condescending. "I am bored at home. Abbu is home in the afternoons and can stay with Ammi. I am free to use that time." I hesitated, not wanting to beg. "I'd really like to try," I said.

Robina tossed her head back, looking all around the courtyard.

"It would be so wonderful, Ujala, but how can I accept such a gift? You know I couldn't afford to pay you."

"Oh, no. It is no problem. You'd be doing me a favor."

"As you wish," said Robina. "But it's not only my children who can't go to school. None of these children can go to school either." I counted eighteen children in the yard. "The prime minister's famous literacy program built a school nearby, but it was open for less than one term when the teachers quit. They were not being paid, and books and supplies never arrived. Soon the politicians made a big noise about who had taken bribes, who had run off with the book budget, and who had not repaired the building. Another scandal and the children suffer."

"You think I could teach these other children, too?" I was stunned by the idea of such a large class.

"I am afraid you would have to. You won't be able to teach mine without the other mothers knowing. They would resent it. As it is, they are jealous because someone like you comes to visit me. You must stop by and visit each one of them while you are here. To do them the honor."

Robina handed me a bowl of hard, pale lentils.

"Would you like to pick through these while I mix the flour?" she asked, squatting and stretching to reach the plastic bowl.

I ran my fingers through the beans, taking pleasure in their cool, smooth texture. I found a few broken stones. I recalled Ammi spelling it out for me, "Teach them."

"Yes. I could teach the others, too," I decided.

"We could set up a school right here," said Robina. "Don't worry. The mothers will do everything to help."

Before I left that day, I visited each cooking area to sit with the other women.

"My son," a toothless woman told me, casting her eyes to the eight-by-ten framed photograph of a young man in uniform. "He is on the border. Kashmir. Ooh," she said, cupping her hand over her mouth and squeezing my hand. I glanced at Amir, who stood by the stove, listening.

Opposite the wall with the family photos, the eyes of a Bollywood poster seduced anyone who looked into their shadows. A child-sized plastic ET peered from a behind a chair. One woman's daughter and her daughter-in-law looked like teenage twins. Their babies were wrapped in sweaters and caps, even in the swelter of Karachi.

"Sit next to me," said the oldest woman. She was a wrapped figure with a smooth face and three teeth. Her eyes oozed like candle wax. She took my hand. Robina sat on my right, and soon another woman with a baby joined us on the cots, each greeting me, "Assalam aleikum." The old woman kept stroking my hand. Finally I wrapped my arms around her body and rocked her like a baby.

"What is it? Why is she crying?" I asked Robina.

"She was a city worker for thirty years and retired two years ago."

"But why is she crying? Does she miss going to work?" Robina shrugged her shoulders and gestured toward the man lying on a cot in the shade.

"My husband," the woman said. "A drug addict all his life, and now his liver fails him."

My stomach felt as tight as the jute on a string bed.

"Shouldn't we discuss their children coming to the school?" I asked Robina.

"No need," she said. "You touched their hands. You held their grandmother. It is enough. They will come."

We watched Ammi die a little bit each day. Finally, one night her neck muscles slackened, her head rolled onto her shoulder, and Abbu carried her to bed one last time. Reshma stayed with us in the women's quarter during those days. I remember her lifting Ammi's limp arm so I could thread it through the armhole of her nightgown. Ammi grabbed the cotton with her good hand and pulled the gown away from her body.

"Ammi," said Reshma. "Ammi, let us do it. Let us cover you."

But Ammi refused to surrender. "Arrrgh!" she mumbled, giving my arm a sharp pinch.

"Ouch!"

I had underestimated her strength again. The agitation was exhausting her, and we were making things worse trying to dress her. What difference did it make if she was naked?

We laid her head on the dark muslin pillowcase, fanned her hair away from her body, and blotted her perspiring brow and neck with cloths.

"I'll stay with her," Reshma said. "I'll cover her if it turns cold."

I looked at Ammi, recalling the vibrant mother of my youth.

"I remember the years before you were born, Uji," Reshma said, "when I was the only child and had Ammi all to myself. She took me with her everywhere. At her Women's Aid meetings, I did homework while they planned their literacy projects.

"'Education is the light of the eye,' Ammi told me. She piled magazines into my lap and told me to trace all the eyes I could find in the pictures, so I would never forget how precious it is to learn. 'And don't forget to put the light in them!' she would say. I never could draw light, but to Ammi, anything was possible . . . now look at her. O, Ammi! Allah, be merciful."

Later Reshma slept by the window. I rocked in the walnut chair that, until Ammi's illness, had remained in Amir's room—he and Meena were the lap babies, the last ones to be cuddled in it. Now we each took turns in the rocker, watching our mother awake or asleep. In her restlessness, she would murmur "oy," and, from time to time, she called out a garbled "Ammi!" wanting her own mother.

September cooled as the changing winds arrived from the sea, cleansing the air of Karachi. At the window I rested my eyes on the glistening sea. I felt the changes around me without judgment, without opinion. I rocked in the chair, while Ammi lay pale against the dark bed linens, resting in a fetal position, her hands fisted together in her naked lap. With a bubble of breath Ammi died that way, wrapped into herself, like a slice of the moon above a starry sea.

When I went to Abbu, he was kneeling by an open window, letting the chill wash over him. He had seen the crescent moon and the stars. He pulled on my hand to bring me to my knees and he prayed.

"May the soul of my beloved rest in the union of her divinity and Yours."

I went to awaken Faisah and Meena. They held each other, crying less than I would have expected. Then Meena pulled away.

"Baji, I'm afraid to look at her," she whispered.

"Oh, Meena. We will send her to God's arms."

I went to Amir. To my surprise, he was in the dark, playing with his video game. He would not look at me.

"Amir, my Amir," I said, lifting his chin, forcing him to look into my face. I put my arm around his shoulder. "Ammi died," I told him, and he cried like a baby.

Reshma took over. Abbu and I telephoned family and friends, who came to be with us in the middle of the night. From the verandah I could see Abbu and Amir spreading out rugs and arranging chairs for our guests. Abbu was trying to comfort his son.

"Amir, pleasure and pain are one set of robes that men must keep on wearing," he said. "Remember when you were a child and broke your arm? Remember how much it hurt?"

Amir nodded.

"That pain passed, didn't it? You must let this pain pass, too."

Reshma had taken a plain cotton cloth and tied Ammi's slack mouth shut. The effect was comical.

"She looks like she has the world's biggest toothache," I said.

Reshma did not crack a smile. She handed me a folded cloth.

"Now place this sheet over her body."

"No," I said, "not yet. I want to see her still."

"We will see her," said Reshma. "First we must cover her, and then we will wash her. You and Faisah, get clean water, shampoo and soap, washing bowls. Meena, bring some camphor and rose water."

When we returned, the four of us began our task, including eleven-year old Meena, who watched Reshma all the while, not looking at Ammi's face.

"In the name of Allah," Reshma said, lifting our mother's upper body forward.

"In the name of Allah," we said, placing our hands on Ammi's back.

"Tie these cloths around her feet and ankles," Reshma said.

We worked at a deliberate pace, speaking only when necessary. We cleansed Ammi completely—her head first—rolling it to one side and then to the other. Next, we washed her torso—the upper part first, and then the lower, the right side first, and then the left, all according to the teachings.

Then Reshma held Ammi's head over a bowl, while I rubbed shampoo into her scalp and through her hair, on the right side. Faisah poured clean water over the soapy mass, and Meena lifted clumps of hair, running her fingers through, rinsing until it squeaked. We completed the washing and rinsing on the left side, then repeated the entire process. In the end, Ammi's hair was washed three times. We took turns holding her head and fingering her hair for the last time. Then we divided her mane into nine parts, braided each part separately first, then braided the nine into three, and placed them underneath her body.

She looks refreshed, I thought. As if she's been swimming.

When the body and the hair were completely cleaned, we tapped every centimeter of her skin with cloths, anointing her with camphor and rose water until the fragrances overwhelmed us. Reshma again covered Ammi with the white sheet, and then removed from fresh brown paper five white cotton cloths: two sheets, a long sleeveless shirt, a cloth cincture, and a head veil. We lifted Ammi up so we could pull a sheet under her and lay her down on it. Our tears sprinkled the cloth. Ammi was wrapped, cloaked, shrouded, and draped in death's shawl. We placed the veil last, then put her hands across her chest, her right hand on top, and folded the edges of the top sheets over her and fastened cloth ropes around her body. One rope was wrapped lengthwise, from her head down under her feet, and two ropes were wrapped around the middle. Finally, we lifted the package that was our mother and placed it onto a common string bed.

Then Reshma handed each one of us a clean white dupatta, and, as we covered our heads to pray, the four of us climbed onto the poster bed and gazed at what we had done. We knew we were different for having done it.

12

Adiala Prison, 1996

Ujala heard a rustling of plastic bags under Rahima Mai's desk and wondered what gift she had brought this time. Then Rahima Mai handed Ujala a block wrapped in thin paper. Ujala sniffed the fragrance of lavender. It was scented soap.

"And one other thing," Rahima Mai said, handing her an unwrapped pink and orange dupatta.

"It is identical to the one I gave to Khanum!" Ujala said. She was both touched and confused by Rahima Mai's thoughtfulness, her strange cheerfulness.

"And like the one you gave to Robina," said Rahima Mai, smiling ear to ear. "I am officially bribing you—now that's a reversal!" She laughed, picked up the two plastic chairs and placed them near the teakettle again. This time she did not have to ask.

"So let me tell you at last what actually brought me to Adiala."

◆　◆　◆

One afternoon after my return from Chitral, I drove to the WASP office from a training session in Gujranwala. I followed the Chenab River to the GT Road. I remember now how the setting sun was reflected in the copper pots that hung from stalls along the road.

Melamine dishware and piles of second-hand clothing were stacked on dhurries under a line of poplars. The road was littered and the river was choppy.

It was early evening when I climbed the staircase of our office building. It was hot, and I was weary. But even the stuffy corridor was preferable to the intensity of the sun.

Then I saw him.

Standing in the hall outside of our office was the man I had seen in the striped shawl with Aga Ji in the compound. There was no one else in the hallway, and he had not yet seen me. As he turned around, I reached into my bag for the revolver.

"You stole my daughter!" he yelled, shaking his fist over his head. He ground his feet into the floor to block my passage.

With my eyes on him, I stepped back toward the stairs. He reached into his pocket and pulled out a small bottle. He uncorked the cap and tried to splash me, but I jumped away. I extended the revolver, gripping it in both hands, as I had practiced. But he faced me down, his moustache quivering. He held the bottle's mouth toward me as if it were a gun.

I fired once, aiming above his head, hitting only the wall. He jumped back.

"You stole my daughter!" he repeated, spitting in the air. "You stole my daughter!" He stayed frozen where he was, with his hand extended. Acid dripped out the bottle, down onto his hand. When he raised his forearm in response, the chemicals rolled along his arm into his loose sleeve. He grimaced with pain and dropped the bottle.

"Get out!" I commanded, gesturing with the gun toward the staircase behind him. I could hear his body tripping down the stairs and his last words, screaming: "Next time, you devil, you will not see me coming!"

◆　◆　◆

Ujala was squinting and shaking her hands as she dramatized the moment for Rahima Mai. Then she realized that this was her last story. She settled into the molded plastic that hugged her hips.

"So that is how I started out on Clifton Road and ended up in Adiala Prison, Baji—jailed the next day for kidnapping Chanda and for brandishing the revolver at her father, attempted murder."

Rahima Mai's chair scraped the floor as she rose.

"I see," she said. "I see." Then she turned to face Ujala. "But how . . . I mean, why . . . what was it that made you so sure, so willing . . ."

Ujala listened to what Rahima Mai was struggling to ask. "Because I became their mother," she said.

"Their mother? Whose mother? Faisah, Meena, and Amir?"

"Yes. And the others."

"Bilqis, Khanum, Taslima, and Chanda?" Rahima Mai repeated their names.

Ujala was surprised she recalled them all. Rahima Mai knew their names, and in chronological order.

"Yes . . . their mother, but more so, their older sister. Like you have become my baji, I became theirs."

Relatives and children swarmed the visiting room, filling it with aromas of curry, biryani, and dal. They spread cloths over concrete and ate with their fingers.

Rahima Mai signaled Ujala, snapping her finger and pointing to the far wall. It had been weeks since Ujala and Faisah had talked.

"Over there," Ujala told Faisah. The sisters sat on their haunches in the corner. Faisah leaned her lower back against the wall.

"We could have mounted a better defense under civil law than we can under Shariah," Faisah said. She sounded worried. "We will need major Islamic legal experts to defeat these charges. But we will find them. Don't worry."

But Ujala was not worried.

"Where are Chanda and Khanum now?" she asked. "Are they OK?"

"We know where Khanum is, but Chanda has disappeared."

Ujala realized that Faisah was not revealing exactly where the other women were. Rule number 1, she thought. Tell no one.

"Could she be with the dancers?"

"We don't know, Baji. We don't know." Faisah shook her head. "But we need her testimony. Since Chanda accompanied Amir on the plane out of Chitral, she could testify about her rescue. But Baji, they may make her testify for the prosecution."

Ujala did not look surprised.

"You know, Chanda's face would be a compelling piece of evidence against them, no matter what words come out of her mouth," said Ujala.

"True." Faisah's fingertip probed the line of her scar as if searching for an exit. "Amir has people out looking for her. Don't worry." Faisah saw loss written on Baji's face. Prison changes people, she thought. Something is changing with Baji.

"I have been missing Amir and Meena," Ujala said, thinking of the shared soul of her baby brother and sister, her son and her daughter, the boy, the girl, the man and woman they had become. She recalled them as toddlers, sitting in front of Ammi's bookshelf—straight backs topped with thick heads of hair, each with a pudgy knee bent, one foot in the crotch of the diaper, the other foot pointing away. How straight Meena's back was! She would pull the books down from the shelves and stack the smaller ones all around her until she was entirely encircled. Then she would wail because she couldn't get out of the trap she had built for herself.

Amir became studious, pouring over the open books and spending hours in his room at the mail-order computer he had built. And now, he'd become a man so like his father. In the Northwest, away from the habits of home, she thought she had seen in him what young women must see. She knew they would want him, would be jealous of his attention to others, and would wait for his small, telling gestures of affection. She could understand how a young woman would want to lay her head on his chest and inhale the scent of Amir.

"Amir shouldn't visit you, Baji," Faisah said. "They could charge him as a coconspirator."

"I know. But ask Meena to come soon."

Faisah nodded. Worried that Ujala was sinking into depression, she changed the subject.

"Baji, reports have been pouring in about honor crimes. We're finally getting solid local documentation." Faisah stopped rubbing her scar. It was a compulsive comfort she allowed herself, but it was distracting. She was determined to get it under control before the trial began.

"At least something good has come of this," said Ujala.

"Oh, and protesters will be making an even bigger noise. This afternoon there is a rally outside Faisal Mosque. Jabril Kazzaz has agreed to attend, and a member of the Human Rights Commission will speak, and Yusuf, too."

"How are Jabril and Yusuf?" Ujala brightened at the thought of the two different men in her life—the aging saint and the Gen-Xer.

"Well, Jabril is the same, of course, and Yusuf is angry," Faisah said. "He may be able to help us gain support from some of the organizations that have been keeping their distance. He has the facts at his fingertips, but he makes no pretense of objectivity when it comes to the topic of honor crimes and you."

"What about you, Faisah? Are you speaking at the rally, too? After all, they did name the mosque after you, didn't they?"

Faisah forced a laugh at Uji's bad joke about the landmark erected by Saudi King Faisal.

"Yes, I will have my say," Faisah said, and her voice was sad. She met her sister's eyes. "But should I speak in public, Baji? Or do I look too much like a monster?"

She blinked to soothe her eyeball—the salt was a bearable sting. Her good eye glistened, wetness clinging to the line of her lower lid. Then a tear formed as the thought of looking like a monster did its dirty work. The tear appeared, whole and guileless, without a consciousness of its own. It was the same tear she would cry if she stubbed her toe, or if she were a young child who wandered away, or if she recalled once losing her first mother, and now faced losing her second. The tear arose, fresh and solitary, until its twin appeared, forcing the first to take the fall. Then the second one slipped into the crevice of her squint and spread across the tiny lines, softening the corners of her eyes.

"Of course you should show your face," said Ujala. "A rally

would not be a rally without you." Seeing Faisah's tears, she slowed her enthusiasm. "What are you afraid of?" she asked, stroking her sister's cheek.

"I don't want to scare people away. They will be afraid that what happened to me might happen to them." She lowered her voice. "On the other hand, I don't want those who did this to me to keep me behind closed doors either."

"The two horns of a dilemma," said Ujala, a line she often heard Faisah use. Faisah grinned.

"I could just keep the bandage on."

"Oh, Faisah, forget about it. You're just not that scary. Think of it like the Girl Guides—the mark on your face is a badge of honor you earned."

"*Honor*," Faisah said. "What does it mean? I've come to despise that word," she said and her mouth began to harden. "OK. OK. I'll do it. I'll speak at the damn rally."

It was the first time Ujala ever heard her sister curse. Must be spending a lot of time with Lia, she thought.

Ujala untied the cloth in the baskets Kulraj Singh had sent. Inside were chapati, spiced lentils and tomatoes, a jar of milk tea, and two pieces of dark chocolate. She tore off pieces of flatbread and stuffed each one into her mouth, chewing slowly, deliberately, as Faisah talked.

"Jabril knows professors at the university who are willing to be our experts—to give an alternative interpretation of the Q'ran to the one the prosecution will present. The religious law on obedience, ta'ah, is untested in this context. But academics are suspect as witnesses— too secular in the eyes of the court. We need someone else."

"So our witnesses would say what is Islamic, what is anti-Islamic, and the state's witnesses would do the same?"

"I'm afraid so. It is extremely problematic, but that is how it is done."

Ujala understood at once. "And it all depends on the judge, of course?"

"If you have a progressive judge, he'll interpret the concept progressively; and if not, he won't. We have law students trying to find the better interpretations from other court cases."

"To me, that is not what a court should be," said Ujala. "Honor crimes are like slavery. Nobody quibbles over Q'ranic interpretations of slavery."

But, then again, she thought, ending slavery had been a political decision, hadn't it? She turned her head to rest it on her hand, sitting cross-legged, her elbow on her knee. Faisah continued to parse their arguments.

"We can argue that a person either has human rights or does not. The political leaders want it both ways—at the U.N. the government claims to respect human rights, but at home they act like honor crimes are private matters—especially if the mullahs are involved."

Ujala sighed.

"But how can they prove the assault charge against me when Chanda's father was the one with the acid?"

Suddenly Faisah saw her sister as a client—with the plainspoken questions of an intelligent client, but, as with clients, Faisah was becoming impatient.

"You were the one with the gun, Baji," she reminded her. "I told you to give it to the police when you first picked it up from that killer." Faisah wanted to end the conversation. "Never mind. Leave the legal strategies to me."

But Ujala would not abandon her questions. "So I led Khanum astray? Is that it?" She squinted. "Isn't there an exception to every rule, including the rule of wifely obedience—a woman is allowed to visit her own family without a husband's consent."

"That's right," said Faisah. "It is arguable. Ta'ah is not a hard-and-fast rule, but one that must be considered in light of the circumstances. We need expert testimony to give the judges a hook to hang their hats on—if they are inclined to rule our way. If that is not what they want to do, then we are out of luck anyway."

Ujala saw Rahima Mai lifting her brow and tossing her chin in the direction of the door. It was the end of visiting hour. Faisah gathered her papers and picked up the basket.

"It seems like whatever we try to discuss, we always end up talking politics," Ujala said.

"And it has always been so, Baji," Faisah smiled, hugging her goodbye.

"Your brains are beautiful, Faisah. I know you'll find a way out of this for us."

"Inshallah," Faisah whispered. "God willing." But she was not so sure.

13

Islamabad, 1996

Dominating the skyline was the Faisal Mosque, with its four minarets pointing with certainty to the promise of heaven. Set against loden pines, cedars, and palm bushes of the rolling Margalla Hills, the modernistic mosque bewilders— as if it were an eight-faceted diamond laid in an emerald, or a heavenly tent for one hundred thousand worshippers. A spaceship preparing for liftoff, or a giant bug trapped on its own back. Its front yard entombs the despised General Zia, who died in an exploding airplane, and people joke that the relics in the grave are not Zia's at all, but the tailbone of an ass.

The hundreds who gathered for the rally on the mosque's lawn that day were only a peep of dissent in the body politic. When Faisah arrived at the demonstration, she hid along the side of the crowd, away from the stage, with her dupatta pulled across one side of her face. Meena introduced the speakers and each ascended the few steps to the platform, spoke for five minutes, and descended again. Jabril Kazzaz finished his comments and handed the microphone to Sister Nasreen Francis from the Peace and Justice Commission. Wearing the white veil made famous by Mother Teresa, the young nun looked up from her papers.

"Whether legal or illegal, Baji Ujala's actions to save those girls were just," she said. "They were destined to live tortured lives. She is a model for all who seek justice. May God have mercy on Pakistan."

Sister Nasreen returned to her chair as the crowd politely pumped up and down the signs they had tacked onto sticks. Standing at the microphone with her fist in the air, her pregnant belly high and round, Meena roused the chanting, "Free Baji! Free Baji! No honor in honor crimes! No honor in honor crimes! Free Baji! Free Baji!" The crowd responded, loud and intense, as if the volume of their voices alone might make a difference in the social conditions they protested.

Mynah birds with white-tipped feathers were feeding on seeds in the lawn. At a distance the gun barrels of a line of Kalashnikovs pointed into the sky. From beneath a cascading orange jacaranda, a group of thirty women in black burqas watched the protest from afar. Bearded men from Islamic University milled around two idling motorcycles. Several wore the green turbans of the Islamist political party. They looked hostile and seemed to be shouting at the protesters in front of the mosque. Yusuf watched them but could not hear exactly what they were saying. In his pocket he fingered the revolver Ujala gave him when he guarded her door at Nankana Sahib.

Meena lifted her chin to Yusuf, signaling that he would speak next. He climbed the stairs and stood at the podium in a white caftan and skullcap. He riffled his notes and brought Ujala's face to mind. Adjusting his glasses, he looked out over the crowd.

"My statement today reflects jihad," he began, "the struggle I have engaged in, as a Pakistani, as a Muslim, as a man. I come from an old family, from the hills above Karachi, where my grandfathers taught me. My father's father built the first mosque of this century in his town. My mother's father was from Lahore, a patron of art, education, and Q'ranic scholarship. From them I inherited a love of God and confidence in the word to express both new truths and old.

"Eleven years ago I left this country to work in America as a journalist. But today in Pakistan I have found a story I cannot stop telling—one that was invisible to me when I lived here. It is the story of the suffering of women under the harsh rules of our society, an injustice that contrasts with the compassion of the Q'ran I learned at the tables of my grandfathers.

"It is because I am a Muslim that I will tell these stories. To be a Muslim is to surrender to the will of God by living in such a way that one can always know what the will of God is. Then one can act on that will, even at the risk of losing one's own freedom, or reputation, or even, one's life. It is not hard to be a good Muslim when we have models of goodness such as Ujala Ehtisham—a teacher who has followed the path God directed her to. May the light of Allah bring peace to those who are persecuted."

Then there was a mysterious event that Faisah would try to describe later, but she would never succeed completely.

From the sidelines she heard a commotion in the back of the crowd. A migration of crows began—tens, hundreds, thousands, tens of thousands of black wings silhouetted against the hazy sky. Magnificent, they raced from the void, fast, and with great intention, as if the kernels of their hearts might pop open. The crows swept by the crowd for many minutes, blackening the day, and the experience carried the people away to something they knew, something they needed to remember, something older and even larger than the courage it took for them to demonstrate their beliefs in public.

The ground to the south of the mosque became a carpet of crazed, calling crows. Faisah stood under a tree so full of birds that it seemed to blacken and tilt forward from their accumulated weight. Only the sound of overhead jet planes drowned the birds' complaints. Then, as quickly as the spectacle appeared and darkened the sky, the last bird sped by, and the mystery dissolved like an image on film.

Faisah waited for the effect of the birds' drama to subside before she mounted the platform. When she reached the top step, she tugged her veil down onto her shoulder and faced the crowd, leading with her chin. The air emptied of words, as her friends saw the extent of Faisah's injuries. Over one eye she had placed a hospital-green patch fastened by an elastic cord tied around her head. She wore round, wire-rimmed sunglasses for protection.

The scars on her cheek and neck were ribbons of flesh welded to her bones. Someone in the back of the crowd began a slow, rhythmic clapping. Others joined in one by one, but Faisah interrupted their nervous, ambivalent tribute. She could not bear the tentativeness of the crowd's response. She did not want them to linger on her face.

"Today in Islamabad," she began, "in the shadow of God's house, we are outraged by the crimes of violence committed against women in our country. Last year, here in Punjab alone, nine hundred women were murdered in so-called honor killings. In Sindh, in the first three months of this year, over a hundred were reported—that is one per day. For many women the pain of being female is so great that suicide is their only relief."

Faisah lowered her voice.

"People of conscience must continue the work my Baji has begun—and we must do it even if we are afraid. We must listen to our conscience, not to our fear. This is what we face."

At the mention of the word *face*, Faisah hesitated. With her good eye, she could see another crowd growing near the wild jacaranda across the park. She inhaled and continued. "And do not be frightened by what you face. This woman you are looking at is yourself. Yes, these scars are not mine alone; they were intended not only for me, but also for you. I was merely selected to receive them. We earn these scars together because we value our consciences more than our faces, our daughters more than our selves, freedom more than security."

For the first time, Faisah smiled as she spoke.

"They say that a lion knows danger like an old friend. And a lion with one eye is to be respected—she's tattered and a little crazy."

As Faisah grinned and Meena reached for her, the protesters broke into applause. All at once a frightening popping sound split the crowd into pieces, as people ducked and hurried apart.

If God had been watching from the minaret He would have seen one body of people explode into pieces, winging apart, a churning mix of movement and emotion. He would have seen people yelling and running to avoid a spray of bullets.

But there was no spray of bullets. There was only one shot. Meena! Not Meena!

If it was intended for Faisah, it missed its mark. A single, hot bullet drove into Meena's chest, and, standing next to her, Faisah felt the impact, too. Meena felt a numbing burn that tunneled in. Faisah pulled her down to the platform. Meena gasped for air as her quiet eyes surveyed the blood pooling beneath her. It was as if her eyes were untouched by the shock wave that rocked her body. Faisah felt the heat of Meena's blood saturating her clothes, and she knew what it meant.

She and Sister Nasreen curled themselves around and over Meena, covering her with their bodies. They had nowhere to go, nowhere to run.

The rustling and calling of people to each other continued in the lower ranges of sound. The high-pitched war cry of police sirens came closer and closer. The pile of people protecting Meena moved aside so that Yusuf could lift Meena carefully and carry her from the platform.

Armored vehicles circled a patch of grass. Uniformed police streamed out of the vans and lined the street between the protesters and the students. Every other policeman pointed his weapon in the opposite direction, half at the protesters, half at the students. Several officers began a foot-chase around the mosque, searching for the shooter. Others followed on motorcycles, and their sirens split the air. Meena lay on the grass with her head in Faisah's lap while Yusuf scanned the crowd for an ambulance. Meena groaned as she bled.

"I'm here, Meena," Faisah spoke through her tears. She could see the entrance wound where Meena's clothes were ripped apart. Her flesh was seared, a gash, open like a pocket. Meena swooned with pain. "The ambulance is coming. The hospital is nearby. Hold on. Breathe with me. Look at my face."

Meena's eyes gripped Faisah's, who inhaled Meena's desperation, as if she were drawing out the remaining breath from her sister's lungs. Meena tried to follow Faisah's lead, but she could only cough and cough.

"Here," Faisah said. "Watch me again. Just a little breath, like this." She pinched Meena's cheek. Meena rested her eyes on Faisah's, trying to puff her breath. Her lips stuck together and a teaspoon of air slipped through one corner of her mouth. "Stay with me, Meena. Oh, stay with me."

"Ammi," Meena whimpered, staring at the blazing jacaranda.

"Here they come!" shouted Yusuf, waving his arms above the crowd to the hospital truck. Two porters lifted Meena onto a gurney.

"Call Zeshan," Faisah whispered to Yusuf as she climbed into the truck, "and Abbu and Amir."

Faisah looked where Meena had been staring. In a flash under the jacaranda, she imagined she saw Nafeesa there—a silver-haired woman in black with a scar at her hairline. Faisah froze in that moment, utter sadness filling every pore for the five motherless children that they were, for all the motherless children everywhere.

"How has the world come to this, Ammi?" she asked.

Nafeesa watched and whispered, "It has always been so."

Faisah snapped out of it.

"And tell Baji," she said to Yusuf. "You have to tell Baji."

The ambulance sped along the brick wall lining Airport Road, past rows of simple signs extended like open hands. Each sign bore one of the ninety-nine names of Allah. Faisah read them to Meena as they flew by: Allah, the Merciful. The Wise One. The Only One. The One Who Brings Good News. The One You Can Expect Something From. God of Our Ancestors. The Giver. The Omnipotent. The Greatest One. The Innocent One. The Righteous One. The Alpha and the Omega. The Inner and the Outer. God of the Orphan. One Who Talks About God. The Friend. The Just. The All-Seeing. The Protector . . .

Meena died at midnight. Minutes later, surgeons separated her baby from her womb. Meena's final act in this world was to give birth to a daughter.

"You are Nafeesa Zeshan," Zeshan said to the infant when he first held her. "Welcome to the world and bid goodbye to your mother." He curled the squalling baby into Meena's neck, between her cheek and her shoulder. "She has given her life for you, a martyr for all the daughters of Pakistan."

Then Zeshan placed his face next to his child and wept like a baby. It seemed the room was filled with the pain of birth, the pain of death, and of all of the suffering of life between the two, all the pain of Pakistan.

"Give her to me," Abida said, placing little Nafeesa into the arms of Kulraj Singh.

Zeshan permitted Meena's body to be transported from Islamabad to Nankana Sahib for ceremonies and burial, and the family entered the formal mourning period.

"The best thing for you and Yusuf to do," Faisah told Lia, "is to keep the radio station operating and to keep visiting Baji. I can take care of things here at home. We washed and wrapped Ammi's body ourselves so long ago. Maybe it will come back to me."

How odd, Faisah thought, that the house is full of men—this house that has been dominated by women. I'm the only daughter at home now. Meena dead, Ujala in prison, Reshma gone for so long, and so far away in Karachi. I do not want anyone to call Reshma, to tell her what has happened. It is extremists like Reshma and Muhammad who killed Meena. I will rely on Abida and the village women to help me remember the laws on preparing Meena's body. But we are short of Muslim hands for this work. Zeshan and Abida can shroud her, but, as non-Muslims, Lia and Abbu cannot.

Zeshan laid his wife's body down on the bed of her childhood. Her chest and abdominal wounds were bandaged to keep the blood inside her body, as required. Abida brought pitchers of water and large washing bowls. They filled the room with fresh-cut eucalyptus leaves and rose petals. Zeshan held his sleeping baby in his arms and stood by while the women worked.

"Bismillah, In the name of Allah," they prayed. Abida placed a bowl under Meena's head while Faisah supported her neck and squeezed shampoo onto the black mass of Meena's hair.

"Everyone shall taste death," Zeshan prayed aloud, reciting the scriptures. "The life of this world is only the enjoyment of deception.

No one knows when and where she will die, or knows how. May God forgive her sins and grant her eternal happiness in paradise."

The fragrance of lavender tickled Faisah's nostrils as she divided Meena's hair into sections and squeezed the lather through. As she worked, she could see her father embracing someone outside the open door. Then Reshma walked into the room. She carried white cloths folded across her arms.

"Baji! You have come," said Faisah, wrapping her arms around her oldest sister. Relieved of the duty she did not want, she collapsed onto the bed next to Meena. Forgiveness suffused her soul. She cried out loud and lay her head down on Meena's breasts.

Reshma wailed, too. Meena had been hers, a gift Ammi left behind for her. She looked up from where Faisah lay and confessed to Kulraj Singh.

"I abandoned Meena," she said. "Ammi left Meena in my care, and I went on with my own life without her. I did not even give my blessing to her on her wedding day." Her voice was desolate.

"Now you are with us, now you are here. You can bless her baby," he said.

Reshma felt her father's wisdom. He always knew that this terrible day might come and had prepared by a lifetime of surrendering his broken heart.

"You are more of a Muslim than I," she said.

She joined the ritual and dried Meena's body with pure cloth, all the while quoting the Q'ran. Her voice comforted them. It was a mother's voice telling a story to a young child.

"Little Meena," she began, "Do you know what the angels say when Death takes the life of a righteous one like you? They say, 'Enter paradise because of the good deeds that you did during your life.' Right now, with faces like a thousand suns, the angels are coming for you from heaven with the perfume of paradise. See them there, so far away? See them coming now?"

Kulraj Singh stood outside the open door, listening, watching Reshma move around Meena's bed. She looks so much like Nafeesa, he thought. Faisah and Abida followed Reshma's lead. They had had no words for their feelings, and now they were grateful for the poetry of the scriptures.

"Then the Angel of Death comes and sits at your head, Meena. He will coax you, 'O good soul, come out to forgiveness and acceptance from Allah.' Your soul will appear as a tear, and the angel will seize it right then. Then the other angels will shroud your soul, as we do your body, but they wrap you, not in cotton, but in the shroud of paradise, perfumed with the sweetness of night jasmine and honeysuckle.

"Then, my baby Meena, then they take your sweet-smelling soul up to paradise, and whenever they pass by a group of other angels who ask, 'Who is this good soul?' your angels will reply, 'This is Meena, Mother of Nafeesa, the Daughter She Bore in Death,' and 'This is Meena, Daughter of Nafeesa Who Birthed Only Strong Children and Taught Them Well and Left Life Too Soon,' and 'This is Meena, Wife of Zeshan Who Loved Her For a Short Time But Loved Her Well,' and 'This is Meena, Daughter of the Dear and Holy Kulraj Singh,' and 'This is Meena, the Treasure of Her Sisters, Faisah and Ujala and Reshma, and the Twin Soul of her Brother, Amir,' and 'This is Meena, the Voice of Many Women Who Has Given Her Life Like a Martyr Promised Paradise.'

"Meena, when you reach the first heaven, Allah will ask, 'Who are you?' and you will reply, 'I am my own good deeds.' And Allah will say, 'Record the book of my daughter in the highest place, spread out carpets for her, clothe her in the splendor of heaven, and open the gates of paradise.' Rejoice in these garments and perfumes, Meena," Reshma said, as they finished the third round of cleansing, "for this is the day which you have been promised."

Meena's hair was shining, blotted by the soft hands of her sisters. It was damp and parted in three pieces—each one impeccably braided and placed behind her back, as is the custom.

"Meena?" Ujala asked when Yusuf told her. Her voice was almost soundless, less than a whisper. She shook her head and looked into his eyes. Yusuf held her gaze and nodded. Ujala looked down. Yusuf wanted to hold her, to console her, but he could not.

There will never again be a moment like this one, he swore to himself, when I am unable to touch her, to console her. I will make her my wife. Inshallah. God willing.

Ujala sighed.

"Oh no. Not Meena. Not Meena." Her heartache was doubled by her separation from the family. They were all in Nankana Sahib, and she was behind prison walls.

Rahima Mai, too, was at a loss to comfort Ujala. She could put in a requisition for her temporary release for the funeral, but she knew that the central office was watching her. Dare she risk making such an unprecedented request?

"Thank God for Kazzaz," she whispered when word came over the phone that, with Jabril Kazzaz's intervention, the Court permitted Ujala twenty-four hours to offer dua, supplication prayers for Meena.

"You can go for one day," Rahima Mai told Ujala, standing at the door of her cell. She looked through the bars into Ujala's eyes, wanting some recognition, some contact, some light. But Ujala's eyes only looked inward, as her soul swam in the dark.

Jabril met Ujala at the prison and they rode the bus to Nankana Sahib with a female guard, as required by the Court and arranged by Rahima Mai.

The eyes of Ujala and of Jabril Kazzaz held one unspeakable pain.

"I don't understand how it can be such a glorious day," Jabril said. They sat on the backseat of the bus, careful to keep an empty space between them.

"Yes," said Ujala.

"It is hard to understand Allah's will," Jabril said. "—perhaps He is telling us that now Meena is in a heaven as beautiful as this day."

Ujala's voice was bitter.

"I take no solace that she may be in heaven, Jabril. You are a spiritual person. I am not."

"Oh, no," said Jabril. "It is the nearness of angels like you, like Meena, or your mother, that raises the spark of God on earth." He dared to look at the starkness in Ujala's face. He sighed. "My words sound hollow," he admitted. "I am not such a spiritual person. I am more like a cave, echoing the sounds of someone else's thunder."

Ujala smiled at her friend in his long robe and trimmed beard. It comforted her to be with him and to be going home.

"I am eager to see the baby. And Reshma," said Ujala.

"And I am eager to get you out of Adiala and out of Pakistan," Jabril whispered. Ujala looked at him in surprise, and did not lower her voice.

"And where would I go? And who am I without my family and my country?"

Ujala's questions dangled between them. She thought of the untouched dessert on the table that evening she had shared with Jabril Kazzaz beneath the neem tree. It seemed so long ago now, that day when she thought she and Jabril might have a future together. He seemed not to mind that their romance had become instead an uncomplicated friendship. They rode the rest of the way to Nankana Sahib in silence.

The guard with her pistol sat in the seat next to the bus door.

"We will follow Zeshan's wishes," Ujala said, resuming her role as mother of the family. They assembled under the neem tree in the courtyard. Kulraj Singh passed the tea and a plate of chapati to the others. He was fasting.

"But I want to go to the cemetery with Meena," Faisah said. She looked at Reshma and whined. "Reshma says I cannot."

"And I cannot either," said Reshma. "Women are not permitted at a funeral. Only male relatives may carry her body."

"Yes, only Muslim men may attend," Kulraj Singh said in a neutral tone.

"Even in death, men control women," said Faisah. "So who will carry her? We are just women and infidels."

"I'll go," Amir said. "Zeshan and I are her relatives. We can go."

"And, Jabril, you are like family to us," said Ujala. "Will you carry Meena, too?" Jabril nodded. "What is most important is a peaceful burial for Meena," said Ujala.

"The men will go for everyone. Yes, Baji?" Amir asked.

"Yes," she said.

At sunrise Ujala and Faisah covered Meena's shroud with rose petals. Then Zeshan, Amir, and Jabril lifted her from the bed onto a pallet. From beneath the neem tree, where Reshma fed Baby Nafeesa a bottle of boiled milk, Kulraj Singh and the women of his family watched the procession move down the tractor path and through the sunflower fields toward the peeling walls of the cemetery at the edge of Nankana Sahib. The people carried strings of tinsel to spread over her grave. The tinsel glinted in the light.

14

Nankana Sahib, 1996

The family's grief did not stand at the door and close off the world. It was like water that seeped through the ceiling when it rained, or an apparition reflected in a mirror, or an insistent backbeat driving an unfamiliar tune.

In the shrine room, Kulraj Singh's chanting would stop, as his hand froze on the harmonium. Instead, a memory of Meena glowed in his mind. There she was, running her fingers along the edge of her dupatta, moving it out of her way like a curtain of beads, as she squatted to light the stove. A moment later the music would start up again, and his voice hummed a tune.

Amir slipped into the driver's seat and reached for the gearshift. Intending to push it from neutral to first gear, instead he saw his twin in the windshield, and threw the engine into reverse.

Faisah's grief flashed like heat lightning and struck without thunder. At times it would dull her mind; at other times it shocked life back into her.

The pages of Reshma's texts crinkled when she turned them, so coated were they with dried tears.

But the way that grief and Ujala met one another was like two old women stooped over by the grudges they had carried through the years. Grief would crow in the dark before dawn.

"Assalam aleikum," Ujala said, "you stubborn old rooster. You always have to be the first to have your say. No wonder you never let anyone rest."

Work became the mortar between the stepping-stones of their heartache. Around the family, a barrage of activity was raging. Pakistan was in an uproar.

Lia brought news into the kitchen at Nankana Sahib.

"Women are wearing eye patches everywhere," she said to Faisah. She could not disguise her excitement. "They say they want to share the badge of honor that you wear. You should hear them— in Multan, in Hyderabad, even in Swat. Women say they want to be in solidarity with the 'She-Lions of Punjab.'"

"She-lions?"

"Yes. You, and Meena, and Baji," said Lia.

"Which Baji?" asked Amir, but he knew the answer.

"Baji Ujala, of course," Faisah said as if the answer was self-evident.

"Look, you started the lion thing, you know," Lia said, elbowing Faisah, "with that line about being a tattered old cat." Amir stopped grinding spices long enough to growl and claw the air.

"Will Baji Reshma be staying?" he asked.

"If I can talk her into it," said Faisah, "she will be our secret weapon at Baji's trial, our expert witness on Shariah."

"But she's an Islamist, a fundamentalist," Lia said.

"Which will give her testimony even more weight."

"And she's a woman," Lia said. "They will discredit whatever she has to say."

"Just the opposite," said Faisah. "We will propose Reshma as the jurisconsult, the sole expert for the case—for both sides. Reshma thinks that the recent publicity will cause the judges to select her. They will want to appear sympathetic."

"I don't know," Lia said. She sounded skeptical.

"I agree with Lia," said Amir. "The court will discount her testimony because she's Baji's sister. Actually she is Baji's baji, so of course she is biased."

"Look, we talked about this at length in the legal team, and everyone agrees that it's a risky strategy, but our best hope. Once the court accepts her as jurisconsult, they have to also accept that she is objective and unbiased. That is part of the oath she takes."

"My promise of paradise would be on the line," said Reshma from the doorway. The three turned to see that Reshma had been listening in. "Testifying for Ujala will be the test of my scholarship, my integrity, and my faith."

The toughness of her voice reassured them.

"You are so like your mother," Kulraj Singh told Reshma during their walk to the Gurdwala. "Such a fine mind and so wise."

"I don't know, Abbu. Was it wisdom that kept me away from the family for so many years, or pigheadedness?"

"You had your reasons, Buttercup," he said, using the pet name he and Nafeesa had called her as a baby. He took her hands into his own, as he had when she was a child, before she had judged him, before she went her own way. "You were our first love in the years when life was fresh and we lived inside a globe of happiness." He cupped her hands and she squeezed his.

Allah returned me to my family when he took Meena away, Reshma thought. *I see now that I am as connected to them as the wisteria is to the neem tree.*

"You are part of this family, you know," Kulraj Singh said. "God brought you back to us when he took Meena."

"You knew what I was thinking!" Reshma said, dropping her father's hands, stopping on the path. "Were you reading my mind again, Mr. Singh?"

"No. I can't read minds. We both were sharing God's mind for a moment," he said. "Both of us are listening to the same voice."

They crossed the sunflower field. Reshma dug deep inside herself for the worn resentments she had carried for so many years, but they were gone. Now she had a father to lean on again. She didn't know how she would explain it to Mohammad. Would he encourage the twins to respect their grandfather? Would the twins be cold and harsh, as she knew they could be? Her eyes followed the light that danced on her father's beard. She relaxed to a depth she had not felt for many years.

"I'm sorry I called you an infidel," she said. "You are a better Muslim than I."

"Let's not talk theology," he said.

"But it was an awful thing to say. It is so evident that God is in you."

"Let's not talk politics, either . . . but, Reshma, you do need to have that conversation with this family's mother."

"You have to be a feminist, not a fundamentalist," Ujala told Reshma as they began hammering out trial strategy.

"Shariah is not incompatible with democracy or human rights," Reshma said. "What Islamists reject is the idea of separation of church and state. Government should be run according to God's laws."

"So there are fundamentalists and there are fundamentalists? Is that what you are saying?" Faisah asked. "I have to understand exactly what your testimony will be because I will be the one to question you in court."

"Then above all you must understand that there is a rich discourse among those who believe in the sanctity of the Q'ran. Frankly, as Muslim women, you should know better." Reshma sucked her tongue against her front teeth to keep from showing her disgust at her sisters' ignorance. "Some feminists blame Islamic law, when they are not familiar with its early history. Do not assume that Shariah is oppressive. It may be the quickest road to the freedom of women."

"Now you sound like our mother's daughter," Ujala said.

But she was not sure exactly what Reshma meant.

At precisely nine o'clock the three associate judges took their seats. The prosecutor entered the courtroom with a short woman in a blue burqa who walked directly to her brother, Sadiq. You could no longer see the light in her eye or the sequins on her nose.

"So now we know where Chanda has been," Faisah whispered.

"A Pathan woman answers to her brothers and her father. They are the great Khans, no?" Faisah could hear resignation settle into Ujala's voice. "She will testify against me. She has to do it. To save her life."

"No. She will not have to testify. They will present her affidavit only. They have brought her here only to demoralize us, to let us know she is under their control."

The president judge began the session in a formal tone.

"The district court of Lahore has sent a reference to the Federal Shariah Court. This matter is being considered under a special statute that permits this court, in extraordinary circumstances, to give interpretative guidance to the trial court in matters of Islamic law. We accept jurisdiction.

"Pursuant to the Constitution of the Islamic Republic of Pakistan, this court has invited a person well versed in Islamic law to assist in its decision. Mrs. Reshma Mohammad is a person of the highest scholarship and unquestioned integrity."

Reshma's twins sat in the audience with their father. They smiled with pride at the judge's respect for their mother and watched their father's reaction. He sat calmly, fixated by the courtroom scene.

"Pay attention!" he whispered to them. They listened to the judge's remarks.

"It is unusual to have a jurisconsult who is related to a defendant—here she is the defendant's elder sister. This is very unusual indeed. Has the prosecution no objection?"

The prosecutor had been examining the edge of the scar on Faisah's face. Distracted by his curiosity, he fumbled, jumping to his feet.

"Uh, no objection, your Honor."

"Well, then," continued the judge, "in the absence of objection and in light of Mrs. Mohammad's well-known piety and fairness, as well as her professional stature, this court nevertheless finds she is the best-qualified jurisconsult to testify on the issue presented. We ask her to come forward to take her oath."

Dressed in a dark blue shalwar kameez and a white cotton dupatta, Reshma approached the bailiff who held the Q'ran in his hand.

"I, Reshma Mohammad, do solemnly swear that, as jurisconsult to the Federal Shariah Court, I will discharge my duties and perform my functions honestly, to the best of my ability, and faithfully in accordance with law; and . . ." she paused dramatically to look at the judges, as if promising each one personally, "I will not allow my personal interests to influence my official conduct or opinions."

She took her seat in the witness chair, and Faisah walked up to the podium.

"Madam, please explain to the court the historical basis of your interpretation of the concept of, ta'ah, a wife's duty of obedience."

Reshma cleared her throat.

"For many centuries, a wide range of judicial interpretations of ta'ah has existed, varying according to two things—first, the society in which the interpretations were made, and second, according to the judge's intention to permit certain freedom of conscience to individuals. However, modern Islamic nations have codified family law, and in doing so, have selected particular schools of thought and discarded others, thus eliminating the richness of our organic jurisprudence. This limited selection of law has weakened the fundamental freedom of conscience that the Prophet—Peace be unto him—encouraged and which was well known to jurists of the past."

"Exactly which jurists do you mean?" barked the Chief Justice.

"Imam Al-Shafi'i, for example, revised his early jurisprudence to account for the social customs of Egypt when he moved there from Baghdad," Reshma answered and returned to her point. "Many customs today, including ta'ah, are not in the original personal law. Rather, those customs were superimposed on the holy verses, distorting them with a patriarchal view of the relationship between husbands and wives."

Reshma was trying to be understood by the audience and the press, as well as by the judges. Reshma was addressing Pakistan itself.

"Another example comes from Morocco, a Maliki jurisdiction. Today its personal code states that taking care of the house is part of the duties of the wife. Imam Malik, also in the eighth century, rejected the view that marriage was a service contract and concluded that the woman was not obligated to perform housework."

"Women in Pakistan do the housekeeping," said an associate judge. "What does this have to do with this case?"

Reshma was unflappable.

"My point, Sir, is that the history of Islamic jurisprudence, until 1947, supported the sanctity of individual conscience and valued diverse interpretations according to particular societies. In my expert opinion, in 1947, in the rush to create an Islamic state, Shariah was codified in Pakistan without due consideration to these historical realities.

"But here today," Reshma said, turning to the judges, "with the Islamic world watching, the court has the benefit of experience to look broadly at the law as it applies to women—in order to correct these errors of the past."

Faisah was a little disoriented. Was Reshma's argument too remote and theoretical for these judges? Or was it too close and threatening? She tried to move the testimony forward.

"What did the Prophet—Peace be unto him—have to say about ta'ah?"

"Nothing," Reshma said.

"Nothing?" Faisah asked again, to emphasize the point.

"The Prophet—Peace be unto him—was silent on the subject. After all, we know that two of the Prophet's wives, Khadija and A'isha, surely moved freely in their work. We also know that the Prophet—Peace be unto him—did household chores, and did not demand obedience at home. The egalitarian model that he created was one based on cooperation and consultation, an unusual model in his day, and rare today . . . but it is reported in the texts."

"So exactly what is ta'ah?"

"There is Ta'ah with a capital T, and ta'ah with a lowercase t. Strictly speaking, ta'ah is the obedience due only to God, not to a husband or a ruler. God's law is the highest, which is the reason for the existence of this court—to balance the duty owed to God against the duty owed to the political authority. Household ta'ah, on the other hand, is a small concept—not obedience at all, but merely the idea of consultation and—most important to this case before the court—consent in the private sphere, such as the consent of the wife to the wishes of the husband."

"So there is no support in the Q'ran for the hierarchy of males over females?"

"There is not. That hierarchy is merely a residue of patriarchy, a part of human history."

"And is there any specific verse of the Holy Q'ran to which the concept of ta'ah is repugnant?" Faisah asked, honing the question to match the exact language of the court's legal authority.

"Yes. The Holy Q'ran at 4:1 states that men and women are created from the same soul. How then, can one have authority over the other?"

"Thank you, Mrs. Mohammad. I have no further questions."

"I have some questions for Mrs. Mohammad," said the prosecutor, standing firm.

"As do I." The chief justice spoke with irritation in his voice.

"Please, you go first, my Lord," said the prosecutor. The judge was a former prosecutor himself and famous for the precision of his examination of witnesses. The prosecutor sat back in his chair to let the judge do his job for him. "I'll just sit right here."

"Mrs. Mohammad, does the Holy Q'ran not state at 4:34 that 'men are qawwamun over women'? Are not men the protectors of women because they have more strength?"

"My Lord," Reshma replied without emotion, "the problem with the modern translation of *qawwamun* is that it supports a limited interpretation of the word. According to ancient Arabic dictionaries, the word can mean many things—*head*, or *boss*, or *leader*, or *protector*, or even *manager*, *guide*, and *advisor*. These words can be open to authoritarian or to democratic interpretations. Thus, where a society was authoritarian, it made sense that interpreters colored the meanings with an authoritarian perspective. But today, as the world has changed, modern jurisprudence can regain for the word its original meaning. In light of Pakistan's being a democracy, the Court would do well to opt for nonhierarchical interpretations of the word."

"Interesting, Mrs. Mohammad, but does the Q'ran not also state that man is faddala—superior to woman?"

"My Lord, technically, according to Arabic etymology, *faddala* simply means *different from*, not *superior*."

"So, which interpretation are we to believe—to apply to this case, Mrs. Mohammad?" asked the Chief Judge.

"Under rules of jurisprudential construction, general principles carry more weight than particular ones. Clearly, the equality principle concerning the souls of men and women is general. But this second verse, indicating the so-called superiority of men over women, or of men as protectors and managers of women, is limited only to circumstances where women are financially dependent on men. In those circumstances, the verse informs us, God gave to a man supporting a woman the responsibility of offering the woman advice in those areas in which he happens to be more experienced."

"And presumably the woman is entitled to reject this so-called advice?" the judge asked.

"Well, otherwise advice would not be advisory, now would it, my Lord?" She smiled and the audience chuckled. Reshma was charming them. She said, "This interpretation is consistent with the verse that states that Muslims, male and female, are each other's walis—protectors, allies, guardians."

The Chief Judge surveyed the audience, the attorneys, and his associates on the bench. Sensing that the questioners were satisfied by her answers, he returned to Reshma.

"Mrs. Mohammad, you have the appreciation of the Court." He nodded to a line of police who were pouring into the courtroom with their sticks drawn. "This matter will be taken under advisement and a ruling will be forthcoming. The bailiffs will please secure this courtroom. This court is adjourned."

The judges stepped from the bench and disappeared behind closed doors.

"Go into the holding room," Rahima Mai told Faisah. "I will stay on the courtroom side of the door. We don't want a replay of the riot in Lahore."

"Baji, you were brilliant. Shukriah," Ujala said to Reshma, hugging her. Reshma's sons felt shy in front of these relatives they hardly knew. Mohammad was smiling. Despite himself, he could see God's work in his wife's reunion with her family. *Allah be praised!*

Lia kept trying to be heard, to get a word in the commotion. At last, she jumped up, waving a sheaf of papers in her hand, "The government shut down the radio station this afternoon," she said, and the room hushed. "They locked us out on an administrative directive. Something about inciting violence on the airwaves."

"It's from the Minister of Information," Faisah said, reviewing the papers Lia had been brandishing.

If the government has closed down the radio station, Ujala thought, the next loss might be the judges' decision in her case. Maybe even her life.

Rahima Mai gestured toward the exit, directing Ujala back into the van, while Faisah talked to the press.

"We want to talk to Reshma Mohammad," one reporter said. "It looks like she is the fourth 'She-lion of Punjab.'"

"Unfortunately, it is not appropriate for a jurisconsult to comment on the case," Faisah told the reporters. "Mrs. Mohammad has left with her family. She really is not available."

"Perhaps she would give an interview—not about the case," another reporter suggested. "We want to know more about her, and the changes she sees coming in Islamic law in Pakistan."

The reporters pressed her, one after another insisting on a meeting with the fourth she-lion, and Faisah did not want to alienate them.

Lia could see that Faisah was tired. "We'll be happy to ask her about it and let you know," she said, taking journalists' cards. Finally, the swarm of reporters buzzed away.

"You look tired, Lia. Shall we get a cup of tea?" Faisah asked.

"Not tea," Lia whined. "Please, no more tea." She laughed. "A bourbon on the rocks, that's what I'd like. But where, O where, can I find Jim Beam in Islamabad?"

Yusuf received a phone call from Karachi. It was Ujala's friend, Robina Shahani, with whom Ujala had first started the courtyard school. Robina had an idea.

"Bribe the prison guards?" he said.

"Yes. Do it the old-fashioned way," she said. "The Pakistani way. They expect it. Probably wondering why it is taking so long."

"Maybe you're right. Ujala has made friends with the women's supervisor. I could approach her."

"She is probably waiting for an offer. Make her one. That is why I called. I have a leather pouch full of jewels being sent to you by overnight post."

"Jewels?" he asked. "Where would a school teacher get a box of jewels?"

"Let's say it's from one of Baji's sisters. A woman is always willing to exchange a few bangles or precious stones for freedom."

"Let me talk to Kulraj Singh about it."

"Absolutely not!" Robina shouted. "You want to get him into trouble? No. Tell no one—that is rule number 1."

Yusuf felt naive.

"So if that is rule number 1," he said, "what is rule number 2?"

"Skip rule number 2," said Robina. "Go directly to rule number 3. Do not get caught!"

Rahima Mai was furious.

"What do you think I am, trying to bribe me, to involve me in a prison escape? I should report you to the authorities. I am a professional. Do you think that Baji would want you to jeopardize my job? She cares about me!"

"But she may never get out of here," said Yusuf. "You yourself said it—who knows what kind of evidence they have against her?"

"She never should have carried that revolver. If it had never been fired, she would be free today," Rahima Mai said, looking for someone to blame. "Why did you let her carry a gun anyway?"

"Me? I didn't even know she had a gun. I was in the U.S. at the time."

"In the U.S.? Oh, yes, I forgot, you are famous in the U.S. But here you are nobody." *Who is boy who has never known hardship—this boy that Ujala wants?* "Maybe you believe too many of your own stories about government corruption. You just want to have her all to yourself. To take her away from those of us who understand her, who love her, who need her." Rahima Mai was at the point of tears. She hissed at Yusuf, "You are one whose sweetness is a lie."

Yusuf stepped back. *Ujala shared our story with a prison guard?*

Rahima Mai saw the shock on his face.

"Yes, she told me all about you, Mr. Big Shot. She has told me things she will never tell you. Or be able to tell you—she may not get the death penalty, but she will spend the rest of her life here at

Adiala with me. I am a better guardian than you ever will be! With me, it is a matter of honor."

Yusuf realized he was out of his league. He placed a small pouch on the table between them.

"Take these, anyway," Yusuf said. "If you love her, you will use these in her best interest while she is in your care. Forget about the escape plan. We cannot succeed without your help."

Rahima Mai slipped the leather pouch into a plastic bag beneath her desk and reached for a seltzer to calm the nausea rising in her throat.

"Stupid boy!" she shouted at Yusuf's back. "Whatever does she see in you?"

"I need to give the keys of my soul to someone," Yusuf said to Ujala across the table in the visiting room. "Will you receive them?"

"Yes!" Ujala said, laughing at her own enthusiasm.

"I have another question."

"I hope it's as easy as your first one."

"Will you marry me and come away to London, as we planned years ago?"

Ujala stopped laughing.

"Remember I have a few things I have to do here first? Such as waiting for the court decision, and serving a prison sentence, or being executed?"

She tried to sound light, but in speaking the words, even in whispers, her throat closed.

"You trust the court to be fair?" he asked.

She rolled her eyes.

"Even if we are successful in court, Uji, your life will always be in danger in Pakistan."

"But I must continue my mother's work," she said, realizing that she still thought of her work as being, in some way, her mother's. She thought she heard a distant, unfamiliar female voice, scolding her: Wake up, Ujala! All of the things you want! You want your work, you want your Yusuf, you want Pakistan. Life is a trade-off. Now tell me, what do you want to keep and what do you want to lose? "Maybe I do have to leave Pakistan," she said at last.

"Jabril will come for you in the morning," he said.

"What do Faisah and Lia think about my leaving Pakistan?"

"Amir is speaking to them now."

"And what about Abbu? How can I leave my father?"

Faisah and Lia approved of the plan Amir described.

"Yes, let Yusuf take her to someplace safe," Faisah said. "We should have thought of this long ago. I've been so wrapped up in her case that I haven't had time to think about other options."

"You don't have to think of everything, Faisah," Lia said. "You've been going every which way like—"

"I know—a chicken with its head cut off, as your mama would say."

"Seriously, Faisah, maybe you and I should think about following Baji out of Pakistan?" Faisah did not skip a beat.

"Maybe. But we have to finish what we have started here first."

"You and your plans and your lists," Lia said, happy to hear the *we* in Faisah's answer. "You know, we can have a radio station and a website from almost anywhere, isn't that right, Amir?"

Amir did not move. He was reluctant to get in the middle of their argument, if it was an argument. He couldn't tell exactly.

"You really want to go home, don't you?" Faisah asked.

"No, not so much go home as make a home where we can be safe."

Faisah turned to Amir.

"But what about Abbu?" she asked.

"Jabril's talking to him now," he replied, with an immense sadness. "I do not understand this. First, Baji Reshma moves away, then Ammi dies, you are attacked, then Meena is murdered, and now Baji is jailed. If Baji leaves the country, we lose our mother again. If you and Lia leave, too, then what becomes of Abbu and me?"

"What would Abbu say?" Faisah asked.

Amir sighed. "He would say that pleasure and pain are a set of robes that a man must keep on wearing."

"Then whether you are inside Pakistan or not, who better than Abbu to guide you?"

During visiting hours on Friday morning, Jabril Kazzaz entered the Women's Prison with a large shopping bag. He joined the line of relatives waiting to enter.

"Sign in. You must sign in," shouted the guard in a tan uniform. She tapped her finger against the table and from time to time glanced up at Rahima Mai, who stood by the door, overseeing the process. A bound book of signatures lay open on the desk as the people passed a ballpoint pen, one to the other. Jabril had dyed his hair black and shaved his beard, and he was swaddled in a prayer shawl.

The place is busy and crowded today, he thought. God has given us lots of children and distractions. Allahu akbar! *God is great!*

When Jabril's turn came, he scribbled a name and listed the prisoner he was visiting: *Sadia Mirza*, he wrote, *Niece*. He opened the mouth of the bag he carried.

"It's nothing," he said. "A cover for my sister's bed. She says she is cold in here at night."

The guard was not listening to him. She gestured him on.

The indoor picnic began. Two uniformed guards stood in one corner, picking their teeth and watching the children play. Ujala sat in a far corner near the toilet area.

"Assalam aleikum," Jabril said as he approached her.

Ujala bowed her head. "Waleikum salaam, Mamou," Ujala replied, calling him "Uncle."

Jabril smiled. "I have brought you a burqa," he whispered. When she looked into the bag, she recognized that the moment of her release had arrived. She could feel anticipation in her throat and had difficulty swallowing.

"Say nothing and stop looking at it," Jabril hissed, and Ujala complied. "We will simply sit here quietly until we have a plan we both understand," he said. "Then, inshallah, the journey out of Pakistan will begin."

"But I have not said good-bye to anyone."

"It must be that way. Your father sends you every prayer for safety."

Ujala's heart ached at the mention of her father. *Will I never see your face again? Good-bye, my gentle Abbu.*

Jabril continued, "If everyone came to see you all at once, it would attract attention. Now listen to me. We wait until one of the guards leaves the room, which we have arranged to happen in about ten minutes."

"You arranged to happen? How could you do that?"

"Many people love and admire you, Baji." He returned to giving her instructions. "As the guard leaves the room, you will go into the toilet with this bag and put the burqa on. I will stand by the door to see that no one else enters. There will be a commotion."

Ujala stared. "How do you know there will be a commotion?"

"As I said, there will be a commotion. When you hear it, you leave the toilet and accompany me to the door, as if you were my sister. Follow behind me. And say nothing to anyone, no matter what, until you are safely in the car with Yusuf."

Ujala's pulse rose at the thought of being outside of the prison walls with Yusuf.

"I understand," she said, repeating the instructions in her mind. *Guard leaves, go to toilet, change clothes, hear commotion, follow Jabril, say nothing, Yusuf.* "Yusuf," she whispered softly.

No sooner had Ujala spoken Yusuf's name, than Rahima Mai called one of the guards to the door. They surveyed the room and signaled to the remaining guard, who nodded and left the room. Ujala slipped into the toilet. She had just pulled the burqa over her head when she heard a slamming sound and children crying. The commotion had begun! She rushed out to follow behind Jabril Kazzaz, as planned. She saw that a plastic table had collapsed onto the concrete floor, frightening the children and sending food flying in all directions. The guards, the prisoners, and the visitors were all busy trying to restore order and clean the mess. Kazzaz opened the visiting room door, which someone had left unlocked, and they joined a line of visitors exiting the prison. They passed by the table where Jabril signed in.

"You!" One of the female guards shouted, pointing at Jabril. "You must sign out over here."

Ujala followed him to the table where the guard was running her index finger down the page of the book, looking for his name.

"My sister and I were visiting my niece, Sadia Mirza," he said.

"I do not see it here, Sir. You will have to stand over there," she said, pointing to a holding area next to the visiting room.

"I will do no such thing!" Jabril said. "Who do you think you are? Ordering me about!"

Rahima Mai pushed through the crowed, shouting at the guard. "Idiot, what is the problem? Let them through."

"But, Madam, his sister is not on the list," the guard protested.

"And who failed to put her name on the list? Hmm?" Rahima Mai asked. She pressed a cloth into Ujala's hands. Jabril escorted her through the exit, down the narrow hallway, and out the prison door.

Yusuf sat behind the wheel of a rusty Nissan. He jumped out to open the back door while Jabril's eyes scanned for Rahima Mai, who watched from the gate. She stood with her arms folded across her chest.

In the backseat of the car, Ujala unwrapped the cloth that Rahima Mai had forced into her hands, an orange and pink shawl. Ujala recalled the words she had spoken to Robina, "If you give a shawl to a woman, she is forever your sister and you have the right to protect her."

Inside the shawl was a leather pouch of precious stones—lapis lazuli, pearls, rubies, topaz, and tourmaline. Underneath the gems, she found a folded paper—a map to Muzzafabad, where Rahima Mai had marked an old donkey path into the back hills marking a way through Kashmir to the border.

Ujala looked back at Rahima Mai. Around her head she had wrapped an identical orange and pink shawl.

The car pulled away, and Rahima Mai's prayer was lost in the wind, "Allah hafiz, Baji." *May Allah protect you.*

Acknowledgments

Almost eight years ago I met a remarkable Pakistani, a woman whom I will call Aisha, a grassroots teacher for twenty-five years, a woman who had been involved secretly and personally in rescue efforts for a number of women condemned in so-called "honor crimes." As I listened to her stories, in my mind she became the "Harriet Tubman of Pakistan." As for myself, I had spent years as a lawyer activist in the early battered women's movement in the United States, so the details of the abuse Aisha described were strange, but strangely familiar at the same time. On the evening that I met my new friend, as we washed dishes after a small meal, we recalled the courage of the abused women we had known, and, with our hands in dishwater, both of us silent, we began to weep. Impulsively, I quietly asked her if I could write her story. She agreed at once, and over the following months, we met every other week over cups of tea while I read and she commented on my first drafts of this story. After awhile, her story became mine as I turned it into fiction, both to protect her and to give me the freedom to create the particular story that seemed to want to be told. Over the next six years I traveled to Pakistan, conducted extensive research, became involved in Pakistani human rights support, and completed this novel with the help of many others.

So first I must acknowledge Aisha, whose stories about the courage of Pakistani people inspired me to begin this project. Her generous family hosted and sheltered me during my research in Pakistan, and I thank each one of them with all my heart, as well as many Pakistanis who welcomed me into their homes and into their lives—Asmari, Ayub, Catherine, Behzad, Bilal, Daniel, Farhada, Imran, Kanny, LeShan, Maan, Malik, Maria, Mariba, Mira, Mohammad, Moon, Mumtaz, Najma, Nosheen, Philip, Pricilla, Reena, Ribka, Rifat, Rubina, Rufina, Sabah, Sachel, Saima, Shabana, Shazia, Shazzad, Swinder, Tomas, Umara, Yaqub, Yusuf, and Zahida.

I hold in my heart the human rights workers and lawyers of Pakistan who remain publicly steadfast in their commitment to the rule of law and liberation of women and children under increasingly difficult political, social, and economic circumstances. They are an inspiration to the world: Asma Jahangir, Joseph Francis, Zia Ahmed Awan, Justice Majida Rizvi, Farida Shaheed, Tahira Khan, Shahid Anthony, Samina Benjamin, Tomas King, Amna Buttar, and Sabira Qureshi.

I acknowledge my writing mentors and many friends who have read drafts and guided and encouraged me over many years: Andrea D., Anita G., Brian C., Chris A., Claudia G., David K., Debbie and Matt P., Diane H., Dick A., Dorothy A., Eileen W. H., Elise P., Erika K., Fawn G., Fawzia A., Jean J., Lana H., Jeff O., Jennifer W., Kay W., Kristine T., Laura H., Libby C., Linda F., Lisa and Jason M., Marilyn K., Mary and Jim A., Molly M., Nina S., Pam K., Paul B., Penelope B., Phil W., Phyllis G., Rhonda S., Rita S., Ronnie S., Sally M., Sandra S., Sharon and Ray P., Sheryl J., Sonya U., Sue A., Susan S. C., Suzanne K., Syed E., Thrangu R., and Steve S.

I appreciate the support given to me by various writing programs and communities where I was able to commit undistracted time to writing and receive support and valuable insights: Colorado Council on the Humanities, Vermont Studio Center, Centrum, Wild Acres, Rocky Mountain Women's Institute, Denver's Lighthouse Writers, Julia and David White Artist Colony, and the University of Colorado Creative Writing Program.

I thank Ramanand P., for allowing me to borrow some of his words to transform into the voice of Kulraj Singh, and who assures me that he probably borrowed them from someone else who in turn borrowed from someone else and so on. I acknowledge Azizah Y. al-Hibri, a legal scholar whom I have never met. Her writings helped me to understand Islamic jurisprudence related to women's rights in order to write about trials in the Pakistani civil and Shariah courts. I also want to honor here the influence of and appreciation I have for the writings of Pakistani novelist Bapsi Sidhwa, who points a way, a writer's way, of writing truthfully and lovingly about Pakistan in all of its complexities. I appreciate the work of Fouzia

Saeed in her book *Taboo: A Ph.D. Girl in the Red Light Area,* and Tahira Khan for her book *Beyond Honour.*

I thank my editor, Robin Miura, for her enthusiasm and expert guidance, and Kevin Watson, whose vision of Press 53 has allowed the work of little-known writers such as myself to find their audiences.

As wide as my extended family has become in my life, I owe the most, the very, very most, to those who always remain the closest: my children, their spouses and children, and also their dear father.

Recently I spoke with Aisha, who is now back in Pakistan working with women's and girls' programs and helping with the development of a girls' school. She told me they need a shelter for women and children attempting to escape abuse. Half of the gross proceeds I receive from the sale of every copy of this book will be donated to a nonprofit organization in Pakistan for the purpose of constructing a safe shelter there. May all beings benefit!

Jacqueline St. Joan
2010

JACQUELINE ST. JOAN is an award-winning poet, travel writer, teacher, and lawyer. She has worked as a domestic violence activist, county judge, law professor, and children's rights advocate. Her writings have appeared in *Ms.*, the *Bloomsbury Review*, *Harvard Women's Law Journal*, *Empire Magazine*, *F Magazine*, the *Denver Post*, the *Denver Quarterly*, and other anthologies, scholarly journals, and online publications. She is the coeditor of *Beyond Portia: Women, Law, and Literature in the United States*. Her first novel, *My Sisters Made of Light* was inspired by a Pakistani teacher she met in the United States, who has since returned to Pakistan where she helps women who are survivors of honor crimes and other injuries. Jacqueline traveled in Pakistan to interview victims of human rights violations, including some who were in hiding or living under extreme duress. She met with human rights workers in many organizations, and later became public education chair for the Asian American Network Against Abuse of Human Rights, a U.S.-based NGO that works to support Pakistani efforts to end human rights violations, including sexual violence. She currently teaches "Women and the Law" at Metropolitan State College of Denver, where the germ of this novel was nurtured by her students during a 2002 course titled "Women Writing about the World after September 11th."

JACQUELINE ST. JOAN is an award-winning poet, travel writer, teacher, and lawyer. She has worked as a domestic violence activist, county judge, law professor, and children's rights advocate. Her writings have appeared in *Ms.*, the *Bloomsbury Review*, *Harvard Women's Law Journal*, *Empire Magazine*, *F Magazine*, the *Denver Post*, the *Denver Quarterly*, and other anthologies, scholarly journals, and online publications. She is the coeditor of *Beyond Portia: Women, Law, and Literature in the United States*. Her first novel, *My Sisters Made of Light* was inspired by a Pakistani teacher she met in the United States, who has since returned to Pakistan where she helps women who are survivors of honor crimes and other injuries. Jacqueline traveled in Pakistan to interview victims of human rights violations, including some who were in hiding or living under extreme duress. She met with human rights workers in many organizations, and later became public education chair for the Asian American Network Against Abuse of Human Rights, a U.S.-based NGO that works to support Pakistani efforts to end human rights violations, including sexual violence. She currently teaches "Women and the Law" at Metropolitan State College of Denver, where the germ of this novel was nurtured by her students during a 2002 course titled "Women Writing about the World after September 11th."

Cover designer **SONYA UNREIN** is a freelance editor, designer, and small press publishing consultant living in Centennial, Colorado. After earning a B.A. in English from the University of Colorado at Denver in 2001 and an M.A. in Digital Media Studies from the University of Denver in 2003, she won the Colorado Book Award for her anthology, *Open Windows 2006*, which she designed, compiled, and edited when she was a co-founder of Denver's Ghost Road Press. Visit her website at sonyaunrein.com.

CPSIA information can be obtained at www.ICGtesting.com
Printed in the USA
BVOW070057070613

322679BV00002B/8/P